Praise for *Games Women Play*

"Crown's debut will appeal to a wide variety of urban fiction
fans. Writing with power and from the heart, Crown is a
promising author to watch." —***Library Journal***

"Zaire Crown totally astonished me with an action-thriller
that had my imagination racing as fast as my pulse."
—***The Washington Informer***

"*Games Women Play* is an exciting, twisty thrill ride that'll keep
you turning the pages to its jaw-dropping conclusion."
—**De'nesha Diamond**

"*Games Women Play* goes in hard and heavy straight from the
gate! Zaire Crown is a bold new voice in urban fiction!"
—**Noire**

Books by Zaire Crown

Games Women Play

The Game Never Ends

The
GAME
NEVER
ENDS

ZAIRE
CROWN

KENSINGTON BOOKS
www.kensingtonbooks.com

DAFINA BOOKS are published by
Kensington Publishing Corp.
119 West 40th Street
New York, NY 10018

All Kensington titles, imprints, and distributed lines are available at special quantity discounts for bulk purchases for sales promotion, premiums, fund-raising, and educational or institutional use.

Special book excerpts or customized printings can also be created to fit specific needs. For details, write or phone the office of the Kensington Sales Manager: Kensington Publishing Corp., 119 West 40th Street, New York, NY 10018. Attn. Sales Department. Phone: 1-800-221-2647.

Dafina and the Dafina logo Reg. U.S. Pat. & TM Off.

ISBN-13: 978-1-4967-2521-9
ISBN-10: 1-4967-2521-2

First Kensington Trade Paperback Printing: September 2020

ISBN-13: 978-1-4967-2523-3 (ebook)
ISBN-10: 1-4967-2523-9 (ebook)
First Kensington Electronic Edition: September 2020

10 9 8 7 6 5 4 3 2 1

Printed in the United States of America

Prologue

"You don't catch feelings!" For twenty years, Tuesday had lived by this one unbreakable commandment. From her small strip club in Detroit, she and her team of ex-dancers would target all the local drug dealers. Their M.O.: robbery through seduction. She had been the mastermind behind the successful planning and execution of countless heists. Until she met her match.

During her last mission, she went after the most powerful and reclusive boss in the Midwest: the infamous Sebastian Caine. Tuesday broke her own rule by falling in love with her target and this earned the betrayal of her crew. An attempt was made on her life after they murdered her best friend. Tuesday had to flee Detroit, but not before she got revenge on her former associates.

For three years she had been living in California under the name Tabitha King, married and raising two children with Caine. Like her, Sebastian had also put his old life behind him. The former kingpin now lived as Marcus King and was completely legitimate. The couple owned Abel Incorporated, where Tuesday served as the CEO. A small venture once used to launder Caine's drug profits had grown to become one of the largest importing companies in America.

Tuesday had come up from the stripper pole to the board room. After years of being in the struggle, she now enjoyed a comfortable life with luxury cars and private jets, all while living in a Beverly Hills mansion with the man of her dreams. Tuesday seemed to have achieved the fairytale ending.

However, when dangerous enemies resurfaced, Tuesday learned that happily ever after only happens in children's books. She and Sebastian may have changed their names and gone legit, but that didn't erase their criminal pasts. Being done with The Game doesn't mean The Game is done with you.

Chapter One

Tuesday checked her watch to learn that it was fifteen minutes past eight. She was late *again.* She cursed out loud and scrambled to get dressed.

Over the past few weeks she had gotten sloppy and careless. Careless was something she had never been. Sloppiness was something she never tolerated.

When she was back in Detroit, every minute of her day was meticulously planned, every decision weighed to the point of torment. It was the same neurosis that gave her the ability to analyze all the angles to a situation, and was the primary reason why her team pulled off so many successful licks.

Now she was barely able to keep track of time and doing something so reckless that it could cost her life.

She jumped into her panties and pants. She slipped her feet into her Marc Jacobs heels. Since she didn't feel like taking the effort with her bra, she just shoved that into her Chanel bag after going headfirst into her shirt.

Tuesday had received the storybook ending that most little girls dreamed about. She got her Prince Charming in the form of Marcus and lived in a big white castle in Beverly Hills. Prada,

Gucci, and Dior were overflowing in closets large enough to get lost in. She had cars and jewelry and more money than she could spend. Most importantly she had Danielle and Tanisha: finally a family.

So why was she at a low-rent bungalow in West Hollywood putting it all at risk?

Like most transplants, Tuesday soon realized that Los Angeles was the most image-conscious city in the world, where every waitress, check-out girl, and parking valet was a model-slash-actress in waiting. Tuesday had always been thick, so the thirty-five pounds of baby weight she picked up carrying Tanisha did little for her self-esteem. Neither did turning forty. So the millions she poured into renovating the entire thirtieth floor at Abel to create a first-class gym just seemed like a conscientious move for her and the employees.

Tuesday only hoped to reclaim some semblance of the banging body that had been as much a trademark as her color-changing eyes. She knew she would never again be the same bad bitch who used to cause thunderstorms when she danced at the Bounce House but wasn't ready to let it all turn to pudding. Building the company gym had only been about keeping herself tight for her husband. She never intended to meet anyone.

She never intended for her and a co-worker's innocent flirting to lead to an innocent lunch date. She never intended for their innocent friendship to become a not-so-innocent relationship.

There was nothing innocent about what just happened in that bungalow, and what had been happening several times a week for the past four months.

Tuesday left Shaun sleeping on the bed, grabbed her purse, then rushed into the adjoining bathroom. Inside she checked her phone to find twelve missed calls. She hissed a string of curse words then bit her lip in frustration.

As expected, most were from Brandon and the office sprinkled in with a few random numbers that were unimportant, but the final three were from her husband. Those haunted her. He had started calling at fifteen minutes after seven and tried two more times in fifteen minute intervals. Seeing this was like a gut-punch that dropped Tuesday onto the toilet.

She pulled up her event calendar and saw that it was clearly marked there: *Danielle's School, 7 pm.* She had saved it in her phone, and had her secretary give her a verbal reminder, only to forget still. Tuesday had totally lost track of time, which was happening more and more often while she was with Shaun. It was bad enough that she was lying to Marcus, and being late for (if not altogether missing) board meetings and appointments at work, but now she was even flaking on her daughter.

And for what? Flawless caramel skin, an amazing body, and exotic features. Shaun was new and exciting but Marcus was her heart. It wasn't even a contest.

Tuesday stood and when she caught a glimpse of herself in the bathroom mirror, she frowned. She was ripened by time but still had the luscious lips and gray-green eyes that made her a dime. Her skin had been bronzed some by the California sun. She eventually got her body right thanks to exercise, a low-carb diet, and a little bit of cosmetic surgery. It was not her appearance that had Tuesday put off by her reflection.

She said, "Bitch, you fuckin' up!" And the twin staring back at her nodded to agree.

It was time to end this shit and she knew it.

When Tuesday came from the bathroom, Shaun was sitting up on the bed waiting. Nude, twenty-two years old, and perfect. This byproduct of a black father and Peruvian mother had a body toned by discipline and good genetics. Shaun's mind had earned that degree in accounting, but the looks had helped to pay tuition. The brief stint as a model had resulted in a few magazine spreads and video shoots as well as three hundred and fifty thousand followers on Instagram. Shaun was a gym rat whose dedication had helped to spark Tuesday. One of Tuesday's favorite pastimes was smoking some good California kush and just watching the youngster walk around the house naked.

Shaun was an Amazon, at close to five feet ten inches. When they met in the center of the room, Tuesday's four-inch heels only put her at eye level with Shaun, who was still in bare feet. Shaun's one hundred and thirty-seven pounds were always beach ready. What accentuated her figure was a pencil-thin waist and eight-pack abs. She had small up-thrust breasts with rubbery nipples that Tuesday loved to feed on almost as much as the pretty shaved pussy which always smelled and tasted of something sweet.

Tuesday took it all in, knowing that this was going to be the last time. Tuesday grabbed an ass that was well-toned from squats and leg-lifts. Their lips met for a long, slow kiss, and when Shaun tried to pull her back towards the bed, Tuesday had to stop her.

"Bae, just stay the night," Shaun said in that whiny little voice that could be cute or annoying depending on Tuesday's mood.

Tuesday gave her a look that expressed she didn't find it cute at the moment. It was a stupid comment because Shaun knew better.

"Shit, I was supposed to be home like three hours ago." She shrugged her bag onto her shoulder. "I missed another meeting with the board members today. Worse, I missed Dani's competition! My husband and daughter probably flippin' a coin right now to see which of 'em get to kill me."

Shaun pouted the way she always did when Tuesday brought up her family. "I'm beginning to think you and him ain't gone ever have that talk."

Tuesday rolled her eyes. The talk Shaun wanted her to have with Marcus was never going to happen. Tuesday had only said it would to placate her, and Shaun was finally starting to realize that. Even if she did like to fuck a bad bitch once in a while, to Tuesday her family was, is, and always would be first.

Shaun went to the bed and yanked off the sheet to cover herself. It was to say that Tuesday had lost the privilege of seeing her beautiful body.

Tuesday turned to leave. "I gotta go."

There was a finality in those three words that Shaun could

pick up on. She snatched off the three-carat diamond earrings that Tuesday bought for her a week prior and threw them at her.

"Here, I don't want 'em and I don't want *you*. Bye! D'you know how many women and men try to holla at me every day? Shit, look at me. Just on my floor I got six or seven people lined up for a shot at me. You think a fine muthafucka like me can't do no better than a bitch who old enough to be my momma?"

Tuesday didn't feed. She understood that it was just Shaun's youth and immaturity giving vent to her pain. Tuesday didn't even bother to pick up the earrings. She stepped over them on her way out of the bedroom.

"Maybe I should go see HR in the morning. Tell 'em that the chief executive officer came on to me in the gym, told me that if I didn't go out with her, I'd lose my job. What if I did that?"

Tuesday stopped and threatened her with a look.

While the company had no official policy against employees dating, her and Shaun's relationship was inappropriate, which was why they took great care to play it low-key at work. Outside of Tuesday's marriage, their respective ranks within the company did violate the unwritten rules of the corporate caste system. If a low-level drone from the accounting department went to human resources and claimed that the owner's wife and CEO used her position as leverage, it could cause a scandal. Bill Cosby and Harvey Weinstein's accusers had opened the floodgates, only to be pushed wider by the #metoo movement. Powerful people making unwanted sexual advances against their subordinates had embroiled many celebrities and had recently become the media vultures' favorite carrion.

"Going to HR wouldn't be the smartest thing you did," said Tuesday. "My family doesn't like unwanted attention, and you'll be surprised how far we'll go to keep our names out of the press."

Tuesday saw in Shaun's face that the message was received. She turned and continued her exit.

"Wait." Shaun ran down the hall after her.

Tuesday was in the living room a few feet from the door when

Shaun came and wrapped her up from behind. Shaun was a big girl and Tuesday was too old to be fighting. There was a Heckler in her bag; her alias Tabitha King had a license to carry in the state of California. She liked Shaun, but if she tried to go *Fatal Attraction*, Tuesday wasn't above shooting this bitch.

"Please, baby, please. Just listen to me."

She spun Tuesday to face her. Shaun needed all her beauty and the sincerity in those sparkling brown eyes to make her final plea. "Tabitha, that nigga will *never* love you as much as I do. NEVER."

Tuesday stared back at her with eyes that were hard and gray. All the green had vanished from them.

"And I will never love you as much as I love HIM."

Shaun stumbled backwards, holding her chest as if the words were a gun blast. Her face contorted, her lips quivered.

Tuesday saw the buckling of the emotional dam and could pinpoint the exact second when Shaun's heart had broken. Tears spilled in a steady stream. She ran to the couch, flopped down hard, and began to bawl like a child.

Everything Tuesday had in her wanted to go and console her friend but she couldn't. This was always going to end ugly, and Tuesday knew it even if the youngster didn't. She left that cheap bungalow in West Hollywood. Tuesday pulled the door closed to the sound of Shaun calling her a thousand different kinds of bitch.

Chapter Two

By the time Tuesday made it home, dusk had descended and the landscape lighting bathed the limestone facade of the big Grecian mansion in a luminous white. The portico over the front entrance was supported by huge columns with decorative acanthus capitals. Out front, statues of Aphrodite and Athena stood post on either side of a wide, reflecting pond where a fountain sprayed water jets into the air that resembled arcs of gold coins when dazzled by the moonlight. Tuesday often thought that their house looked like something that should sit atop Mount Olympus rather than be a home for ordinary mortals.

She parked her white SLS AMG Benz beneath the portico behind Marcus's black G Wagon SUV and the two-tone Rolls Royce Wraith they shared. The rest of their toys were kept in the attached garage. She sighed when she saw her stepfather's Bentley Mulsanne, only because she had hoped to avoid him until tomorrow.

Tuesday killed the engine but didn't get out. She wasn't quite ready to face her family. For a second she just sat there behind the wheel of her two-hundred-thousand-dollar car, looking out over the grounds of her thirty-million-dollar estate.

Life was good. In fact, life was so damned good that it was easy to forget how hard things used to be. Just three years ago, Tuesday would spend months plotting a lick that might only net her twelve grand when now she could easily spend ten times that in a single trip to the Hermes store. She had forgotten about those lonely nights in her one-room condo, eating microwave dinners with only her cat for company: no family, no man, and so horny that she was going through fresh batteries every few days. She promised herself that she would never take Marcus and the girls for granted, but that was exactly what she had done. That was why she had to cut Shaun loose.

Tuesday never hid the fact that she was bisexual; she and Marcus had even tag-teamed a few thots. Those times had been just for fun but Tuesday broke the rules when it came to Shaun. First, she had kept her a secret, and second, she had gotten emotionally attached. She knew it was no excuse, but the past few months had produced a change in her husband. He was more reclusive, opting to work from his home office rather than be at Abel. Marcus had never kept many friends but he was being less social with the few people in his inner circle.

While he was physically more available to Tuesday and the girls, spending lots of time with them, mentally he still seemed to be elsewhere. Even when he was laughing and playing ticklemonster with Tanisha, there would flash a far-off look in his eyes that gave Tuesday concern.

Their sex had even suffered, but only because Tuesday felt like he wasn't connecting with her emotionally. There was no drop-off in his skill or stamina, in fact, over the past month Marcus had been wanting her more than ever, and he still earned a standing ovation from that ass whenever he hit it from the back. Still, Tuesday didn't enjoy it as much because she sensed he was only using her as a distraction from some problem he was secretly dealing with.

Tuesday's repeated inquiries were met by casual dismissals. A few times he offered simple explanations that she knew were only to shut her up.

Although Marcus was being distant, Tuesday knew that it didn't justify her creeping with Shaun. Marcus had done so much so for her that she felt he could ignore her for a year and it didn't warrant her sneaking behind his back. This was selfish and potentially dangerous considering what happened to the last woman who cheated on him.

Her husband did so well at disguising himself as Marcus King, respectable entrepreneur and philanthropist, that Tuesday sometimes forgot about his alter ego, Sebastian Caine: ruthless drug lord. An ex-fiancée had done him dirty in the past and gotten her head chopped off because of it. Tuesday didn't think Marcus was that person anymore but knew betrayal could bring the worst out in people.

Many women who went both ways often used the saying "eatin' ain't cheatin' " but Tuesday didn't subscribe to this. She knew if she caught Marcus with a young side-piece, Tuesday would kill that bitch even if she was only sucking his dick.

But she never had to worry about this because Marcus was fiercely loyal. She knew how rare that was in a man and it made her feel even worse.

A flawless fourteen-carat cushion-cut diamond dominated her left hand. She glanced at it, feeling unworthy of the ring or the man who gave it to her.

After a little more self-loathing, Tuesday finally let up the gullwing door on her AMG and entered the house. They had twenty-two thousand square feet under one roof: eight bedrooms, fourteen baths, two elevators, two indoor pools, a gym with a sauna and a home theater. Carrera marble ran throughout the first floor, and the grand staircase in the foyer was adorned with custom brass balustrades designed by Versace. From the ceiling, twenty-five feet above, hung decadent chandeliers made in Paris by some designer with a name Tuesday still couldn't pronounce.

There was a time when Tuesday had been intimidated by the big white house, but it quickly became as comfortable as an old slipper.

All the staff had already gone for the day so the house was quiet and still.

Tuesday had been gone since breakfast and had eaten nothing the entire day—except for Shaun. They had two kitchens, a gourmet kitchen plus an executive chef's commercial kitchen, which they only used to cater formal gatherings. The first was the smaller of the two and where Tuesday immediately went for a snack.

The granite countertops were spotless and the stainless steel appliances shone like polished chrome. Dinner was typically prepared by their personal chef and Tuesday figured that the family already ate without her. She found a veggie lasagna in the refrigerator and reheated a slice. For dessert she stole four of the walnut chocolate chip cookies their housekeeper Esperanza baked especially for Marcus. Tuesday was at the center cook island nibbling on one with a glass of milk when Brandon entered the kitchen.

To the world, Brandon King was Marcus's father and the face of their legitimate empire. In truth, he and Marcus were not even related—a secret known to no one outside the three of them. Brandon had played the right-hand and enforcer to her husband back when he was known as Sebastian Caine. People would look at this handsome elderly gentleman with his tailored pinstriped suits, salt-and-pepper curls, and friendly smile, thinking he belonged on the cover of *GQ* magazine. They would never suspect that he had once been one of the most notorious hit men in the country.

He perched himself on the stool next to hers. "We missed you today."

"Sorry, I had an appointment that ran long." Tuesday was staring straight ahead trying to avoid the judgment in his eyes. "When I knew I wouldn't make it, I sent you a text and told my secretary to take notes. I'll look 'em over tomorrow."

The appointment she was referring to was at the salon. Tuesday just wasn't in the mood to deal with work this day. While the rest of Abel Incorporated's senior staff was taking care of business, Tuesday was out with her girlfriend getting their hair and nails done.

His tone was sympathetic: "Hey look, I get it. Boring ass three-hour meeting and you decided to play hooky. Who wants to listen to stuffed suits go on and on about Pakistan's changing export regulations and how they'll affect our market share? Shit, I wish I could skip 'em too. But as the chief executive officer, and one of the Kings to boot, that's not a good look for the company or the fam."

Guilt slumped her shoulders; she offered a nod. She knew that what she did at Abel reflected back on Marcus and Brandon, which was why fucking with Shaun was doubly stupid. The two of them had worked extremely hard to conceal their pasts and build the Kings' reputation. They were proud of the name even though neither of them were born with it.

Tuesday swallowed more milk. "Why is he doing this? He knows I don't have the slightest fuckin' idea of what I'm doin.' Most of the time I'm just sittin' in my office, looking stupid and signing shit I barely understand."

"It was his decision," Brandon said, breaking himself off a piece of her cookie. "It's not like he listens to me. Just made me pour another hundred million into the scholarship program. I told him it would kill our third quarter profits but I'm just the puppet; we both know who pulls the strings."

Being in charge was something Tuesday never wanted. When she first came to California, Marcus hadn't just set Tuesday up with a new identity; he gave her a job in his company. It was an advisory position that basically allowed her to collect a six-figure salary with no actual responsibility. In fact, Tuesday never had to even show up at the office.

Then after years of allowing Brandon to run the company while Marcus played the background, he stepped in and made

Brandon hand the reins over to Tuesday and demoted Brandon to executive vice president. The old man didn't think it was wise and Tuesday was in full agreement but for some reason Marcus had insisted.

She said: "The only business I ever ran was a booty club and it did so bad I still had to rob niggas on the side. Why in the hell does he think I can handle running a big ass corporation?"

"Do you remember the very first conversation you and I had? It was when I picked you up from that police station just as he was going on the run."

Tuesday remembered. It was three years ago, her last night in Detroit. The feds had held her for an entire day sweating her about Marcus but she gave up nothing. When she saw the suave assassin pull up in that Maybach, Tuesday had first thought Brandon was there to kill her.

"One of the first things I told you about my boss is to never try to figure him out," he reminded her. "You'll never be able to do it and you'll only drive yourself crazy in the process." Brandon playfully nudged her with his shoulder and Tuesday smiled because he was right.

"He been actin' weird lately," she said, serious again. "It's something he ain't tellin' us."

"Of course there's something he's not telling us," the elder said laughing. "Did you forget who he is?"

Tuesday understood that her husband was better than most at keeping secrets. He had survived the game at the highest level for over two decades by being clandestine. Sebastian Caine had done business only through intermediaries; buyers and suppliers never got to see his face. Even the people within his organization never dealt with him directly. This was how he eventually became known as The Invisible Man.

Brandon pecked her cheek then stood to leave. "And if I gotta' sit through those meetings bored out my mind then you do too. If he asks, tell 'em I got on your back about not showing up."

Tuesday agreed that she would.

Even though he wasn't Marcus's real father, Brandon had come to be a father figure to her. He was the one who held down Tuesday and Danielle that first year. She was pregnant with Tanisha while Marcus was running from a federal indictment. Since then, Brandon had served as a sounding board and counselor.

She sat there a while longer thinking, relishing the combination of chocolate, walnut and brown sugar. Despite the warning, she couldn't help but try to understand why her husband would hand over his Fortune 500 company to a woman who didn't attend high school. Even Tuesday didn't think her pussy was *that* good. She sensed some angle Marcus was working just beyond her comprehension. Either Brandon couldn't see it either or was in on it and just role-playing. She couldn't decide which.

After the final cookie, she made sure to wipe the crumbs from her lips.

Chapter Three

Tuesday entered the family room to find her husband on the sofa and Danielle on the one that sat adjacent. Like most nine-year-olds, Danielle's attention was consumed by her phone. Tuesday didn't know if she was texting a friend or playing a game.

"Dani, I'm so sorry I missed your thing but—"

The girl just stood up and brushed past Tuesday before she could finish the apology. Danielle left the room without saying a word. She didn't even throw Tuesday a "fuck-you" glance.

Whether justified or not, Tuesday felt totally disrespected by that and started to go after her until she was held up by Marcus.

"You might wanna give that a minute," he said, never looking up from his book. "After the way you left her hangin' today, she straight on you right now."

"I get she's mad but damn, to just walk off while I'm trying to talk to her is some other shit! I'm out here running errands and looking at real estate and just got caught up."

Marcus knew that Tuesday had been looking to open a boutique that sold fashion-forward clothes for women with her body type, and for six months had been checking out different commercial properties. Lately, however, the store search had just been her cover for spending time with Shaun.

He turned a page. "Just lost track of time. Happens to the best of us."

Tuesday wasn't sure if he believed her or not. She thought Marcus would make an excellent poker player because the nigga had no tells.

She asked, "Did her school win?"

He nodded. "They had a little struggle but baby brought it home for her team. She calculated the square root of a number I couldn't even fit in my head."

He switched gears. "See Brandon before he left?"

"Yeah, I talked to 'em." She made a point to add in: "And got cursed out for missing the staff meeting."

"Should've been there."

"I told you I had a crazy day," she said defensively.

Marcus was cool. He just continued reading for a while then said, "I see you got your hair and nails done."

He stated this as if it were just an observation but Tuesday read an accusation into it. She knew how fucked up this looked: on a day where she bailed on work and missed their daughter's academic contest, to then stand in front of him with a fresh hair-do. She couldn't even tell how he noticed, being that he hadn't turned away from his book since she walked in.

Tuesday started to craft a lie that would explain it all then thought better of it. Her husband was the sharpest person she had ever met and anything she concocted would only insult his intelligence. Rather than dig a deeper hole, she just let the matter drop.

Marcus was wearing what had basically become his uniform as of late: a crispy wifebeater, long hoop shorts and ankle socks. He was in the house so much that Tuesday hardly remembered the last time she'd seen him dressed in anything that didn't have a Jordan logo.

She took the opposite end of the sofa, kicked off her shoes, put her feet on the cushions and tucked them underneath his thigh for warmth. Marcus just tossed her a side-glance then kept reading.

" 'Nisha sleep?"

"She crashed around seven thirty." He consulted a Chrono-swiss timepiece Tuesday bought for him last year. "So she gone be up about two in the morning, full of energy and ready to play. Have fun with that."

She rolled her eyes and gave him the finger. When he seemed too consumed with his book to feed into it she asked, "What'cho reading?"

"*Meditations* by Marcus Aurelius. He was the emperor of Rome in the second century, and one of its most brilliant field generals. He was also last of the great stoic philosophers."

"I know who he is," she lied. Tuesday had practically grown up in the strip club and gained her knowledge from the years spent there and in the stick-up game. On the other hand, Marcus had an intelligence that went beyond the hood. While he obviously had enough street smarts to get heavy in the dope game, her husband had also been to college and was a voracious reader. He was never condescending to Tuesday, but talking to him sometimes highlighted her eighth-grade education, and made her feel inadequate.

She said, "It ain't like I don't read stuff too."

"All the time," he agreed. "You ever finish the book I gave you?"

Tuesday couldn't tell if he was being sarcastic or not. "I'm working through it."

"Okay."

"I'm gonna finish it."

He turned another page. "Okay."

She hissed, "With everything I gotta do at Abel, I just don't get a lotta time to read."

He shrugged. "Take your time."

It irritated the hell out of Tuesday when he acted like this, nonchalant like nothing she did or didn't do mattered to him either way.

She erupted, "I'm not stupid, Marcus. I just got a lot I'm dealing with right now."

He finally put down the book to look at her. "Who said you're stupid? Bae, we both know your head is the main reason I'm with you."

Tuesday didn't miss the joke. He did that goofy little grin that brought out his dimples, and it was that easy for him to defuse her attitude, to make her smile.

"Oh, so now I'm just a trophy wife who's only job is to pleasure you?"

"A trophy?" He laughed. "Winners get trophies—you're a punishment. What fucked up contest did I lose to deserve you?"

Tuesday clubbed him with a sofa pillow and their playful wrestling match quickly turned sexual. Tuesday was sitting across his lap while his large hands roamed her body, squeezed her titties and rubbed her thighs.

This was what had attracted her to Marcus from the very beginning: their chemistry. The way they played with each other and slipped one another; for Tuesday it was like being with her best friend. Lately he had been withdrawn, and she could still tell something was weighing on him, but none of that had taken away his appeal. Tuesday was still absolutely crazy about him.

Growing up she had been that light-skinned girl who always crushed harder on the darkest boys. Marcus was a well-built six-foot-three with skin the color of Hershey bar chocolate. He stayed clean-shaven other than a thin mustache and goatee. Healthy living and exercise made him appear ten years younger than his forty-four.

Marcus slid his hands up her skirt but when he went in for a kiss, Tuesday turned away from it.

"Boy stop. What if Dani come back in here? Plus, why you

wanna kiss me if I'm such a horrible punishment?" It was a clever diversion. Tuesday had just been with Shaun and wasn't so dirty as to kiss her husband with another bitch's pussy on her lips.

She wanted him but needed the opportunity to clean up first. So when she said, "I'm going to take a shower," it was an invitation for him to join her.

Her husband looked suspicious. For a long moment he just stared at her, his eyes narrowed. Then he said, "You ain't slick muthafucka. I know why you don't wanna kiss me."

Tuesday's heart suddenly shifted from first to fifth gear. Her mouth went dry and it seemed harder to breathe.

"I know you been in there eatin' my damn cookies," he said through a smirk. "Esperanza make those just for me. Everybody know how I feel 'bout my walnut chocolate chip joints."

"I'm sorry bae," she said after a relieved gasp. She covered her mouth as if embarrassed. "I only got you for a few of 'em."

He shook his head. "Yo' greedy ass."

She grabbed his dick and massaged it through the thin nylon shorts. "Let's go upstairs and I'll show you how greedy I really am."

"Go on up. Just let me knock out the rest of this chapter."

Tuesday snatched the book. "I got something more important I need you to knock out."

"C'mon bae, I'll meet you up there in twenty minutes." There it was again, that far-off look flashed within his warm brown eyes.

Tuesday could feel his stiffness in her hand so she knew he wanted to fuck, but she returned his book also knowing the time he required had nothing to do with his interest in the Roman emperor.

Tuesday didn't press him about it because she wasn't trying to spoil the mood. Instead, she tried to tempt her man with the one thing she knew had always been his weakness.

The only bonus to gaining so much baby weight was that a lot of it had gone to her husband's favorite places. Tuesday always had a fat ass but the pregnancy had basically given her a free butt augmentation without the surgery or silicone.

Working out with Shaun had helped to shed the excess around her stomach while toning the addition to her hips and thighs. The result was a slender waist with an all-natural booty as plump and round as two basketballs: Marcus's kryptonite.

Her tight skirt accentuated her curves, and when she stood directly in front of him, she made a show of picking up her shoes by slowly bending over right in his face. Tuesday twerked a little bit and made her ass bounce like Jell-O.

He smacked it. "You know you gone pay for that right?"

"Whatever. Just read yo' book, nerd." Tuesday strutted off, putting plenty of extra swing in her hips. Before leaving the room, she looked back to catch him staring.

Tuesday smiled to herself. She hoped she had just cut that twenty-minute wait in half.

Chapter Four

Upstairs, Tuesday stopped by the nursery to look in on her baby girl. Tanisha was sleeping peacefully with a thumb in her mouth. Physically Tuesday saw so much of herself and Marcus in their daughter; however, it amazed her that at two years, eleven months, Tanisha had already developed a personality distinct from either of theirs. Tuesday just watched her sleep for a while then tiptoed out through the minefield of toys scattered over the floor.

Marcus had warned her to give Danielle some space, but Tuesday felt what she had to say couldn't wait.

Danielle's room was heaven for a nine-year-old girl. She had an army of plush dolls and stuffed animals as well as a huge LCD television with an assortment of the latest games. In the corner was a six-foot play maze in the shape of a castle that Danielle could crawl into whenever she felt like playing princess. She also had a saltwater aquarium with tropical fish and a cage for her pet ferret.

Growing up in Detroit, Tuesday had shared a bed with her mother for most of her childhood, and had to sleep on the couch whenever her mother had company, which was often. She didn't get her own room until she was thirteen and it wasn't a fraction of the size of Danielle's. The only amenities were a twelve-inch black and white TV, a twin-sized bed supported by milk crates, and piss-stained sheets hanging as curtains. All she could claim for pets were the rats and roaches that came standard with every run-down flat her mother moved them to.

Tuesday was happy that her daughters would never know the struggle but was also a little envious. She spoiled the girls as much as Marcus and sometimes worried over that.

Danielle had a full-sized bed with pink lace and flouncing to continue the princess motif. She was lying on her stomach in her school uniform, hair split into twin pigtails with large spiral curls. Unlike her sibling, Danielle carried none of Tuesday's or Marcus's features. Each year Tuesday watched her grow into a more beautiful young lady, but one whose origins were a mystery.

She studied from a tablet; next to it was a thick open textbook on spherical trigonometry. When Tuesday sat on her bed, Danielle turned and faced the wall.

"Dani, I know I missed your competition tonight and I know you mad at me. I'm sorry if you feel like I let you down."

Danielle had always been a bright girl but about a year back her teachers observed an extremely high aptitude for science and mathematics, prompting Marcus to have her placed in advanced classes. She had become the star of her school's academic team that competed against other prep schools in *Jeopardy*-style quiz battles.

Tuesday continued: "But being mad don't give you no excuse to disrespect me. The way you treated me downstairs wasn't cool and I'm not havin' that. D'you understand?"

Danielle lay on the opposite side of the bed quiet and still. She seemed to be just waiting for Tuesday to leave.

Tuesday didn't appreciate being ignored. "Girl, you hear me talkin' to you! You don't get to disrespect me, Dani. Ever!" It was the fiercest tone she had ever taken with her stepdaughter. "Now tell me you understand!"

Danielle never looked back at her. "I understand. I'm sorry, Tabitha."

That was a low blow and Tuesday felt it. A little more than three years back she had come into Danielle's life as Tabitha Green, but they had long since crossed that bridge. One of the proudest days in Tuesday's life was when Danielle had started calling her "Momma." For her to revert to using "Tabitha" really stung Tuesday. Worse was that Danielle was smart enough to know this.

To Tuesday, the room reflected the struggle of an immature little girl dealing with an adult-sized intellect. Above the plush toys and Barbie dolls were shelves holding books on Newtonian physics and college-level algebra.

Pride wouldn't allow Tuesday to show any pain. "Well congratulations on your win. I'm really proud of you."

When Danielle didn't respond, Tuesday just slipped out of the room thinking perhaps that Marcus was right and she should've waited.

Tuesday still couldn't believe that in such a short period she had gone from never wanting children to not being able to imagine her life without them. It was Danielle who had changed Tuesday's opinions about kids. At six, she had been so much more mature than her years, and the dedication Marcus showed her as a single parent was a big reason why Tuesday had fallen for him. The girl had made such an impression that Tuesday risked her own life to get Danielle back when she was kidnapped.

It wasn't long ago that she and Danielle were tight, but their relationship had slowly changed over the previous year. Danielle's attitude had become more hostile, snapping at everybody, even her little sister. When her face wasn't buried in a book, it was hard to get three words out of her.

Tuesday noticed she changed around the same time Marcus put her in those advanced classes and didn't think it was a coincidence. Danielle started coming home with more homework than Tuesday thought was suitable for a girl her age, and the shit was so complicated that Tuesday couldn't help with it. She believed the pressure was too much. She shared her theory with Marcus, but he dismissed it as a phase.

Tuesday often wondered about Danielle's real parents and how she came to be with Marcus. She knew her husband well enough to know he didn't adopt her through any legal means. Tuesday had heard a rumor involving the murder of his former friend, but Marcus never confirmed this and she never asked. Her husband was better than most at keeping secrets.

Tuesday spent a half hour in the shower waiting for Marcus to join her but he never did. She left the master bathroom attached to their room expecting him to be on the bed waiting for her. When he wasn't, Tuesday figured he was still downstairs pretending to read while dealing with whatever was on his mind.

She started to put on something sexy for him then decided he didn't deserve it. She shed her bathrobe, and after taking a minute to lotion up, slipped into an oversized Detroit Tigers T-shirt.

If he was going to preoccupy himself with a book, Tuesday decided to do the same. A few months back, Marcus had gifted her a copy of *The Art of War* by Sun Tzu. It was the small abridged version with only thirteen short chapters, but Tuesday hadn't been able to get past the second. Each time she tried to attack it her attention wandered. It wasn't that Tuesday couldn't read, she just didn't enjoy it that much.

The paperback was on her nightstand where it sat untouched for three weeks. She picked it up and stretched across the bed to get comfortable. Tuesday couldn't understand why Marcus thought this was so great that she needed to read it. Some Chinese man who had been dead for thousands of years discussing war strategy with horses and chariots when niggas had AK's now. It didn't seem relevant. She forced herself to concentrate on the page, on the words no matter how badly her mind wanted to jump to other things.

Tuesday only made it through six pages before she traded the book for the TV remote. She switched on their monstrous ninety-two inch Samsung, more interested in the wars fought between the ladies on the *Real Housewives of Atlanta*.

Marcus had obviously been watching CNN, and Tuesday was about to change the channel when a news report caught her attention. The caption read: "One of the Largest Drug Busts in History," and curiosity made Tuesday turn up the volume.

Thanks to a joint task force between Mexican and US agencies, the number of seizures along the Texas border had quadrupled in the past eleven months, culminating in this record breaker. A shipment containing twelve tons of cocaine had been intercepted. The product was concealed within the filth of three sewage-treatment tanker trucks. On the screen, two uniformed officials wearing proud smiles stood behind a pallet stacked with bundled kilos. A Republican senator credited the President's new wall, saying that it had plugged all the cracks in the border, forcing illegal immigrants and drug smugglers into riskier methods. Several law enforcement experts patted themselves on the back and speculated about the damage this latest blow had done to the Mexican and South American cartels.

Tuesday only gave CNN forty-five seconds of her attention before she switched to Bravo and caught up with the petty drama between NeNe Leaks and Candi Burress.

At the time, she couldn't imagine how that news story was about to change the lives of her entire family.

Chapter Five

Tuesday was thirty-five minutes into her favorite reality show when she heard Marcus approaching from the hall. She quickly shut off the TV and killed the lamp on her nightstand.

He entered their two-thousand-square foot master bedroom to find all the lights out. Tuesday was curled up on their custom ultra-king-sized bed with her back to him.

She ignored him when he called her name. Tuesday knew it was a childish game. It was just like the one Danielle had just played with her, but still, she was mad at him. As a woman she felt she had the God-given right to aggravate her man.

Marcus slid beneath the sheets and closed the distance between them. Tuesday didn't respond to the feel of his warm body against hers. When he draped his big muscular arm around her, Tuesday didn't move.

"Baby listen," his voice was a bass-filled whisper right at her ear. "Don't insult my intelligence by faking like you sleep and I won't keep insulting yours by faking like nothing's wrong."

Tuesday sucked her teeth. It was the only acknowledgement she was willing to give.

He said, "I been trippin' lately because I gotta meeting coming up and I'm really not looking forward to it."

Tuesday had expected something much worse than some boring meeting like the one she skipped out on. "Just send Brandon in your place."

"Can't. It's something I have to deal with in person."

Tuesday turned on him. Even in the gloom the worry could be seen in her gray-green eyes. Without needing to be told, she already knew what type of meeting this was and why he had been sweating it. He was not being called to attend as Marcus King; this was a meeting for Sebastian Caine.

"Who's calling this sit-down?"

"The type of people you can't say no to." He didn't elaborate and Tuesday didn't need him to. As a rule, he had never done business in person, so anyone who could demand the presence of Sebastian Caine was definitely somebody to be feared.

"But I still don't know why they want you. You've been through with that life." Her last statement had the ring of a question just in case there was something Marcus wasn't telling her.

"I've been completely legit for years but I'm also connected to shit you're never really out of. I still have dues I have to pay and obligations I have to meet."

She asked, "Everything gone be okay?"

"Yeah. Just a couple of people gone be there I ain't never want to see again. That's all."

Tuesday appreciated the explanation, but knew there was more. She had watched her husband stress over something for months and now he was trying to convince her that this meeting was nothing to stress over. "If this ain't no big deal then why you been so down lately?"

Marcus rolled onto his back, expelled a heavy breath. "You've never heard of Rene Rodriguez—I know it without having to ask. He's a Mexican immigrant who been living in San Antonio since the sixties, and on the low is one of the richest muthafuckas in America. Rene had control of the border towns in Texas and been responsible for half the product coming up from Mexico since the early eighties.

"When I was twenty-two, I was down there working for his son. I was just a goon but, for whatever reason, the old man took a shine to me. After his son died, Rene became like a father to me—and this was back when a lot of Latinos wasn't fucking with blacks like that. You never wondered how a regular nigga like me was able to get plugged on that level? Rene was my connect— later on, he gave me his blessing to start my own thing."

Tuesday was fascinated because Marcus never talked about his past. Most of what she knew about Sebastian Caine was centered around myths that circulated through the hood, despite the fact that they slept in the same bed and were raising two children together.

She started to piece things together for herself. "Rene's got to be pretty old by now. He's dying. That's what this whole thing is about?"

Marcus rewarded her correct assessment with a brief smile. "Stage four liver cancer—he doesn't have long. A group of us have to discuss how things are gonna shake out after he's gone. I also have to go pay my respects."

Tuesday was hungry for more but knew that even this small scrap of information was like a buffet when coming from him. It still put her at ease somewhat since she could now understand his concerns.

She asked, "When do you have to go?"

"Next week. I'm leaving on Wednesday."

Tuesday moved closer to him. Her eyes were gray and serious when she said, "Thank you for telling me."

He pulled back the silky black hair that hung to conceal part of her face. "Bae, I'm wrong for not telling you sooner. Even with the rings and kids, I know sometimes it just feel like we're playing family. But in order for our thing to be real, we have to let each other in."

Marcus was bathed in the violet glow that filtered into the window, falling across their bed. He stared at her through coffee-colored eyes with thick brows. His neatly-trimmed goatee framed pink juicy lips.

Tuesday didn't know at what point she started kissing them. She just found herself on top of Marcus, pulling off his wife-beater. He had a broad chest from years of lifting weights which Tuesday covered with light kisses.

He stopped her as she pecked her way down his eight-pack abs. "If you gone hook me up, do it right."

Tuesday looked up at him. "What'cho mean?"

"I'm just sayin' if you gone bless me, bless me with the real shit. Don't shortchange me."

Tuesday smirked. "Nigga, I know you ain't sayin' my head done got whack?"

"Not whack because you better than most when you ain't even trying. But you ain't been giving me yo' best either. Lately you ain't been goin' hard."

Tuesday pretended like she didn't know what he was talking about when she actually did. The distance between them had Tuesday capping him off more out of obligation than genuine enthusiasm. She didn't notice the drop-off in her performance but he obviously had.

"Or maybe you was just saving your best tongue work for yo' girl?"

That came out of left field and caught Tuesday totally off guard. Her eyes went buck but she caught herself before she gave away too much. "Boy, what is you talkin' bout?"

Marcus gave her a *bitch please* look. "You really gone sit here and do that?

"At first I ain't give a fuck cause I figure it was just you havin' some fun, relieving some stress. But now it's affecting shit at work and at home. You need to shut that shit down like yesterday."

Tuesday didn't know why she was so surprised that Marcus knew about Shaun; since she had known him he made it his business to know about everything that happened around him. She didn't think he actually had people following her but couldn't rule that out either. Her husband had enough clout to have somebody in the CIA watching her with a satellite.

Tuesday was busted but still tried to play dumb. "Bae, for real. What'cho talkin' about?"

Marcus just smiled. He saw the game she wanted to play and just left it alone. "So what's happenin'? Can a nigga still get hooked up or what?"

Tuesday had always taken pride in her skills and felt some type of way at hearing her man was not satisfied. She wanted to make up for that and remind him of what she could do. So when she tugged down his shorts, she devoured the dick. She took the length of him hungrily, all throat and no hands. Marcus cuffed the back of her head and groaned in ecstasy.

It hardly took five minutes of Tuesday using her special corkscrew technique to push him to a powerful explosion. He cursed out loud, unloaded into her warm, wet mouth while she continued to suck and swallow.

Marcus was lying on his back, head still spinning when Tuesday asked, "Was that my A-game or what?"

"Oh, now you gone get arrogant. Bitch come here!"

He pulled Tuesday on top of him and when he pulled off her Tigers T-shirt, there was nothing underneath because, while he might not have earned the sexy lingerie, she still knew she was going to fuck him. She teased his semi-hard dick back to a full erection then sat on it and began to grind in slow circles.

Most of the rich housewives were flocking to get plastic surgery and Tuesday was no exception. She only got a boob job because nursing Tanisha had left her tits deflated. She selected a modest 36C that looked and felt natural.

She was on top riding Marcus while he matched her rhythm with upward thrusts. That big dick was hitting her spot and she couldn't control herself. He sat up to feed on her nipples while putting fingers in her ass. Marcus stroked her deep and told her the pussy was his and Tuesday moaned in agreement.

What Shaun and many previous lovers couldn't accept was that, while Tuesday sometimes used women for recreation, she could never be a full-on lesbian. She was too attracted to masculinity. With women Tuesday typically took the more dominant role but at heart was a submissive. She loved rough sex and was most turned on when being manhandled and controlled in the way that only a thuggish nigga could.

So when Marcus flipped her onto her stomach and pushed into her from behind, she was already cumming again. He had her face down on her knees, tugging at a fistful of new weave. He pounded her from the back and groaned, "Damn bitch, 'dis ass so fat!" and the sound of it slapping against his pelvis echoed throughout the room.

Forty-five minutes and two positions later, Tuesday was on top again, riding him reverse cowgirl. Marcus had rolled a blunt from their personal stash of premium kush. They passed it back and forth while Tuesday put on a show, tossing her hair, licking her fingers. She knew her husband was enjoying the view of his bad bitch dancing on his dick in slow motion. Tuesday was so hot and wet that Marcus joked that she had a Jacuzzi in her pussy.

She was in a trance with her eyes closed and about to bust again when Marcus suddenly stopped mid-stroke. She knew her man well enough to know he didn't cum. "Bae, what's wrong?"

"You ain't gone believe this shit," he whispered low through a mouthful of smoke. "Guess who standing over there lookin' me right in my muthafuckin' face?"

Tuesday glanced across their spacious bedroom and in the gloom could see Tanisha's tiny silhouette. Their two-year-old daughter stood just inside the half-opened door silently watching them.

"You forgot to lock it," hissed Tuesday. She snatched the sheet to cover herself. "Shit! How long she been there?"

"I don't know, but just be cool. We ain't gotta make this weird for her. She too young to know what she seeing anyway. If we don't act like we doin' nothing wrong then it'll be straight."

He called to her: "Hey, Nisha. What'cho doin' outta bed?"

Tanisha started to whine the way kids do when they think they're in trouble.

Marcus put out the blunt and tried to fan away the smoke. "It's okay Ni Ni, I'm not mad at you. Come here. Come to Da-Da."

Tanisha shuffled over to their bed wearing Wonder Woman pajamas and holding the stuffed toy bunny that was her constant companion. Tuesday slid off of Marcus when he picked up his daughter and kissed her forehead.

"What's the matter wit' my baby? Mommy woke you up makin' all that noise?" Tuesday kicked him under the sheets.

When Tanisha said she wanted water, Tuesday gave her a few swallows from a glass on the nightstand. Then she climbed in bed between them and made herself comfortable. Tuesday and Marcus just smirked at each other because they knew that sex was a wrap. They were back in Mommy and Daddy mode.

Tuesday had named Tanisha after her best friend who had been a casualty of the war she fought in Detroit.

She teased her. "Nisha look like she still sleepy."

The little girl shook her head for an emphatic "no" even as she let out a long yawn.

A few minutes later, Tanisha was resting her head on her father's chest with a thumb in her mouth. Tuesday was playing with the ends of her daughter's braided hair.

"I already ended that situation tonight." Tuesday saw no reason to keep lying to him when he obviously knew the truth. "I shouldn't have let it get outta hand like that."

He asked, "Was she starting to catch feelings?"

It took a few seconds before she confessed, "We both were."

Marcus gave her a kiss for support. It was his way of saying he appreciated the honesty and she would not be judged. Tuesday loved this about her man. If Tanisha wasn't there, that would've earned him some more head.

"If you don't mind me asking, what made you shut it down?"

She looked into his eyes. "She wanted the one thing from me that I wasn't willing to give."

The conversation Shaun pressed Tuesday to have with Marcus was not in regards to Tuesday leaving him. It was about Shaun joining in. She had proposed a polyamorous relationship where the three of them all lived together as one big happy family.

Tuesday pretended to think about it, but knew that was never going to happen. She understood how difficult it must have been for Shaun to see Tuesday pull off in her new Benz and head off to her big mansion while being left to struggle in the hood. Tuesday liked spending time with Shaun but wasn't looking to save a bitch. She damn sure wasn't looking to share her family or her man.

Marcus laughed. "I'm just trippin' cause yo' boy couldn't get invited to the party one time."

Tuesday was serious. "I don't mind bringin' bitches home who come to play. But that bitch wanted to stay."

Chapter Six

Early the next morning Tuesday was back at work simply because she couldn't skip a second day. The headquarters for Abel Incorporated sat in downtown Los Angeles, occupying a gleaming glass high-rise that resembled a twisted piece of art-deco sculpture. For fourteen years, Abel had grown exponentially until it had become a Fortune 500 company employing over twenty-seven hundred with assets approaching six billion dollars.

While Brandon lauded their record earnings, Marcus was most proud of its outreach within the urban community. Abel donated heavily each year to numerous causes that provided entrepreneurial opportunities or scholarships for minorities nationwide. Marcus was very passionate about them giving back. Many times Tuesday had heard him lecture on how it was their civic responsibility as a black-owned company. Her husband and stepfather disagreed on exactly how much responsibility.

While she knew Marcus's intentions were sincere, Tuesday secretly felt that his generosity was motivated by guilt. For years he had flooded those very same communities with drugs, contributing to the crime, poverty and overall destruction.

This was his way of paying restitution. Years back, she peeped the biblical connection between a man who had done so much evil under the name Caine trying to do good using the name Abel.

Tuesday always tried to downplay her sexy at work. She wore a navy-blue custom Dior pant-suit that didn't draw too much attention to her curves. She complemented the look with a white blouse and heels appropriate for the office. Insecurity still made her feel like all the white faces stared at her.

The CEO's office was on the seventieth floor. It was a massive space with plush carpeting and ultra-modern decor. The walls consisted of wooden tiles in a layered herringbone pattern, except for the rear, which was a floor-to-ceiling picture window. Its sliding door led to a narrow balcony, but the potential seven-hundred-foot drop made Tuesday enjoy her scenic view of the Pacific coast from behind the tempered glass.

Tuesday was relieved when her secretary told her she had a light agenda with no tedious meetings; however, that quickly changed when she found a mountain of paperwork waiting on the desk. Brandon's office had delivered thirty different reports from twelve departments that needed to be read and signed by the day's end.

When she first took her new identity as Tabitha Green, Marcus had given her a driver's license, birth certificate, social security card, medical records, along with detailed work and credit histories. Later he added a Master's in Business Administration once he decided to make her CEO. The forged degree from Wharton hung on the wall.

Tuesday had never stepped on a college campus and feared those working under her could sense it.

In their presence she knew to tone down the slang, to speak proper English. She knew so many others within the company were more qualified. The woman she sent on Starbucks runs actually had more education than she.

All these concerns were voiced to Marcus from the start, but as usual, he had convinced her she could handle it by running some smooth shit on her. He explained that a conductor doesn't know how to play every instrument in his orchestra. It's only his job to delegate, to make sure the wind, string, and percussion sections played together in harmony. Like a conductor, it would be her job to oversee the whole.

At the time, that analogy made sense to Tuesday but she soon found a huge flaw in it. They didn't hand a baton to any random bitch off the street who walked into Carnegie Hall.

Over the past fifteen years, rappers and every nigga on the street had screamed "I'm a Boss!" until the word had lost all credibility. Even Tuesday was guilty of this, because back when she was hitting licks, she had the nerve to call herself Boss Lady, as if owning a rundown strip club earned her the right. Being at Abel made her realize that she had no idea of what it meant to be a real boss. Thousands of people were depending on her for their livelihood. Any poor decision on her part could sink the company, costing them their homes, cars, and savings.

Hours later, Tuesday was developing a migraine and was only halfway through the second report. Some division was asking her to allocate nine million dollars for some type of fuel research for their international cargo freighters. At least that's what she got from it because the language barely made sense to her.

At lunch time, Tuesday exploded out of her office, eager to get away from the reading. Her tired eyes were starting to string the words together in an endless run-on sentence of nonsense. She needed a sandwich, a 5-Hour Energy, and a little cardio to recharge. After a cold cut combo from Subway, Tuesday was down in the company gym wearing yoga pants and a sports bra, working on an elliptical.

Tuesday had hardly built up a light sweat when she looked over to see Shaun walk in. Shaun was dressed in yellow Spandex and selected a machine only several away from hers. They always tried to keep things low-key at work but Tuesday didn't know how Shaun would respond after their blow-up last night.

First the mixed-breed beauty did some stretching that advertised her flexibility to every straight male in the gym. Then she took a swallow of Gatorade, pulled out her iPod, and stuffed her ears with music. She started going hard on a stair-climber as if oblivious to all the eyes and erections pointed in her direction.

While Shaun didn't even acknowledge Tuesday, she received the message.

Tuesday wasn't surprised that a young bitch like Shaun was playing games but wondered what else she had up. She didn't know if Shaun would keep things cool or was still planning to put their relationship on blast.

To Tuesday, the most important thing was that Marcus already knew, but still, she didn't want a scandal that would embarrass the family. For the rest of the workday Shaun's threat hovered like a storm cloud.

Chapter Seven

Marcus and Tuesday didn't go out often, especially with her husband playing hermit lately. However, Tuesday talked him into a late dinner at his favorite restaurant. They left a sitter at the house with Tanisha and Danielle, who was still giving Tuesday the cold shoulder.

It was ten thirty when they arrived at Dominic's on Wilshire Blvd. It was a family-owned restaurant that had been serving Los Angelinos the finest Italian cuisine for close to sixty years. Marcus had been a regular and then converted Tuesday when he introduced her to their veal scaloppini.

Even without a reservation, she and Marcus insisted on a table that gave them a view of the entrance without putting them too close to the bathroom.

Sometime after their order was taken, Tuesday presented him with a box containing a new Parmigiani watch from Cellini Jewelers. When he asked why, Tuesday simply said because she wanted to. They met over the table for a kiss.

Of course, the dinner and gift was just Tuesday trying to cushion the blow. She wanted to resign as CEO. She spent the whole afternoon looking for the best way to tell him.

After the lunch break she spent another hour poring over the reports before she finally gave up. The decision had been made right then. For the rest of the workday she just trolled social media and played games on her phone.

She needed to explain to Marcus that he might have changed her name but couldn't change what she was. Tuesday Knight was not Tabitha King. Tuesday Knight was a hood bitch, not cut out for this corporate shit. She was not some lazy bitch who wasn't down to pull her own weight, but she couldn't handle running his company. She just wanted a cute little clothing boutique where girls larger than a size four could come get fly for a fair price.

Because of how they met, Tuesday always felt like she had to prove herself. She came into his life only looking to seduce and rob Sebastian Caine before she fell in love with Marcus King. Guilt over that kept her never wanting to disappoint her man. This made it hard for her to tell him how she felt at times.

She figured the conversation could wait until after they had eaten. Marcus might be less combative with a stomach full of pasta and wine.

While he inspected his new gift, Tuesday looked around the restaurant to notice something odd. Nobody was eating. The place was three-quarters filled with diners, most of whom had arrived before Tuesday and Marcus, but no one had been served. Most of the other patrons were couples, a few were in groups of three or four, but nobody had any food in front of them. Diners were laughing, talking, or in hushed conversation, all over spotless white linen tablecloths that held no Italian cuisine.

Dominic's had a long-standing reputation for fine food as well as excellent service. Two waiters were coming back and forth from the kitchen, but Tuesday didn't see either carrying plates. It also dawned on her that twenty minutes had passed since their order was taken and their table had not even received bread.

What seemed merely strange slowly started to appear ominous. Nobody was complaining or demanding an explanation.

The fact that everyone was chatting and laughing as if totally oblivious made her suspicious.

Tuesday's pulse quickened. Something felt wrong. It became hard for her to breathe. Her anxiety started to build the same way it used to just before she had a panic attack.

But that was impossible because she was over her OCD. She hadn't suffered an attack in almost three years. Tuesday tried to calm herself with deep breaths and rationalize away her fears.

It wasn't like she actually saw anything to trigger her anxiety. In the past, her obsessive compulsive disorder manifested as a need for neatness and order that was mostly restricted to her condo. The rooms had to be spotless and sometimes she would remake her bed six or seven times before it was just right. At her worst it never reared its ugly head in public. Plus there was nothing messy or unsanitary about Dominic's. The dining area was immaculate. The oddity was that they refused to serve food.

Tuesday fought to get control of her breathing. The oxygen helped to beat back the rising tide of panic cresting within. She maintained her cool because she didn't want to bug out over something that might be as simple as a slow night for the kitchen staff. She chalked up the phantom fear to just nervousness over speaking to Marcus about the job.

He was still consumed with his new watch, turning his wrist this way and that way when she grabbed his attention. "Bae, don't you think it's kinda weird that ain't nobody got served yet? Come to think of it, I don't even smell no food cookin'."

Marcus slowly surveyed the restaurant using his peripheral vision then flagged down one of the waiters.

"Hey, is it gonna be much longer? We've been waiting a while for appetizers."

The young Latino server was humble and apologetic. He confessed there was some problem in the kitchen causing the delay but promised it was being resolved. To make up for the inconvenience, he announced to the room that everyone's dinner would be free and this earned applause from all the other diners.

This explanation put Tuesday at ease. She felt silly for letting herself get so paranoid. It may have been a residual effect from all her years in the stick-up game.

As the waiter left, Marcus slowly scanned the restaurant again. He threw his head back for a laugh before he leaned in for another kiss.

Marcus was still wearing a broad smile but his voice was deadly serious when he whispered: "We gotta get the fuck up outta here right now."

Chapter Eight

We gotta get the fuck up outta here right now.

Tuesday knew Marcus had a sense of humor but nothing in his eyes hinted that he might be joking. Instead of giving some type of explanation, he just mouthed the words: "Get ready."

He was still smiling when he called the friendly waiter back over. "I have a question about the *costoletta di vitello.*"

Before the server could respond, Marcus stood and leveled a .45 at the side of his head. The blast sent blood and brain matter exploding from his skull.

Marcus then turned and starting shooting in the direction of the second waiter at the rear of the dining area, who had already pulled his own pistol. There was no chance to return fire. He dove headlong into an empty booth as the .45 punched holes through the cushion right over his head.

When he told Tuesday to "get ready," she wasn't expecting this but didn't hesitate to react. She was already on her feet with the Heckler freed from her Hermes clutch.

Marcus guided her towards the front door. He kept an eye and his pistol turned to the kitchen as if waiting for someone else to come out the rear.

Then he suddenly stopped and Tuesday didn't know why until she saw the valet. The same dude who had parked their Rolls Royce had crept up on them and had an AR-15 aimed at Marcus's head.

"Please sir. I need you and your wife to drop the guns." He was just as cordial as when he had taken the keys to the Wraith.

Marcus let the .45 slip from his fingers and Tuesday followed by throwing down the Heckler. The second waiter Marcus shot at promptly came to collect both weapons.

They marched the couple back to their table and made them sit.

Tuesday was fucked up. She looked around the restaurant wondering why all the customers were just sitting there calmly. It started to make sense when many of them began to pull out assault rifles that were concealed under the white linen tablecloths. They sprang to their feet, barking orders to the rest of the diners. They forced them all to the floor and made them place their hands behind their heads.

Tuesday only then realized what Marcus had already peeped: they had walked right into a trap. None of the other diners had complained about the food because nobody was waiting to eat. Half had been waiting for them; the other half were just hostages to make the scene look realistic.

The valet called out "Lock it up!" and some of the gunmen started to shut down the restaurant before any more real customers could intrude. They scrambled around to lock doors, pull the blinds, and dim the interior lights. A second valet came in carrying an M-11 and locked the front entrance then flipped the sign to CLOSED.

They ordered Tuesday and Marcus to keep their hands on the table.

"So what the fuck up wit' this man?" he asked. "Y'all act like a nigga wasn't gone leave a tip or something."

"Mr. Caine, I think you know this is about a little more than a gratuity."

Hearing them call Marcus by his real name scared the hell out of Tuesday. The way they set up this ambush marked them as professionals, but anyone who would knowingly ambush Sebastian Caine was either well-connected or suicidal. Dangerous either way.

The valet slung the AR over his shoulder and sat at the table with them. "Mr. Caine, seriously, I'm a longtime fan. I'm trying hard not to be on some groupie shit and ask for your autograph.

"I hate to finally meet you like this, but our employer wants to have a conversation and thought this was the best way to make sure it happened in a neutral environment where you both felt safe."

If Marcus was afraid he didn't show it. "Nigga, miss me wit' all that fake ass James Bond shit. My employer. Bitch, I know who you work for and knew it the minute I peeped this whole play. Where the fuck is Guapa?"

Guapa? Tuesday had never heard him mention that name before.

Even though her heart was in her throat, she wanted to show that she wasn't scared either. "All this for a conversation? Next time tell yo' boss just hit us up on Twitter."

The henchman got a text then checked his phone. "La Guapa just pulled in so you can tell her yourself, smart ass. I'd love to see that."

Her? Tuesday wasn't sure she heard him correctly.

Marcus looked at her. "Bae, I need you to listen and do exactly what I say. When she comes in here—no matter what she says, no matter what she does—you stay quiet. Don't say shit."

Tuesday felt like Marcus was trying to check her. "I don't care who dis bitch s'posed to be. As long as she respect me—"

He cut her off. "Tuesday, I know you not some scared chick but trust me, it's not the time to play tough. Not now, not here, and definitely not with this bitch. Don't smile at her, don't frown at her, don't even roll yo' eyes. Please just do what I said."

The fake valet smiled at her. "If I were you, I'd listen to your man."

It wasn't what Marcus said that convinced Tuesday. It was the look on his face. For the first time since she had known him, she saw genuine fear in his eyes.

The lead henchman stood. "La Guapa is at that door, let's go. Clear it out!"

The gunmen along with the fake busboys rounded up the real diners who were still face down on the floor. The hostages were ushered into the kitchen single file. Some with sniffles and sobs, some with delusions of being released. Seconds later, a few short staccato bursts of automatic gunfire quelled all their hopes and fears.

Tuesday imagined the innocent diners were lying dead next to the kitchen staff, the real waiters and busboys, every employee at Dominic's who had the misfortune of having a shift on this night.

The fake waiter went to the front door to unlock it again. He nodded to the valet one who spoke into his phone: "It's all clean, bring her in."

A minute later, four more goons entered the building escorting two women. One preceded the other.

The first was a tall, slender Latina in perhaps her mid-forties. She was incredibly fine despite not trying to play up her femininity. She was in a Ralph Lauren suit tailored to fit with jet-black hair pulled back into a bun. She presented herself as all business and Tuesday thought she looked like one of their lawyers at Abel.

The woman that followed had the same height, build, and face. She was a twin but with a totally different look and swagger. The second was dressed like she had just left a gala. She was in a white mink wrap over a form-fitting tan suede dress that Tuesday thought was fly as hell. The gold shoes matched her belt and bag. Her hair spilled over her shoulders in shimmering cascades of black silk and Tuesday could tell it was all real.

Tuesday was floored because she was looking at one of the most beautiful women she had ever seen, and if it wasn't for the moment probably would've yelled "Dayyummm!" Her dark-brown eyes were fierce and her mouth would tempt Jesus. She had the type of face that would get her the lead role on a Spanish soap opera even if she never acted a day in her life.

The Mexican beauty had her practically seeing stars but Marcus only looked at her with cool detachment.

The two valets fetched extra chairs. The ladies joined Tuesday and Marcus at their table like they were merely dinner guests arriving late due to traffic.

La Guapa looked to Marcus. "It's been a long time. About fifteen years right?"

Whatever reaction she was hoping for, Marcus didn't oblige. He had the face of a statue. "You went through a lot to set this up. I can tell by the look on your face, you're really proud of yourself right now."

"No, not proud. Actually, a little disappointed that you made this so easy. At what point did you realize?"

Marcus shook his head. "I see you still think everything's a damn game."

"But I like games, especially those that challenge the intellect." She flashed a luminous smile with flawless white teeth. "Humor me, please."

"Your boy here gave it away." He motioned to the dead waiter at their feet leaking blood and cranial fluids. "It's Cali, so it's not uncommon to find all Mexican waiters at an Italian restaurant. But two Mexican waiters trying like hell to hide their south Texas accents, who just happen to have bulges under their vests." He pointed to the second waiter who he shot at. "And that one there still got a little blood on his sleeve."

The gunman looked down at his shirt and spotted two tiny drops on his cuff that were barely noticeable.

Marcus said, "Probably splashback from the real waiter he killed to get the uniform. I was slippin' but my wife caught the biggest give away. Your boys shouldn't have killed the chefs before they started cooking. Having some food to put out would've helped to sell it."

"You know what a stickler I am for details." La Guapa threw a nod to one of her personal escorts who immediately turned and shot the second waiter.

She turned back to Marcus. "Those amazing deductive powers aren't as sharp as they used to be. The man I used to know would've sniffed out this trap before stepping out of his car."

She gave Tuesday a smug grin that said, *Yes bitch, your man used to suck my pussy.*

"She's pretty." La Guapa stroked her sable wrap. "She sort of has a Shenahnay-from-around-the-way quality that some men find appealing. I just expected someone with your pedigree to have made a more refined choice."

Marcus snapped, "You don't know my pedigree and you don't know hers. Now watch how you talk about my wife."

Tuesday appreciated him checking her but didn't appreciate that she couldn't do it herself. She obeyed his warning. It was just hard letting this bitch talk about her like she wasn't there.

While Tuesday kept her tongue in check, she didn't shy away with her gray eyes. She sent a clear message to La Guapa that even though she had the ups, Tuesday wasn't intimidated.

The two ladies became locked in a staring match and seemed to be gauging each other.

Tuesday was searching for any flaw, any pimple, blemish or imperfection that she could criticize her for. The problem was that La Guapa had none. Her attitude was shitty but even Tuesday had to admit there was an ethereal beauty about the woman, the kind that inspired artists and poets. Tuesday was a hood dime and used to being the baddest chick in the room, but sitting across from La Guapa made her feel a little insecure.

La Guapa smiled as if able to read that insecurity. It was the look a woman gave to another woman whom she didn't consider competition. Tuesday knew it because she had given it to quite a few bitches in her day.

Marcus broke up the contest. "What the fuck you want, Reina? We both know this isn't a hit."

She sneered. "Don't get cute. You won't be able to hide behind my father for much longer."

"Don't make the mistake of thinking your father is the only powerful friend I have."

"You haven't worn the jewelry in a long time. From what I hear, nobody at the table recognizes you."

His face was grim. "You already know that I ain't never needed protection. So what are we doin' here?"

She leaned back in her seat. "I'm just here to personally extend your invitation to our little gathering. Things are about to change and you play a critical role in this transition."

Tuesday finally disobeyed her husband. "But why? Why he gotta be involved when he ain't had nothing to do wit' y'all for so long?"

She ignored the *shut the fuck up* look Marcus was giving her.

La Guapa laughed. "Oh, so she speaks. And so eloquently I might add. You didn't tell me she was a poet laureate."

Tuesday started to respond but Marcus spoke over her.

"I already made plans to be there. I also wanted to pay my respects to Rene."

"He would like that," said the conservative twin in the business suit who had not spoken.

Marcus quipped, "Roselyn, you still talk too much."

This earned a thin smile from her. "Hello Sebastian, it's good to see you too. I just hate that it had to be under these circumstances."

He shrugged. "I guess we got your sister to thank for that. I thought you would've gotten away from this crazy bitch by now."

It was her turn to shrug. "What can I say, *somos hermanas*."

"I've tried to never hold that against you." And they both laughed.

As they spoke, Tuesday could see La Guapa was annoyed by their banter. She rolled her eyes and made little disgruntled noises. It was obvious she didn't like not being the center of attention.

She broke in: "You are incredible, Sebastian. Rico considered you his best friend, and even after you killed him, my father still embraced you like a son. You've had me in your bed, and after all these years, Rose still looks at you like she's ready to cum in her panties."

Tuesday watched the quiet sister look away, shamed. She and Marcus were going to have a talk when they got home.

La Guapa said: "Tell me your secret. Tell me our weakness. What is it about my family that makes us eat right out of the palm of your hand?"

Marcus stared at her for a moment. His expression was sincere and sympathetic. "Your family was my family, Reina. Rene was a father to me, and Rico was a brother. The saddest thing of all is that you done spent twenty years hating me for something I didn't do. I carry my own guilt about Rico, but not because I killed him. Because I should've been with him."

She shook her head. "There was a time when those brown eyes could've convinced me of anything. But you forget that I know you better than anybody, Sebastian. I know you because I know myself and we've always been the same. Always calculating, always counting the moves. You killed your friend and took his place because it's what I would've done. Sacrificed a knight to promote a pawn.

"And with Rico out of the way, my father opened up the floodgates for you. For twenty years I had to sit back and watch you grow, prosper, earning the name and money that was supposed to be my big brother's."

She smacked her hand against the table. "And now the king of cocaine is retired and living in Beverly Hills with two kids and a goddamn stripper."

She glared at Tuesday. "Yeah, I know all about you, Tuesday or Tabitha, whatever you want to call yourself. Tell me, just between us girls, how does a common hoodrat like you go from fucking in cheap motels and robbing street dealers to being married to a man like this? You must feel like Julia Roberts in *Pretty*

Woman—the prostitute who catches the billionaire. Dreams really do come true, right?"

Tuesday wanted to spaz, but if she went off the way she wanted, she would only end up on the floor next to the dead waiters. She simply said, "Bitch, you don't know me."

"But I know your man, and I know him very well," La Guapa teased. "Let me guess, he told you not to say anything. Ask yourself something. Was it because he was afraid I might hurt you or was he more afraid you might embarrass him?"

Tuesday returned the smile La Guapa was giving her. Inside she was fuming but she refused to let her have the satisfaction of seeing it.

Marcus asked: "How long do you think we can sit here and reminisce? I'm sure the people who work here have family who are starting to call and get worried. Nobody's answering the business line or their personal phones. How much longer will it be before people start knocking on that door?"

Roselyn gave her sister a cautionary look of agreement.

For a moment, La Guapa just glared at him with a look that could cut metal, then conceded. "My father's prognosis is much worse than we've let on to anybody outside the family. He doesn't have months, just days to live. So the meeting has been pushed up to Saturday."

Tuesday frowned. "The day after tomorrow?"

La Guapa said to Marcus: "You'll be leaving with us tonight. My father wants to see you first and sent me to collect you personally. We have a jet waiting nearby."

Tuesday said, "Bitch, he ain't goin' nowhere wit' y'all. And we got our own jet. We'll meet you there."

Marcus said: "I know Rene didn't sign off on this bullshit. This little stunt was all you, Reina."

She gave a guilty grin. "He only said to come and get you. He didn't specify the means."

"We need to leave now," Roselyn reiterated. "We have somebody to make sure your wife gets home safely."

"Fuck that!" Tuesday spat. "Where he go, I go."

"Sebastian, muzzle your pet before I put her down." La Guapa flashed him a warning glare. "Father's protection doesn't extend to your wife." She added with a sinister tone: "Or your kids."

One of her men came and stood behind Tuesday's seat.

Marcus shot him a look. "Bitch you betta back the fuck up unless you 'bout to massage her shoulders."

He cut back to La Guapa. "I'll go with y'all, but let that be the last time you threaten my family. Act like you remember who the fuck I am. I kill shit about mine."

To Roselyn he said, "And I'll be the one making sure she gets home safe. Me and my wife came here together, we leaving together. And any muthafucka who got a problem with that can start shooting shit right now."

Marcus scanned them all. His eyes defiant.

Chapter Nine

The drive home was quiet and eerily surreal. The strangeness at Dominic's—the trap, La Guapa—made Tuesday feel like only that part of the evening had been real, while everything that preceded was a dream. They navigated the streets, passing motorists and pedestrians while Tuesday looked at them curiously. It fascinated her how they were totally oblivious that there was a popular Italian restaurant where the entire staff was murdered and stored in the meat freezer, totally oblivious that they lived in a world where that could happen outside their movie studios.

Tuesday was in the passenger seat continuing the silence Marcus had demanded at Dominic's. She did place a quick call to the sitter just to check on the girls but said nothing else. Every now and then she glanced at the side-view mirror to find the same set of headlights tailing them. La Guapa's men.

Marcus had the Wraith by the wheel and seemed equally content to let silence be the theme. There was no talk or music. The sodium vapor street lamps threw shafts of pale orange light into the car, briefly illuminating a dark face strained with concentration.

After a while he unexpectedly broke the silence. "Reina took over her father's business when Rene got too old and his health started to fail. She was a scholar who was never supposed to be in this life. Usually that would have fallen on the oldest son, but without Rico—" He allowed the thought to trail off.

"What happened to their brother?" Tuesday made sure it didn't come off like an accusation.

"I worked for Rico back when he was being groomed to take over for his father. I was his right hand, and in charge of his security.

"A rival crew caught him leaving a club in Houston. They sprayed over two hundred rounds in his Maserati. I was supposed to be with him that night but got caught up doin' some other shit."

Tuesday said, "Somewhere doin' his sister."

He confirmed it with his eyes. "She was real close to Rico and the loss hit her hard. She blamed me for that shit."

Even though Reina and Marcus were ancient history, Tuesday still couldn't stop the childish game of comparing herself to his ex.

"Why do they call her La Guapa? Is it like guap—slang for money?"

"I actually gave her that name a long time ago." Marcus focused on the road to avoid looking at her. "Rico was teaching me Spanish back then and when I learned *guapo* meant handsome, I thought it had a feminine counterpart. I started calling her La Guapa—The Pretty One."

Tuesday sucked her teeth. "Ain't that a bitch."

"It was twenty years ago. I didn't think it would stick."

"How did she know we were going to be at Dominic's when I only reserved that table a few hours earlier? How tha fuck did she do that?" Tuesday thought about all the scams and heists she'd ever planned, and remembered how she would plot for weeks. "How in the fuck did she do that?" she asked herself more than Marcus.

He said, "Reina is very smart and meticulous."

Tuesday shook her head, rejecting that simple explanation. "We're smart. We're meticulous. I called for a table around four thirty. This bitch somehow found out, flew up from Texas and set that trap in six hours. Nobody's that good."

Marcus sighed. "Bae, Reina was one of those child prodigies. She graduated from high school when she was thirteen and had a Master's degree by seventeen. When I met her she was twenty-three and had already earned her second Ph.D."

Tuesday was already intimidated by her looks, so hearing that she was also smart did not help her self-esteem. "So what, you sayin' she like a genius or somethin'?"

"Well yeah." Marcus was hesitant. "That's exactly what she is."

Tuesday crossed her arms over her chest. She was trying to decide if he was giving that bitch a compliment or merely stating a fact.

"She still got a thing for you. She didn't go through all this just to come pick you up. I know bitches. That was her stuntin'. You see the way she made her entrance. That whole little show was to impress you."

Marcus said, "She wanted to impress me but not for the reason you think. While I've been retired, she's been getting stronger—to the point where she has a few cartel bosses in her pocket. That situation at Dominic's was about showing me her reach, to let me know that she can get to me any time she wants. The only reason I'm not dead already is because she can't do it. Rene won't allow it, plus she kinda needs me."

Tuesday's mind was taking her in the wrong direction. "What the fuck she need you for?"

He explained. "Since forever, the Rodriguez family controlled the border towns—that's where most of the contraband is being smuggled into the country. Lately the feds been crackin' down and the pipeline is getting choked off. Reina and her friends have been taking some big losses this year."

Tuesday remembered the news story from the previous night

and was able to connect the dots. "And you just happen to have a big ass shipping company. They want to use Abel to get their dope into the country."

"And to get their money back out to the cartels."

Marcus maneuvered the Rolls Royce around a slow-moving Lincoln then took a hand off the wheel to rub Tuesday's thigh. However, as the final pieces of the puzzle fell into place for her, she got so mad that she pushed it away.

She glared at him. "You sonofabitch! That's what this this fuckin' meeting is all about. They gone ask and you gone say no."

She gasped. "And when you do, they gone kill you!"

Chapter Ten

Learning that Marcus was going to be assassinated at this meeting wasn't what pissed Tuesday off the most. The anger that shifted her eye color came when she realized that he had known this entire time.

She thought back on how he had been lately: pensive, reclusive. It explained why he was dodging his usual responsibilities to spend so much time with their daughters. He had been living like a man who knew he was on borrowed time.

It also shed light on his ravenous sexual appetite. Over the past month Marcus had been gorging himself on Tuesday the way a condemned man would do a last meal.

She wanted to slap him. "How long did you know?"

He said, "It don't matter."

"What the fuck you mean it don't matter!" she spat. "You just been goin' through the day-to-day with me and the girls, the whole time knowin' you got this hanging over you. How could you not tell me? I'm not just some bitch you fuckin' Marcus. I'm yo' wife. We got a family."

He snapped back at her. "Don't gimme that bullshit cause we both know you been flaky as hell lately. While you been out turnin' up wit' your girlfriend, I been the one at home holding down our family and dealing with this."

That was a deep cut which immediately put tears in her eyes. "You wrong for that Marcus. You know good and damn well if I would'da known—" The rest was choked off by sobs. Tuesday turned away from him and began to weep into her palms.

Marcus dragged a hand across his face knowing it was petty of him to run a guilt-trip. In truth, there had been plenty of chances to tell Tuesday; he had chosen to bear this burden alone. It had nothing to do with the time she was spending with Shaun.

He felt like shit. "Bae, c'mon."

When he reached for her she slapped his hand away. "Pull over. Let me out."

"Look baby, I'm sorry for what I said but we not about to do this soap opera shit. You not about to jump out this car downtown at twelve o'clock at night. It's not happenin'."

That was a bluff and she was happy not to get called on it. She wiped her face then sat in the passenger seat, arms folded, pouting like a child.

For a while the drive was just as silent as when they first left Dominic's. Only this time the Rolls was not filled with a mutually reflective silence. This was a tension-filled bubble heavy with unvoiced emotions.

Tuesday habitually checked her mirror to find the dark SUV matching their turns. What the night had first presented as black, artificial light revealed to be a deep burgundy Tahoe. It and a second SUV that Tuesday couldn't make out kept a distance of about four car lengths.

At some point she didn't even realize, she and Marcus's hands had found each other and laced their fingers. At some point she didn't even realize, Tuesday stopped being mad at him. She was more frightened than anything else.

"So what'cho gone do?"

"I'm going to the meeting," he said flatly.

"Well what'cho gone say when they ask about using Abel?"

Marcus didn't blink. "I'm basically gone tell 'em to kiss my ass."

Tuesday was waiting for him to reveal some plan he had been working on in secret. When he didn't share anything more, Tuesday couldn't believe it. "So you're basically about to walk in there, knowing full well what's waiting for you?"

"If I don't go to them, they're just gonna come to me."

She said, "Just punch it. We could beat them home and get the girls. We could lay low until we figure this out. Hide out for a while on the same island you bought when you needed to dodge the feds."

Marcus shook his head. "That was a different situation. The indictment was only about me. Running puts a target on all our backs.

"And trust me, Reina already got somebody scoping out the house. The clowns following us are just for psychology, a visual message not to try anything. If I mash this gas and try to get light, somebody'll be kicking in our front door before we cut two corners."

"Then fuck runnin'!" she shouted. "We'll go to war. How 'bout that? If she want it wit' us, if she want it wit' Sebastian Caine, we'll give that bitch what she askin' for."

Marcus just stared at Tuesday for a minute with a look that was a combination of puzzlement and pity. "Tuesday, who in the fuck do you think I am?"

She couldn't answer because she didn't know what to make of the question.

"I haven't been that person for a very long time, and the truth is, the Sebastian Caine you believe in never really existed. Even when I was at my worst, I still didn't do half the shit that got put on my name. Now you talkin' bout going to war with not just La Guapa, but the other cartel bosses who's backing her like it's no problem? You've been living with me for three years; do you think I've been hiding an army of mercenaries in the basement?

There ain't no button in my office that makes the walls spin to reveal grenades and rocket launchers. Our tennis court ain't got no supersonic jet hiding underneath it.

"I'm a family man; I own a business; I pay my taxes. I'm an ordinary dude, Tuesday. And I'm sorry if it fucks up the fantasy for you, but that's all I've ever been."

She sat there quietly for a moment, absorbing all that he said. Since she was young, that name Sebastian Caine had been infamous, while the man himself had remained a mystery. Rumors had put his hands into everything from casinos to nuclear weapons.

Even after years of being his woman, she had never been able to separate the man from the myth. Tuesday only realized then how much those stories had distorted her image of Marcus. This was a guy who had succeeded by being elusive and smart but there was nothing supernatural about him.

Her eyes grew misty again. "Tell me you've got somethin' up your sleeve. Tell me you're not just about to go in there and hand them yo' head."

He answered the question with his silence. He avoided her eyes, stared through the windshield as if some televised version of his future played out in the distance.

A sob exploded from her. "I can't believe this! I can't believe there ain't no other way. How are you so cool with this? What about me and Dani and Tanisha?"

"I already took care of that. You and the girls are gonna be super-straight. The financial stuff is pretty complicated but for the most part, the house, the cars, the company—everything will be in your—"

Marcus couldn't believe it when Tuesday stole on him. She punched him in the face and shoulder, causing the Rolls Royce to swerve out of its lane. He corrected the wheel and caught her arm before she could hit him again.

"Girl, what the fuck wrong wit' you?"

"What the fuck wrong with YOU?!" she hissed with heavy breaths. "You think I'm worried 'bout the money? You dumb sonofabitch, I'm worried 'bout what I'm gone tell these girls when they start askin' what happened to they Daddy."

Marcus had known what she meant from the beginning. This was just part of the conversation he was hoping to avoid.

He said: "These last three years been the happiest of my life, and you and the girls are the reason for that. Don't think for a second that I'm cool with this. I've just had more time to deal with it."

Marcus didn't drive slow, just at a speed that showed he wasn't in a rush. Tuesday felt a sickening pain in her stomach when they reached their street and the house came into view. Like Marcus had said, another burgundy SUV was already parked across the street from their home.

When he pulled onto the grounds, the people trailing them remained outside the front gate. Marcus pulled up their driveway and stopped beneath the lighted portico at the entrance. He and Tuesday sat there for a moment; neither of them wanted to leave the car.

"You don't live the life I lived and not expect that shit to catch up to you. There was never gone be a happy ending for me, Tuesday. I always knew I wasn't riding off into the sunset.

"I did a lot of wrong—that company is the one thing I ever did that's wholly about doing good. Sure, it turns a profit, but it's one of the few large corporations that's for the right thing. I can't let that be corrupted, bae. I just can't."

Tuesday shook her head. "I understand how important it is to your legacy that you repair some of the damage you did as Sebastian Caine, but what about your legacy as Marcus King, the father? To your daughters your legacy will be a man who just disappeared out of their lives."

"Tanisha's still young, in time she'll forget me. It'll be a lot harder coming up with something to tell Dani. Of all the slimeball shit I ever done, leaving you behind to have that conversation is right at the top."

Tuesday glanced down at the Chevy Tahoes waiting at the front gate. Tears blurred her vision. She turned away from them but wasn't able to look at him either. "Maybe they'll give you a few minutes just to run in and say goodbye."

Marcus cut the engine and dropped the keys into her lap. "I already did. I've been sayin' goodbye to 'em every day for months."

When he got out of the car, Tuesday followed right behind him. She grabbed his arm as he started down the driveway.

"No. No. I don't believe this. It's not happening like this. Maybe I don't know the truth about Sebastian Caine, but I know you. I know you, Marcus.

"You got a plan. You got some angle you working. You not 'bout to just surrender. That's not you. You got a plan," Tuesday almost seemed manic.

Marcus grabbed her and kissed her lips. He whispered in her ear. "It's up to you to finish what I started. Protect my shit. You will be tested."

Tuesday watched him walk down their drive where two men jumped out of the lead Tahoe to greet him. Marcus held out his arms, submitted himself to a quick pat-down. Then he climbed into the back seat like he was leaving with friends.

Tuesday just stood in front of her house as the three burgundy SUVs rolled off into the night. She had every expectation of seeing her husband again.

Chapter Eleven

The next day Tuesday sent Danielle to school and left Tanisha with a sitter. When Danielle asked, Tuesday told her that Daddy had gone on a business trip and would return soon. Tuesday didn't feel like this was a lie.

It may have been delusion or just the faith she had in her husband. While understanding he was not superhuman, she knew Marcus to be too much of a tactician to simply walk into his own execution. He would find a way to overcome this the same way he overcame the dope game, overcame his indictment, and overcame the odds by transitioning into a legitimate entrepreneur.

Over the next few days, Tuesday went about the business of running Abel and being a mother. The combination taxed her patience and nerves but provided enough activity to fill her days. On the home front, Danielle was still trippin', and it was much worse without Marcus to act as a buffer. At work, she was bombarded with mountains of paperwork, long meetings, and problems that felt like calculus. Luckily, she had Brandon to help steer the ship when the wheel became too much for her to handle.

The days were difficult, but those calm and quiet nights were by far the worst. Lying in their extreme ultra-king, all Tuesday could do was think of Marcus. Being alone on that massive ten-by-twelve-foot bed amplified his absence so much that she opted to sleep in one of the smaller guest bedrooms.

Tuesday did receive a call from Marcus on the second day. He explained that the family had pulled the plug on Rene shortly after the two had made their peace. He said that out of respect, the meeting was being pushed back until the funeral was done.

From what Marcus had explained, La Guapa couldn't harm him as long as her father was living. Despite no longer having that protection, something in Marcus's voice sounded optimistic when they spoke. This helped to feed Tuesday's belief that everything would be fine.

She remained strangely positive even after Marcus stopped calling or answering his phone in the days that followed. Tuesday was sure he would come back with some tale about how he'd out-smarted Reina and her associates then taken them out in one Machiavellian move. They would celebrate as a family, probably spend a day with the girls at Disneyland. That night the two of them would celebrate as a couple by making love in a way that was deep and soulful, reuniting their flesh and spirits.

Even on the fifth day when Brandon came by the house and tried to shatter the delusion, Tuesday still believed.

She was standing in the foyer by the entrance when he delivered the news. Tuesday just stared at him, blinking dumbly. She heard the words but they didn't register. It was if the old man had switched and started speaking a different language.

He said, "It's been done. He's gone. We've lost him."

Tuesday just smiled at him.

Chapter Twelve

Tuesday shook her head. "In three days, five at the most, he's gonna call from some underground bunker. He's gonna send for me and the girls."

The old man's expression reflected his doubt in the likelihood of that.

Brandon confessed his information was secondhand since the meeting was so exclusive that even he had not been able to attend. The gist was that, as expected, La Guapa and the other bosses tried to negotiate a deal to use Abel's importing and exporting network as a vehicle for their product. Despite being offered a generous percentage, Marcus had rejected them. He was determined that his company stay one hundred percent legitimate and that conviction had cost him his life.

Brandon claimed not to be privy to the method, but only knew that Marcus's death had been quick and painless. Apparently Sebastian Caine's standing in the game had earned him too much respect to be tortured. Brandon stressed this as if Tuesday should take some consolation in the fact that her husband had not suffered.

"You know him, Brandon. You know him better than any-body. He always comes up outta this shit. It's what he does.

"In a week I'll take the girls to see the new Pixar movie and Marcus'll surprise us by popping up in the seat behind ours. You know how he do."

Concern drew lines in his face. "Tuesday, I don't think that's a healthy attitude to have. We're better off trying to figure out how we move forward, and what you're gonna tell your daughters.

"Personally, I think a plane crash is the best story. A small charter jet goes off-course and gets lost over water—I'll have to call in some favors, file a bogus flight plan to make it look good, but I can sell that to the public. That'll explain why there's no wreckage. It'll also explain to Danielle why we haven't got a body to bury."

Tuesday wouldn't budge. "We don't have his body, and until we do, we don't know what happened. I'm not tellin' Dani and Nisha anything more than what I been tellin' 'em. Their daddy's away and he'll be back. Until I know for sure, that's what it is." Brandon disagreed but Tuesday didn't exactly leave that open for discussion.

Once he left, Tuesday felt a compulsion to start cleaning and just couldn't stop. Her OCD resurfaced with a vengeance. The house was already immaculately kept by the staff but Tuesday wasn't satisfied. She went behind them with sanitizer, scrubbing surfaces that were already spotless. She tried to reorganize every cupboard and pantry. Danielle was still ignoring her and Tanisha barely got any attention. Tuesday didn't sleep or eat, just cleaned for the rest of the day well into the night.

It was three o'clock in the morning and she was on Marcus's side of their walk-in closet. Tuesday had already sorted his shirts according to color, function, and brand.

She was doing the same with his shoes when she stumbled across something hidden in the toe of an old pair of Timberlands. A jewelry box. Inside were two ugly little rings that she had never seen her husband wear. Both were identical, only one silver and the other bronze.

Tuesday was still reshuffling shoes when something inside her snapped and she threw one of his Jordans at the wall. She threw another shoe and another then snatched all his clothes down from the hangers. She exhausted herself destroying his side of the closet then sat amongst the designer piles of cloth, silk, and fur, breathing hard.

She raided their weed stash then rolled a blunt way too fat for a solo burn. She sat on the floor while she baked herself.

She picked up one of the watches from his collection and put it on. The rose-gold Louis Moinet seemed too bulky for her slender wrist. It forced Tuesday to think about the Parmigiani she gave him at Dominic's and that sparked other thoughts she didn't want to entertain. How that might be the last gift she would ever give him, that he might have died with it on his arm.

She tried to silence those thoughts with more kush. She tried to smoke herself dumb.

But the strand was potent. After just a quarter of the blunt, she had to put it out. Tuesday was already so high that her face felt too heavy.

Her blood-red eyes surveyed the result of her little tantrum. She told herself that she was going to have to do something special for Esperanza. The housekeeper was going to have to handle this one because Tuesday definitely wasn't about to clean that shit up.

Chapter Thirteen

Brandon advised her to take a few days off from work but Tuesday refused. While she didn't enjoy being at Abel, it was the principle. To accept bereavement days would be to acknowledge the unacceptable.

The next two weeks were hectic but Tuesday went to work each day and powered through, working hard even if uninspired. This company was her husband's dream, and for her husband, Tuesday was doing her best.

Brandon was pressing her about the need to declare Marcus dead so that his estate, the company and all his assets could be transferred to her. Tuesday wasn't quite ready to do that, but with each day she didn't receive a call from her husband, Brandon's position seemed more logical.

On this day Tuesday was in between meetings when her secretary announced someone from accounting was requesting to see her without an appointment. Tuesday agreed and Shaun was escorted into her office looking awed and intimidated by the spacious five thousand square feet of marble, glass, and wood.

Even dressed for work, Shaun was nothing less than a stunner. Her blouse was imitation silk, the skirt that hugged her curves was only a polyester-blend, a no-name pair of mules completed the look, but the cheap clothes couldn't negate the natural beauty.

She and Tuesday kept things formal until the secretary closed the door on them.

"Girl, what the fuck you doin'?" Tuesday beamed fury at her from behind the desk. "You know this ain't the time or place for this shit."

"Look I'm not here for the drama," Shaun said on approach until she stood before her. "I'm only here to say sorry. Been wanting to come for a while but—"

She didn't need to explain because they both understood how important it was to keep up appearances at work. There were about six layers of management between them. This was a total breach of protocol that could actually get Shaun fired if reported to her superiors.

"I tried calling you a few times but you didn't answer." Over the past two weeks Tuesday had received several calls and emails which she deleted instantly. The only call she was interested in was one from Marcus.

Shaun looked out on the seventy-story view as if ashamed to meet Tuesday's gaze. "I know I said some hurtful and disrespectful shit the last time we spoke." Her tone was apologetic.

"Just disrespectful." Tuesday said dismissively. It was a petty little barb to let the youngster know that only her feelings had gotten hurt.

"And all that stuff I said about going to human resources, I didn't mean it. I was just in my feelings."

"I understand." Tuesday stood, a polite way of indicating that it was time for Shaun to leave.

However, when Tuesday tried to escort her to the door, Shaun pushed her back against the desk and kissed her.

She was caught off-guard but after a second of Shaun's tongue swimming around her mouth, Tuesday pushed her away.

"What the fuck wrong wit' you? You gone try this shit right here in my office, especially now?"

"I'm sorry. I'm so sorry." Shaun grabbed her hands. "I just miss you so much. I've been missing you like crazy. I've been sick without you."

Tuesday snatched away from her. "I ain't got time to care about your hurt feelings." The words poured out of Tuesday before she had time to consider them: "I don't know if my husband is dead or alive and he dropped this company in my lap, and I'm trying not to run this bitch into the ground but I don't know what the fuck I'm doing. I spend ten hours reading documents I barely understand then go home to one daughter who won't speak to me and another who won't stop crying for her daddy." Tuesday's eyes flashed gray. "Miss me wit' yo' shit right now, Shaun."

"I know baby. I can see you're stressin' like crazy." She took Tuesday's hips into her hands and stroked her thighs. "Let me fix it for you."

"Girl, get the fuck outta here. I gotta bitch sittin' right outside my door and a meeting in twenty minutes."

"Please, baby. Let me fix it." Shaun's brown eyes found hers and softened them from gray to green. "Just let me fix it for you." She continued to beg as she pecked Tuesday's lips again then left a trail of soft kisses across her cheek, around her ear, down her neck. "Let me fix it?" she asked in a throaty whisper.

"No, we can't do this here. Stop." But rejection without conviction was essentially invitation. Those weak refusals only encouraged Shaun's advance to Tuesday's breasts, where Shaun's swift fingers undid her blouse. She freed a plump titty from its lacy prison and devoured the nipple.

Tuesday moaned "No, don't," but allowed Shaun's hands to push her skirt to her waist. She whispered her worries about the secretary and the meeting but helped Shaun to hoist her onto her desk and permitted her legs to be pushed open.

During their relationship Tuesday had typically been the dominant one, but this time Shaun was driving. She pushed the computer and a stack of department reports out of the way, then reclined Tuesday onto her back. Bubble gum lip gloss made Shaun's mouth look irresistible. Tuesday moaned breathlessly, receiving kisses on her stomach. By the time Shaun made her way down to her inner thighs, Tuesday was beyond even fake protests. She was snatching down her panties before Shaun had the chance to make the effort.

Tuesday's legs were in the air, her head hung off the edge of the desk looking toward the glass wall, where one hundred and eighty degrees of the Hollywood Hills, the California coastline, and Pacific Ocean were presented to her upside down.

Shaun's lips pecked hers, then she traced slow circles inside her labia with the tip of her tongue, causing Tuesday to broadcast her pleasure in soft falsetto mews. Then she sucked the clitoral hood and teased the clit by drawing figure-eights on it. Tuesday shuddered like something electric had passed through her body. She grabbed a fistful of Shaun's hair and started to grind her crotch into her face.

"Bae, I miss you so much." Lick, lick, lick. "I love you, Tabitha." Lick, lick, lick. "Please baby, I need you." Lick, lick, lick.

It wasn't long before Shaun's talented tongue drew undulant cries from Tuesday's quivering lips. She was twisting and thrashing wildly atop the desk, back arched so severely it seemed her spine should snap. An intruder would burst into the office and think that Shaun was performing an exorcism, trying to pull a demon out of Tuesday rather than a stubborn nut.

Eventually Shaun found the right frequency to trigger that eruption. Tuesday trembled and shook as waves of pleasure broke against her shores over and over. She released her juices, grumbling praise and curses to God. The young lover continued to lap at her sticky sweetness until Tuesday forcibly pushed her head away. She lay across the desk panting heavily, heart knocking against her ribs, head spinning.

When Tuesday finally sat up and checked her watch, she realized she only had minutes to get to her meeting.

"Shit!" She snatched up her underwear on the way to the private bathroom attached to her office. She washed herself then stepped back into her panties.

Orgasms were transcendent experiences, but the fall back to Earth was typically hard and fast. With it came all the problems and responsibilities that vanished temporarily during the moment of passion. Tuesday's return brought back the scattered papers smeared across her desk, and the meeting she had in two minutes where those reports would need to be referenced.

And then there was the one who helped to take her to that special place. The emotional needs and expectations of her partners were always waiting in the aftermath.

"You gotta go. Now." It was an authoritative command that indicated that Tuesday was speaking as her boss and not her lover. "And don't ever pull up on my office like this no more."

If Shaun thought the sex was prelude to reconciliation, Tuesday shattered that illusion like a brick hurled through a pane of glass.

She responded with a solemn nod. "Look, it's not like I want you to—"

Tuesday hurried to shuffle the papers back in order. Her impatient glare said she didn't give a fuck what Shaun wanted.

Tuesday could tell Shaun wanted to cry and was praying she didn't make a scene. It was suspicious enough for her to have entertained a peon-level subordinate who shouldn't even be on her floor, but if Shaun left out blubbering and bawling like she did at the house, Tuesday would have too much to explain to Brandon and the other members of a board that already had little faith in her.

However, Shaun stayed composed, kept herself together. Tuesday couldn't guess if it was pride or the forty thousand plus benefits keeping her afloat until the modeling thing took off.

"Glad I could be of service to you, Mrs. King." Shaun turned on her heel and strutted out of the office.

Tuesday watched her go, feeling like shit. She felt like she had used Shaun, like she had betrayed Marcus. For that reason she was able to excuse the *Fuck you* glance Shaun threw back at her.

But damn, sometimes a bitch just needed to get her rocks.

Chapter Fourteen

Tuesday's workday ended with a headache-inducing ninety-minute meeting of the executive staff. A dozen different department heads boasted about performance and expectations, and after the first twenty minutes, it was all white noise to Tuesday. These meetings were too much of a reminder that she didn't finish school and why. Stuck there pretending to be interested while somebody talks forever about shit she barely understood or cared to. She fought to stay engaged through heavy eyelids and multiple yawns. Shaun's stress-reliever had her ready for a nap, and the boring suits droning on in a flat monotone was making her start to nod. As much as she wanted to, Tuesday knew it would embarrass Brandon if she put her head on the desk and fell asleep like she did back in eighth grade.

When five o'clock came, Tuesday rushed to get out of the building like it was on fire. The executive elevator descended straight into the underground garage that was reserved for senior staff. Martellius was already waiting when she stepped off, parked and holding the door open for her.

A perk of being CEO came in the form of a company car, a Mercedes Benz S600 with a personal driver. Tuesday slumped in the back seat, slipped off her heels before he could close the door on her. Tuesday's feet and eyes needed a break so she shut them while Martellius pulled from underneath the Abel tower and navigated the surface streets of downtown Los Angeles.

Tuesday appreciated that her chauffeur was quiet. After a perfunctory greeting of, "Mrs. King," they typically rode in silence. Tuesday hated annoying cab and Uber drivers who tried to force conversation or use music to fill that space when it failed. Martellius seemed to get that at the end of the day that all she wanted was a few moments to decompress. He was courteous and professional for the most part; once in a while she caught him sneaking a peek at her ass when she climbed in or out of the car, but Tuesday didn't mind that. Niggas was gone be niggas.

She felt the turns and pauses of the vehicle but still had her eyes closed, wrapped in a cocoon of her own thoughts. Tuesday didn't even realize that the easy glide suspension and soft purr of German engineering had lulled her into sleep until she was suddenly startled awake by the impatient blast of a car horn.

The Benz was stalled at a green light. Tuesday scanned around, half dazed, trying to understand why they were holding up traffic on Wilshire Blvd.

Then realized it was only her holding up traffic. Martellius was gone. The car was shifted into park, key still in the ignition, the driver's door hung open. Tuesday looked around until she spotted him on the sidewalk down the street walking fast. The driver threw back a nervous glance when he reached the corner then climbed into the rear of a burgundy Tahoe that was waiting to collect him.

Tuesday was a game-conscious chick but either it was sleep or the years of not being involved in gangster shit making her too slow to process things. She didn't connect the dots until she noticed the brown wrapped package on the front passenger seat.

Her eyes went wide.

She thought, *Oh shit!*

Chapter Fifteen

She scrambled to be free of her seatbelt, snatched her bag, left the shoes. She darted out of the back seat into traffic where she tried to warn the drivers stuck behind her. She ran along the side of the cars, narrowly missed getting hit by a delivery van, waving her arms and shouting for them to leave their vehicles and run.

All she received for her efforts was the courtesy you would expect from L.A. commuters during rush hour. Those who didn't bombard her with profanities, offered a one-fingered thanks.

Tuesday couldn't guess the weight of the package but figured there could be enough C-4 in it to leave a crater in the middle of Wilshire the size of a swimming pool.

Tuesday finally said fuck playing hero, and put as much distance between her and the Benz as she could. She hurried to the other side of the street, now regretting the tight knee-length pencil skirt that restricted her leg movements. The best she could manage was an awkward shuffle in her stocking-clad feet. Looking back at the car, she expected it to erupt into a fiery ball.

It never did. She watched and waited from halfway down the block. The Mercedes just sat in the middle of the street with the doors hanging open, frustrating motorists. Many of them had already started to pull around it.

After two minutes Tuesday considered if it was safe to return to the car. The box might have been harmless, but that didn't explain why Martellius bailed on her.

It also didn't explain why two men climbed out another familiar burgundy SUV at the opposite corner and were walking towards her with determined steps.

Two Latinos, early twenties, dressed too well to be street thugs. They were clean-cut in dark slacks and expensive leather loafers. These were the type of clothes young men only wore when they were on trial or had a job that demanded a professional vibe, although to her they killed their own swag by wearing tacky loud pastel-colored button-up shirts. One in blue, the other in green.

Tuesday locked eyes with them both and saw malice. Then looked to both of their waists and saw pistols.

The duo was approaching from the same direction as the Benz, removing the option of running back to the car even if the bomb was a dud. She turned and walked away from them at a desperate pace but didn't run. Tuesday feared that trying to run would only cause them to do the same, in which case she would be chased down instantly. She moved through the foot traffic on the sidewalk, many of whom stared at her like *what the fuck* for not wearing shoes.

Tuesday threw repeated glances back to the gunmen. They were causally stalking her from half a block but weren't looking to close the gap. With all the pedestrians out she figured the eyewitnesses restrained them.

Tuesday cursed herself when she realized she never replaced the Heckler they had taken from her at Dominic's. Tabitha King was licensed to carry so buying another pistol was a simple matter. She had been so distracted with seven different kinds of bullshit from work and home that it totally slipped her mind.

Luckily she had not left her bag in the car because then she would have been without her phone. She pulled it but rifled through the bag, searching for anything that could be used as a weapon. She carried nothing more threatening than a metal finger-nail file.

She chose to call Brandon rather than the police. Without Marcus, he was the only adult family she had on the west coast. She grunted in frustration when she only got his voice mail.

Tuesday left an urgent message, recounted all that she could about the driver, the box, and the goons in that short window his inbox allowed.

The idea was to stay in the safety of the crowd, but the foot traffic started to thin out on her side of Wilshire. More people were going in and out of the shops across the street, but just when she intended to switch over at the crosswalk, two more men were coming from that direction to meet her.

They practically announced themselves as being with the other two by being dressed identically in dark slacks and bright shirts with the same style. The man in red and his partner in pale violet were crossing at the corner, forcing Tuesday to turn left on the side street to keep from being boxed in.

She slipped into the alley that ran behind the businesses on Wilshire. After pulling the file from her Chanel bag, she ripped a thigh-high slit along the seam of her skirt to free her legs. In the same moment the second pair stepped into the alley at the corner and Tuesday struck out at a full sprint.

Her phone rang from inside her bag, most likely Brandon returning her call, but she couldn't answer it. She barely had a head start on her pursuers and it was hard enough trying to maintain that lead in bare feet while navigating all the broken glass and debris littering the ground.

Tuesday was headed back the way she had come on Wilshire. She figured if she could beat them back to the car then she could get away in the Benz. Tuesday had run track for a semester in middle school, and even though she wasn't as lean, still retained a portion of her speed.

She was redlining, yet the two giving chase were easily out-pacing her. The one in the red shirt was faster than the dude in the purple; Tuesday looked back and saw that Red was only about ten feet behind her and closing. Tuesday's foot landed in a puddle of cold brown liquid she didn't want to identify; she stumbled but kept her balance, cringed with disgust but didn't slow down.

Then for whatever reason, both men began to slack off. Tues-day couldn't tell if they were exhausted or what, but they slowed their pace from a sprint to a jog and allowed her to extend her lead. Tuesday didn't question it, just zipped past the huge indus-trial garbage dumpsters until there was about forty yards between them. As she neared the outlet, she planned two quick lefts to double back onto Wilshire and the Mercedes.

One more glance at the duo behind her showed them moving at a brisk walk, and when Tuesday looked forward again, she under-stood why they could afford not to hurry. The first two she en-countered on Wilshire, Blue Shirt and Green Shirt, had rounded the corner and cut off her exit. Both had guns in hand.

A set of killers were approaching from both ends of the alley while the scarred brick and graffiti-laced rears of commercial real estate flanked her on either side. She was trapped.

Chapter Sixteen

The colorful quartet slowed their approach as if sensing she were stuck. All were armed but not one had fired a shot. Tuesday didn't know if their plan was to kill her slowly or take her somewhere else to possibly be raped first. She had no intention of being easy prey. A talented artist had spray painted "Get down or lay down" on the wall in elaborate script. Tuesday refused to do either.

They closed in on her and Tuesday thought she had nowhere else to run. She was ready to make her stand right there. She would force them to kill her, choosing death over whatever violation they may have had in mind.

Then she noticed a narrow fence to her right that separated two closely-set properties. It was ten feet high and capped with razor wire, but a gap had been cut into the chain-link as if with bolt-cutters. Tuesday rushed to slip between the breach and safely made it through, aside from her blouse getting ripped.

She found herself in a narrow gangway that separated large warehouses. She took off in search of help.

As she ran she could hear the metallic rattle of the rainbow boys coming through the fence behind her. The sound was punctuated by several shots from a large-caliber gun which pushed Tuesday's fear-driven legs into a higher gear.

After running down a long straightaway, she made a right and then another before realizing she was in a system of these gangways. The abandoned industrial complex held dozens of two-story warehouses. She tried to find her way back to the street but each turn took her deeper into a maze of identical structures.

Tuesday ran by large cargo doors used for loading and offloading trucks. Frantically she tried the service doors, but each one that she came across was secured with a padlock.

While she no longer saw the armed men, she could feel them stalking her. They were only a turn or two behind her. She had to keep moving. The phone started to ring again and she snatched it out her bag, still at a run. Tuesday scrambled to answer quickly for fear the noise would give away her location.

Before Brandon could ask about her message, Tuesday whispered the situation in between gasps. Men were chasing her, she was somewhere off Wilshire lost in what appeared to be the grounds of an old factory.

Tuesday took a right and saw the one in the blue shirt coming at her from that way. She turned and fled down that aisle in the opposite direction.

Brandon was in her ear trying to guide and calm her, not doing well at either. Tuesday kept running, taking random lefts and rights, changing her course when she saw one of them. She couldn't fathom how she still hadn't reached the perimeter. She knew the complex was huge but guessed that she was going in circles.

She darted into an intersection, had to turn left to avoid Purple, and left again to avoid Green. She barely escaped the second; she bent a corner just as he raised his pistol.

Brandon said, "Look, I'm going to track your phone. If you can, try to find a place to hide until I get there."

Tuesday killed the line and sought to do just that, but every door she encountered was locked.

Tuesday was breathing heavily. She hadn't been working out with Shaun and her cardio had suffered. If she didn't get to rest soon, they would be able to track her by the sound of her asthmatic wheeze.

Tuesday finally spotted the fence-line about two hundred yards in the distance and took off for it, until Red appeared in the cross section ahead of her. She had to brake quickly in her bare feet, turn and go back the way she came. She fled down the gangway, went left at the opposite corner, planned to go around him. After she ran past two more structures, she tried to go right again, but Blue was standing in that aisle waiting on her. Before she could respond, Purple was coming from the east to flank her.

She dodged them but had to retreat deeper into the complex. Tuesday detected a strategy at play. They seemed to be working together to keep her away from the outer fence.

She passed one of the buildings decorated with more graffiti. The gold and jeweled headpiece of an English monarch was rendered with expert skill, the words "Down for my Crown," spray-painted under it in block lettering.

She sprinted into another intersection, and didn't see the goon in green coming from the perpendicular aisle. He apparently didn't see Tuesday either. They slammed into each other hard. The contents of Tuesday's purse spilled on the cement when she dropped it.

The collision stunned them both. But in that moment Tuesday saw the gun in his right hand coming up and reacted without thinking.

She didn't even realize she had been holding the nail file this entire time until she jammed it into his throat. She shivved him three quick times like an inmate on a level-four prison yard.

He stumbled backwards into the wall, his trembling fingers reached up to the leaking holes in his neck. The youngster's brown eyes stared into her gray, his look one of disbelief. He went limp and sagged to the ground, his blood smearing the brick. A grisly creation of her own art.

Tuesday didn't wait for him to die because the crimson stain spreading across his shirt in tune to his pulse was proof he wasn't long for this world. She didn't bother to collect all the items that fell from her purse. She only grabbed her phone and his gun before she bolted.

Those narrow passages were starting to feel claustrophobic. The constant fear that one of them would be waiting at each corner taxed her nerves as much as all the running taxed her legs.

They were getting close. Tuesday could hear one of them screaming and assumed they had discovered Green's body.

After a pained cry, he shouted, "Bitch, I'm gonna fuckin' kill you. I'm not fuckin' around anymore. Hear me bitch!"

Tuesday heard but kept moving. There was one less to deal with but fatigue wouldn't let her keep running.

She shot by another warehouse, or perhaps she had passed by this same one several times, but it was the first she saw that had a service door without a lock. It opened when she tested the knob. Her legs were tired and her feet were aching so she hoped she had found a place to hide until Brandon came for her. She hurried inside, closed the door behind her.

The interior was dark, but a few dust-covered skylights allowed her to trace the outline of huge machines whose purpose she could not define. She stood still for a moment, listening for the sound of scurrying rats; without shoes she was cautious for anything that may come along to gnaw at her toes. She crept around those rusty metal relics of the industrial revolution, prehistoric beasts rendered extinct by Google, Amazon and Facebook.

When someone snatched the door open, Tuesday hurried to hide behind one of the machines. She watched as Red and Purple split up to search for her. She guessed the one in blue might be waiting outside in case she got slick and tried to slip out behind them.

But she had Green's gun and that changed everything. She could do more than just play defense now. With each one she killed, she tilted the odds more in her favor.

Towards the rear of the building there were no windows, and

there the darkness was nearly pitch black. Tuesday intended to use that as her ally. She retreated into those shadows and searched for a place to set up her ambush. She hoped for a storage closet or a maintenance locker.

Tuesday was moving by touch when she suddenly was blinded by harsh light. She heard a lot of feet approaching along with the distinctive sound of guns cocking.

Tuesday blinked her sight back into focus to see she was caught up in the high-beams of three burgundy SUVs. A dozen men with assault rifles surrounded her in ski masks and black tactical gear. She threw down her gun and kicked it away when they commanded her.

A woman jumped out one of the SUVs overdressed in a stylish Dior romper and short leather jacket.

"I expected you twenty minutes ago."

La Guapa stood before her.

Chapter Seventeen

"It's easy to control people. The hard part is giving them the illusion of choice." Reina stood, backlit by the high beams of two more cranberry-colored Tahoes and a Range Rover with the same paint. "Every turn you could've made or hurdle you could've jumped had already been factored into the equation. It was cold, hard math and my math is never wrong."

Another elaborate trap, just like the one she set for her and Marcus at Dominic's. And just like at Dominic's, Tuesday had realized too late. From the moment she jumped out of the car she had been herded. The alley, the slit in the fence, this unlocked building; it was all a manipulation to bring her right to that spot.

Someone brought up the building lights, giving the ladies a clear view of each other. Tuesday knew she had to look a mess: sweaty, hair tossed, ripped skirt, runs in her stockings. Of course, La Guapa looked ready to grace the cover of *Vanity Fair*. Black hair spilled over her shoulders, her makeup flawless.

Seeing her uncorked all the negative emotions Tuesday had been holding back since Marcus stopped calling. "What happened at the meeting?"

"The same thing that's going to happen here. I'm going to make you a very generous offer and hopefully you'll be smart enough to accept it.

"Sebastian left you as the majority shareholder of Abel Incorporated. I don't know if you're aware, but those shares are extremely valuable and I represent a consortium of investors who are willing to pay you a fair price for them."

Tuesday frowned at her. "You and yo' little cartel buddies ain't 'bout to put the squeeze on me. I saw the news, I know the feds all up in y'all ass right now. Well you can suck my dick from here to San Francisco, 'cause ain't shit for sale."

La Guapa shook her head. "Oh sweetie, I know how convincing that man can be. Let me guess, he slid that ten-inch python in you and whispered in your ear all this flowery nonsense about his legacy and making amends for his past ways."

She smirked. "Trust me, I know how potent that dick is. The last time I saw him, I just sat on it for two hours."

Tuesday didn't feed. She bit back her lips in a way that looked like she was returning the grin. "Don't even try to play mind games wit' me bitch."

"Funny you should say that, considering I just had you playing one of my favorite games without you even knowing."

Tuesday got impatient. "Whatever this is right here, we ain't finna do this cheesy shit where we try to match wits with each other." She scanned the black-clad men surrounding her with automatic weapons. "So whichever one of y'all is supposed to put the bullet in my head, bring it on. Or else I got places to be."

La Guapa combed her fingers through her hair. "You are such a tough little hoodrat, aren't you? Tuesday, even you should be able to see that I could've killed you any number of ways before now if I wanted you dead. The driver while you slept, an actual explosive placed in your car. Any one of my ghosts who pushed you here could've accomplished that with a well-placed bullet. Do you really think you're fast enough to out-race a gun, especially with those thighs?"

The remaining members of the Loud Shirt Crew had joined them, and when La Guapa motioned for it, the one in blue passed her his gun. She pointed it at Tuesday's face and pulled the trigger three times.

The loud bangs made Tuesday jump, flinch, and cringe. The muzzle flashed but nothing came from the barrel but short coughs of warm air.

"It's a prop just like they use in the movies." La Guapa put the pistol to her own head, pulled the trigger then tossed it back to Blue. "Gunpowder but no lead."

"She killed Emilio!" Red Shirt stood over to the side. His broad shoulders rose and fell with each breath. "She stabbed him in the fuckin' neck."

Tuesday remembered the stunned expression on the face of Green Shirt, as if he never intended for their little game to become deadly. His blood still coated her hand. "I guess she didn't factor that into her math."

Red said, "La Guapa, I demand a life for a life."

La Guapa turned a cold eye to his insolence. "You don't get to make demands here. If your brother is dead it is because of his own carelessness."

She turned back to Tuesday. "Sebastian was a brilliant man, but still, he was just a man and all of them are the same—they reason through their penises then use their minds to justify the choice. He saw those sparkling green eyes and that big ghetto booty and fell in love. Then he attempted to justify that choice by trying to transform an uneducated girl from the streets into something respectable.

"But in being honest with yourself, you know you belong at the head of that corporation as much as I, with my two Ph.D.'s, belong in a strip club twerking for dollar bills. He may have given you a fake name and a forged Master's degree, but even you know you're in over your head. You're not smart enough to run Abel, and deep down, I don't think you really want to. He's forcing you to be a prop, Tuesday, just like they use in the movies."

Tuesday let her gaze drop just for an instant. It wasn't much, but enough for a predator like La Guapa to see weakness.

She took a step closer. "Abel was his vision, not yours. Reflect back on those nights lying with men who disgust you just for a chance to steal their crumbs. From the start, your vision was only about making a huge score—and now you've done that. The number we agreed on for your shares was three hundred and twenty-five million. You can add to that another four percent of our annual profits from the incoming shipments in perpetuity. But between us girls that number is negotiable. We're willing to go as high as six."

The calculation on Tuesday's face made the Mexican Barbie flash her luminous smile.

She continued: "And the entire deal will be above board, no back-alley cash drops or shady offshore accounts. We've already formed a legitimate company funded with enough assets to perform the buyout, even pulled some strings inside the Security Exchange Commission to get the deal pre-approved. All you have to do is sit down with the attorneys and start the paperwork."

Tuesday wasn't trying to do the math to see if she could squeeze out a few more percent. She had only heard everything La Guapa said up until three hundred and twenty-five million. After that her words turned to static.

Chapter Eighteen

"Sebastian made a decision with his heart; I need you to use your head."

Tuesday seemed to be considering her offer in the silence that hung. "My head tells me that if my stake is worth three hundred million now, in a company that's trending upward, then it'll be worth a lot more in the future. My head also tells me that if your shipments can't make it across the border then your business can't survive for much longer, so all I have to do is bide my time and wait for you to die out.

"On the flipside, my heart tells me not to sell out my husband for any amount of money. It's not my company anyway. He told me to protect it and I'm gone do that 'til he comes back."

La Guapa looked at her with pity.

"The company is yours to sell. Sebastian is gone. It was probably the most difficult thing I ever had to do."

Tuesday peered into her pretty brown eyes and saw something that resembled pain. The combination of anger and regret in her stare provided more proof for Tuesday than anything La Guapa could've said. Marcus was the type of man who could stir emotions so deeply within a woman that after twenty years she would still want him dead then be crushed by the loss. Tears sprang up in La Guapa's eyes; Tuesday figured hers had to look the same when her vision blurred.

"What happened to his body?"

"Please, Tuesday, don't travel that road. I can promise you it won't make you feel any better to know the details."

She sneered like a rabid animal. "So you were there? Was you at least woman enough to do it yo'self? Did you have the heart to look him in the eye while it happened?"

La Guapa wiped her cheeks. "Would it make you respect me more to know I did it myself? Would I earn some level of street credibility with you, or do you just want the validation from knowing I thought so highly of him that I stooped to do it personally?"

Her face tightened as anger trumped regret. "Well I'm sorry to disappoint you, Tuesday, but I don't adhere to your thug codes or share your little ghetto sensibilities about what it means to be a gangster. I graduated from Oxford and I'm a classically-trained pianist—I don't even pump my own gas."

None of the armed men standing around expected Tuesday to go after their boss. La Guapa sprang back terrified when Tuesday lunged. The soldiers grabbed Tuesday before she could get a hand on her.

They twisted her arm so hard Tuesday thought it would snap in two. Then someone thumped her on the head with the butt of their rifle. The blow brought Tuesday to her knees.

La Guapa stood over her but at a safer distance. "If you can check your emotion, you'll see this is the easiest decision you'll ever have to make: a large nine-figure check versus a situation that puts those two beautiful daughters at risk."

"Bitch, don't threaten my family." Tuesday looked up at her, blazing hatred.

La Guapa returned the glare. "He's the only reason you're not dead already. Killing you might complicate things but it doesn't mean you're untouchable.

"Fight me, Tuesday, and I won't just destroy you, I'll destroy his precious legacy. I'll leak his true identity to the press with all the juicy details, let the world see Marcus King for who he truly is. All the good work he's done with Abel will be washed away in a tidal wave of controversy when the people learn that beautiful glass tower was built with bullets, blood, and heroin bricks.

"And think about your kids. Is little Dani starting to ask what happened to her real mother yet? I'll make sure she finds out on Headline News along with everybody else at her school."

Tuesday spat, "You slimy ass bitch."

"Take the money, hoodrat. Go buy yourself all the gaudy jewelry, luxury cars, and strip clubs you want. Just know that it'll never buy you class."

She added: "And just so you know: after we put a bullet in your husband's head, his body was dismembered and fed to four-hundred-pound hogs at a farm my family owns outside of Port Arthur. Does that make you feel any better?"

La Guapa seemed to expect some measure of defeat in Tuesday, but when she was yanked back to her feet, Tuesday's eyes had the color and hardness of steel.

"Listen to me." Her voice was so calm yet commanding that even the men holding her came to attention. "Somehow, some way, I'm gone get you alone in a room where it's just you and me—no lawyers, no goons, no guns. Just you and me. In that room, all yo' money, all yo' power, all yo' fancy degrees won't count for shit. Then we'll see who's the better woman."

La Guapa put on a seductive smile. "And once we are all alone, what do you fantasize about doing to me?"

"FUBAR—I'm gonna fuck you up beyond all recognition. I'm gonna punch and punch you 'til every bone in your skull is broken, 'til that pretty li'l face look like hamburger meat. Then I'm gone put my hands around your neck and stare you right in the eye as I choke the life outta you. I'm gone kill you with my bare muthafuckin' hands."

She leaned closer. "I will get you in that room, Reina. I'm

gonna dedicate the rest of my life to this purpose. I won't rest until I accomplish this."

La Guapa seemed more amused than frightened. She shook her head, looked at Tuesday the way a patient parent would a petulant child in the throes of a tantrum.

She started in a scholarly tone: "You would seek to reduce our contest to a simple street fight because you're a simple street person. You're used to being poor, and for poor people, the only type of power at your disposal is physical. You have no comprehension of real power, because you have no experience with its various forms—industrial, political, institutional—other than being on the subjugate end. Tuesday, power doesn't lie in your ability to beat me up. It lies in my ability to send a text from Monaco and have your throat slit in Australia."

With a gesture La Guapa signaled to her troops that it was time to leave. All the men in black and the few in colorful shirts began to pile into the two long Chevy Tahoe ESVs. A few came out of hiding that Tuesday didn't even know had taken up sniper positions in the warehouse. The two men holding Tuesday didn't release her until La Guapa was far away from her.

"And by the way," La Guapa said. "The only way you'll ever get in that room with me is the same way you came to be in this one: I will have led you there every step of the way just like a little rat through a maze. Did Sebastian tell you that when I was thirteen years old, I became the FIDE's youngest female International Chess Master? That means I will always be nine moves ahead of you."

Tuesday scoffed, "Bitch, we ain't playin' board games."

The cargo door rolled up letting the afternoon spill into the dank building, stirring the stale air. La Guapa was headed for the rear of the sleek new Range Rover when Tuesday called out to her.

She said, "You like calling me 'hoodrat' and 'ghetto.' Ask yourself if that makes me more or less dangerous."

La Guapa paused, nodded thoughtfully as if she were pondering that for a second then fired back: "I'm stronger than you, I'm smarter than you, and I no longer have the great Sebastian Caine to worry about. Ask yourself if that makes me more or less dangerous."

Tuesday could only stand there in the gloom staring daggers in her direction as the trio of shiny burgundy SUVs backed out of the warehouse to be burnished by the pre-evening sun.

Chapter Nineteen

"You're still alive because Sebastian was clever enough to protect you and the girls."

Brandon handled the wheel of his Bentley sedan. He had found Tuesday limping down Wilshire Blvd. looking like a homeless person. Although they discovered no bomb in the Benz, he insisted she ride with him and called for the company car to be towed.

"If something were to happen to you then ownership of the shares would split equally to your daughters, only they'd sit in a trust until Danielle turns twenty-four. Now if something were to happen to all of you, then the family trust would become its own legal entity and assume ownership of Abel. Because the trust can't make decisions or facilitate running the business, it would function much like a limited partnership. The shares would be trapped in this sort of lock box for the entire life of the company. I just found out myself but apparently he set this trust up months ago."

He glanced over at Tuesday who was staring out the passenger window, her expression vacant. From behind her left ear, a thin trail of blood trickled down her neck. Being struck with the rifle had probably given her a mild concussion but she dismissed it when Brandon asked about taking her to a hospital.

She appreciated his concern and the explanation of the trust, only she was too distracted by her own thoughts to be engaged.

"I'll see to it that something particularly unlucky happens to Martellius." Brandon held the wheel tightly, flexing his hands in expensive leather driving gloves as if eager to do lethal work with them.

With everything else, Tuesday hadn't considered her chauffeur until then. Martellius drove her for nearly four months and she couldn't know if he were a mole La Guapa planted from the jump or at what point he came to be on her leash. Tuesday thought back on all the times she had been alone with him in the car: eyes closed, guard down, vulnerable.

"Don't even bother," she said in response to Brandon in a voice that sounded far away. "He'll turn up dead in a couple of days. He's not important enough to protect and she's not gonna leave a loose end like that."

Brandon announced his agreement and frustration with a heavy breath. He navigated the Bentley along the Pacific Coast Highway where the descending dusk triggered the head and tail-lights of commuters. Tuesday continued to stare out her window, eyes still focused on something invisible in the distance.

Tuesday always took pride in being a planner. Her ability to read the strengths and weaknesses in people and a mind cursed to be obsessed with details allowed her to stay ahead in the robbery game. She was used to being the smartest person in the room—that was until she met Marcus.

Back when her crew had targeted Sebastian Caine, the mysterious street king had been several steps ahead of Tuesday the entire time. He read her like no other man had been able to do since her first love, A.D. Using men had always come so easy, but Marcus was just the second she ever met who she couldn't manipulate.

She hated to admit it but La Guapa was a female version of her husband. Smart, calculated, with an ability to see straight through her. But what Tuesday couldn't get over was how she had toyed with her, literally played her like a video game.

The maze, the colorful shirts, she had even given a clue when she referred to them as ghosts; Tuesday only put it all together during that ride home. La Guapa had made her play a real-life game of Ms. Pac Man, and that fact pissed off Tuesday more than anything La Guapa had said about her or Marcus.

Tuesday sat there humiliated, chewing on the inside of her cheek. "I'm killin' dat bitch!" The words left her mouth like a viper spitting venom.

Brandon leaned back in his seat. A bit of the anger over Martellius drained from his face. "You'll be jeopardizing the very thing he gave his life for."

She ignored him. "I need you to tell me how we can beat her."

Brandon was silent long enough for her to turn and give him an expectant look.

He finally said: "Tuesday, you're a wonderful woman, I see why Sebastian chose you, but I need you to understand something. Reina Rodriguez isn't like any of the enemies you faced back in Detroit. She's not some low-level gun dealer or some dancer from the club looking to come up. This woman has very powerful friends and a very strong team. She is the most dangerous type of individual: extremely high I.Q. with no moral code."

Brandon relayed a story from back when La Guapa had first taken over her father's business. He explained that a Colombian family of smugglers out of Medellin stopped respecting the Rodriguez family after they put a woman in charge. They challenged her for control of the border towns but after eleven months of bloodshed, the two regimes had fought to a stalemate.

"Somehow Reina learned who would be catering their granddaughter's fifteenth birthday party and hid twenty pounds of C-4 in the girl's cake. After her little present, the Colombians and the Mexican cartel bosses fell in line."

Tuesday spoke the words slowly, emphatically. "She put a bullet in the back of his head, cut up his body into pieces, and fed them to pigs!"

Brandon tried to calm her. "It's natural to want revenge, but going at Reina doesn't bring back your man. Just like her wanting revenge for her brother is what started this whole thing and didn't bring him back either."

"Marcus told me what happened to Rico wasn't his fault."

Brandon pursed his lips in a way that said "don't be stupid." "I loved Sebastian, worked for him almost from the beginning, but that man wasn't no saint. He always wanted power, knew Rene Rodriguez had a seat at The Table. Sebastian was always a helluva puppeteer, used the son to get to the father. Then got rid of Rico when he had the old man's favor—who do you think told their enemies which club Rico would be at?"

"You're saying Reina was right and Marcus sold out his best friend?" Tuesday looked at Brandon suspiciously. "Why are you telling me all this?"

"Because life is a series of serious choices. Because in the game, you have to make choices like that. Hard choices, and then you have to live with them. Back then he chose to be a boss rather than a goon. Just like he chose to protect his family and keep Abel clean."

Tuesday shook her head. "He chose to die."

"So that you and those girls could live. And live well! The trust he put in place ties La Guapa's hands, but the knots are really loose. If you test her—"

"So what am I s'posed to do?!" she roared at him. "This bitch killed my husband, the father of my children, and I'm s'posed to just take that shit?"

The old man's patient tone provided ice for her fire. "I don't know what you're supposed to do but I do know one thing. Three twenty-five up front and four percent of the flip is a damn good deal."

Tuesday frowned like he had just committed blasphemy.

"Look, I'm not telling you to betray him. I'm just saying you have your own choice to make. You never wanted the company and you walk away with enough to give your children an amazing life."

"I made my choice." Tuesday turned her attention back to something outside her window. "I'm killin' dat bitch. And just to be clear, I'm not askin' yo' permission."

"Tuesday, we're family. I'm on your side and I stand by whatever decision you make." Her stepfather ran his gloved hand over the thick curly hair that now boasted more salt than pepper. "And just to be clear, you never needed my permission."

Chapter Twenty

Miles away, just outside of Los Angeles County, the burgundy SUVs pulled onto a small private airfield purchased through a dummy corporation. The secluded ten-acre parcel had a landing strip long enough to accommodate an executive-class jet; however, it was unknown to the FAA or any regulatory industry, so the two luxury King Air 350i planes awaiting on the runway had landed illegally. This place served several wealthy owners who might need to discreetly fly themselves or their product in and out of California without the scrutiny received at a large commercial airport.

Within minutes, La Guapa, most of her men and their weapons, would be in the air and headed back to Texas. A small group would stay behind to handle unfinished business in L.A.

The Range Rover traveled with two Tahoes in the front and rear of it. In the back seat, Reina and her sister sat in silence, each absorbed by her own interest. Through her phone Reina was on a fashion site previewing the spring couture collection from Galliano. Her sister Roselyn's attention was on a worn, dog-eared copy of *Atlas Shrugged*.

Reina frowned her disagreement over a studded ball gown

with a feathered train getting positive reviews from the fashion bloggers. She said, "You think I'm being reckless."

She never looked up from her phone. "I can do the math, Rose. I can calculate to a thousandth of a cent how much this entire demonstration cost us in money and manpower. And it wasn't all just so I could taunt her."

Through her stylish wooden frames, Roselyn peered down at her book. Roselyn was present for everything that took place in the warehouse. She witnessed the exchange between her sister and Tuesday from behind the Range Rover's tinted glass.

Reina said, "Taunting someone is a proven psychological ploy. Athletes will often prod their opponents, make them angry to affect their performance. Empirical data shows that people do not function at optimal ability under duress. It's nothing personal.

"And if this were anyone else we would proceed in the same manner. Precisely the same. This isn't about him—it never was. I explained that from the start."

Roselyn quietly turned a page in her book.

"My objectivity is *not* compromised," Reina said angrily. "I'm not arguing that we couldn't have hidden behind a veil of anonymity and purchased the company without her ever knowing. It's not that I'm so vain that I would've never been satisfied with just cutting her check. I'm aware that I humiliated her today but it was necessary. I'm not some sadistic bully picking on the weakest kid in class.

"I know what I'm doing, Rose. I don't have to explain myself to you."

The twin never looked up from Rand's wisdom. They sat in silence for a beat, swaying in their seats when the Range passed over a divot in the road.

It was only a few seconds before Reina started again. "Yeah, I have been beating this 'Revenge for Rico' drum for twenty years, and now we have it, but I'm not just going after Sebastian's family in a blind rage. I'm not jealous. We need the company and she has it. It's cold, hard math and she's just a variable to be extrapolated, a thing to be solved and moved past. Inconsequential."

Roselyn crossed the pleated pant legs of a pinstripe men's suit by Sergio Hudson that had been tailored to a woman's physique. She wore a lacy blouse under the jacket to feminize the look.

Reina looked up past the driver and passenger in the front seats to the two large blue-and-white dual prop planes awaiting them on the runway. Her expression grew pensive.

"Sebastian Caine easily had the most tactical, far-reaching, disciplined mind we've ever faced, and it would be a mistake to assume he married someone strictly for their looks. And don't even say it Rose: after all, he didn't even marry me. Ha ha ha."

Roselyn's lips stretched into a thin smile. Her eyes never wandered from the page.

"And of course I know there are examples of rare people for whom pressure makes them focus. Her whole soliloquy about the room was amusing but did you see the look on her face when she threatened me? I saw fire and focus. I better than anyone should know not to underestimate a scorned woman."

She brooded over that for a moment then shook her head as if to dislodge the idea. "She's just a hoodrat that he found and took pity on like some stray animal—part of his new magnanimous persona. She's nothing to be concerned over."

Reina studied a Gautier dress with a sweetheart neckline then tucked her phone. She looked over to Roselyn who was turning another page, still wearing a content little smirk.

"What could you possibly glean from that book that you didn't get the first twenty-nine times you read it? I found her analysis trite and unremarkable when it was assigned to us in fifth grade; the cynical observations of a closeted lesbian who was mad at the world because the social constraints of her time wouldn't permit her to openly suck all the pussy she wanted."

"Your mistake was that you misjudged her motivation." Roselyn adjusted her glasses and Reina knew her sister wasn't talking about Ayn Rand. "You offered money to a woman who already has wealth. She's not motivated by greed; she's motivated by survival. We'll have to adapt our strategy accordingly."

Chapter Twenty-one

By the time Tuesday made it home, her adrenaline had waned, starting a chorus of aches from her lower body. Without shock absorbing shoes, her ankles and knees had suffered for all that running barefoot on concrete. She also intended to swallow a few aspirin for the throbbing in her head.

From her tub Tuesday looked over that spacious master bathroom she used to share with her husband: platinum basins set into beige marble with olive-green trimming, his-and-her vanities sat side by side. Marcus's remained a shrine with his toothbrush, beard trimmers, and shaving mirror untouched since he cleaned up for their dinner at Dominic's.

She used to love watching him groom himself. She could still see him shirtless, back and arms swollen from the day's workout, as he lined his goatee. He would catch Tuesday's reflection staring at him like a schoolgirl with a crush then give her a curious look that asked: "What the fuck are you looking at?" He would smile at her as if she were crazy then go back to what he was doing, not knowing how horny he was making her.

Her husband never understood that women do this type of

weird shit when they're deep in love. Sometimes they liked watching their men do ordinary stuff, man stuff. They also did weird things to feel closer to their man, which was why Tuesday finished her bath and put on one of Marcus's T-shirts and a pair of his baggy sweats that still held his scent.

Outside of the blow to her ego, the most painful thing that came from her run-in with La Guapa was the fact she couldn't keep lying to herself about Marcus. During the drive home she and Brandon had talked about setting up the plane crash scenario then starting the paperwork to have him legally declared dead.

If she couldn't lie to herself, that meant she could no longer lie to her daughters. The line: "Daddy was away taking care of business," would temporarily placate Tanisha's whining but not Danielle's growing suspicion. The girl was old enough and smart enough to know that no business, no matter how important, would keep a loving father ignoring his phone when his daughter called. Whenever Danielle confronted Tuesday on this, Tuesday came up with some excuse that sounded weak even to her. The constant lying only produced more friction between them.

It was time for the truth to come out and Tuesday agreed to drop that bomb in the morning. It was a conversation that she didn't look forward to, but she didn't just put it off out of cowardice. It was eight and Tuesday didn't think a little girl should learn her father was dead ninety minutes before bedtime. She would allow her girls the gift of blissful ignorance for another ten hours and would enjoy that with them.

Tanisha was in a playful mood this evening and her musical laughter was contagious. Tuesday found herself on the floor in her daughter's room, crawling on all fours chasing her and playing with Barbie dolls. Spending time with her baby helped to soothe her wounded pride as much as the bath helped to soothe her joints. Tanisha tired herself out and was asleep ten minutes into *Frozen*.

Lately, stepping into Danielle's room had been like entering enemy territory, but Tuesday brought a peace offering to show she wasn't coming for a fight. She carried two bowls of ice cream set over a few of Esperanza's homemade cookies. Tuesday was trying to play the cool mom even though Danielle had already had dinner and it was way too late for sugary snacks.

Danielle was playing a fighting game with realistic graphics and Tuesday just asked to play without bringing up that it seemed too violent for a nine-year-old. For the most part, the bribe worked because Danielle gave up a controller, showed her how to select a character, how to punch and kick. Then she chose a sexy female ninja in a bikini and mercilessly beat Tuesday's ass in twelve straight matches.

Tuesday didn't get the warm and fuzzy moment she hoped for; Danielle was mostly as cold as the dessert she scooped into her mouth between beatings. However, for the first time in a long time they didn't argue. Tuesday took that as a win.

Tuesday returned to her room, climbed into bed. At first their huge mattress had felt too lonely without Marcus, but sleeping in the same spot where they had spent so much time and shared so much passion felt right. She curled up on her side of the bed. Some delusional part of her still expected him to slide in next to her, wrap her from behind, press his warm body against hers, then start grinding his hard dick into her soft ass like he often did.

Tuesday got ambushed by a montage of memories but didn't want to feed into it. She chased some Xanax with some Remy XO to fight off the loneliness and still drifted off with tears on her pillow.

Tuesday couldn't remember much of the dream. What she did recall involved Marcus, her best friend Tushie who had been dead for three years, and several four-hundred-pound hogs that smelled like burnt flesh. She experienced those sudden and inexplicable shifts in location that happens in dreams. Tuesday figured that the combination of Remy, Xanax, and ice cream right before bed triggered a strange head trip.

The dream was scary but not as frightening as what she saw when she opened her eyes.

She first thought the acrid stench was a carryover from her nightmare until she heard the smoke alarms blaring.

The house was on fire.

Chapter Twenty-two

Tuesday jumped out of bed, stumbled a bit. Sleep and Remy still weighed her. She found her house shoes, slid her feet into them. Then she found the .40 caliber Marcus kept in the nightstand.

Both kitchens were on the first floor and in a different wing of the house; the smell of smoke was too strong to come from anything Esperanza might have neglected on the stove. Tuesday confirmed this when she opened the door to the master bedroom and a noxious gray cloud assaulted her. She fought her way through it, down the hall, screaming for her daughters.

She burst into Tanisha's room to see her tiny bed was empty. Tuesday thought the smoke and blaring alarms might have scared a three-year-old into hiding so she checked the closet and under the bed. She scoured the room, kicking and stepping on plastic toys.

Tuesday considered that her baby girl might have run to her big sister in a time of crisis but in Danielle's room all she discovered was another unmade bed. Neither daughter was in their room nor answering to the repeated shouting of their name.

Then Tuesday saw something that dropped her heart into her stomach. Large grimy boot prints stained Danielle's carpet.

She scrambled down the foyer stairs, blinded by panic and the thickening smoke. On the first floor the acrid gray vapor became a black beast, stinging her eyes, trying to choke her. Tuesday's mind tortured her with images of the girls trapped somewhere in the fire: hurt, unconscious, or worse.

Tuesday felt her way forward into the great room. The smoke was heavier there. She was closer to the source of the fire because she could feel its heat.

Tuesday screamed their names at her highest pitch then paused for a moment. Her ears were attuned, hopeful for a response or the sound of crying children. Twenty-two thousand square feet offered too many places where the girls could be.

Tuesday groped around blindly when she tripped over an unseen object. Her house shoe slipped off; her bare foot landed in something sticky and wet. It took a few seconds for her blurry, burning eyes to bring the shapeless mass on the floor into focus. The body had a dark crimson stain pooled around it.

The live-in housekeeper Esperanza was facedown, head cocked, eyes wide. Three bullets left exit punctures in the back of her nightgown.

Tuesday thrust the pistol forward with both hands, elbows locked, just like she had learned from A.D., who had given her her first gun. She swung the barrel from left to right then a full three-sixty degrees. Black smoke swirled around her, blocked her vision, possibly concealed the murderer.

"Dani? Nisha?" It was a desperate plea capped by rough coughs. She inched ahead into the poisonous mist, praying that she wouldn't trip over a smaller body.

She moved into the main hall and saw flames at the far end climbing the walls, devouring the ceiling. Crackling, hissing like a snarling beast, and Tuesday figured it had probably been birthed in the rarely-used commercial kitchen. The fire had grown large enough to make the entire north side of the house resemble a Christian's worst fear of Eternity. It consumed studio portraits of Marcus and the girls which felt strangely prophetic for Tuesday.

She continued to search all the rooms and spaces on the first floor yet to be touched by the blaze.

The home theater was at the southernmost side of the house and one of the last rooms to be checked. Tuesday eased inside, allowing the .40 to lead her through the door. Their theater was modest when compared to some of the more elaborate estates in Beverly Hills: one-hundred-twenty-inch screen with comfortable seating for twelve.

At a glance Tuesday could see the room was empty, but through the haze of smoke she glimpsed a quick shadow moving behind her. Before she could swing the pistol in that direction, someone hit her. Hard.

Chapter Twenty-three

Tuesday didn't know if she was hit with a fist or a bat. All she knew was that something impacted her jaw hard enough to send her eight feet into the room. She skidded to a stop at the foot of a sofa, stunned, her world spinning.

The silhouette of her attacker shifted and blended from one person to three. Tuesday fired wildly, barely able to lift the big pistol which suddenly felt like a hundred-pound dumbbell. She couldn't tell if she hit him or not because he seemed to disappear like a phantom after the third shot.

Her head was ringing from the smoke she inhaled and the blow she took. The irritating screech of the fire alarms pierced her skull. When she tried to stand, her legs wouldn't cooperate.

Then Tuesday heard two large booms that sounded like they came from a cannon. A sofa cushion exploded a few inches from her head. She scrambled over the couch to shield herself behind it.

She had to flatten her body on the floor as bullets tore through the upholstery, the wall and the movie screen overhead. She stuck out the gun, bust four more times in the direction of the shooter.

Her head was still ringing but she had enough sense to stop wasting bullets. Marcus's .40 was a nine-plus-one weapon and she'd already spent seven. She didn't intend to fire again until she had a face to aim at.

Smoke poured into the room at a faster rate. The fire was drawing closer.

Tuesday was afraid to peek out from her hiding spot for fear she might catch a bullet in the eye. Her head was on a swivel, expecting the man to try to creep around either side of the sofa. She didn't expect him to dive over the top. Tuesday was caught by surprise when a big body landed on her.

She was belly-down and scrambling to overthrow him. He pinned her arms above her head and she felt his lips on her ear. "La Guapa says hello." His Latino accent was as strong as the smell of shit and cigarettes on his breath.

Tuesday couldn't use her gun hand but luckily he couldn't use his either. He needed both arms to secure hers but he was battling for a more dominant position. If he mounted her back, used his knees to lock her arms, his hand would be free to strangle her, pound her face, or deliver a kill shot from his gun. Dealer's choice.

"Bitch, this is for Emilio. Where I'm from, it's blood for blood."

Tuesday grunted, "Where's my girls?"

"Saving them for something special," he whispered. "Gonna take them to Guapa, but first they'll meet a few friends of mine. The type of guys who really like girls that age."

While he was bigger, stronger, and easily overpowering her, his words put another level of fight and fury in Tuesday. She whipped her head back as hard as she could, smashed his face with the back of her skull.

For her it hurt like hell but Tuesday knew it had to be worse for him because he let go of her arms. Through his pain he called her another bitch and whined about his tooth being broken.

She tried to slither from underneath him but he caught hold of her legs. Tuesday kicked at him, tried to wiggle free. He held her ankles and started to crawl back onto her.

Meanwhile, flames had crept in from the hall, clawing at the walls and chewing up the floor. Tuesday looked back and could see the face of her attacker tinted orange in the firelight. Red Shirt was now dressed in all black. Blood smeared his mouth and nose, hatred reflected in his eyes.

Tuesday still had the .40 but her angle prevented her from getting a good shot. She had to awkwardly reach the gun down, back and around her.

Tuesday couldn't line up the muzzle with his face, but the pistol was just to the side of his head. She fired anyway. Even though she missed him, he screamed like a wounded lion. She hoped the loud gun blast had burst his eardrum. He clutched the sides of his skull.

Tuesday tried to aim again but this time he was quick enough to take control of the gun. He grabbed her wrist, twisted her arm into a chicken wing, then put his hand over hers and forced her to squeeze the last two shots into the wall. Once multiple clicks indicated the pistol was empty, he ripped it from Tuesday's fingers and tossed it away.

He pulled Tuesday to her feet then slammed her face first into the wall. He spun her around, slapped her across the face with his own pistol and the blow sent Tuesday back to the ground.

She was on her back, writhing in pain, holding her cheek. He stood over her, and with the fire spreading across the ceiling over him, looked like Death incarnate.

He kneeled over Tuesday. He ran his tongue over his chipped front tooth and winced at the pain.

He pulled out the clip and showed it to Tuesday. "No games. Real bullets this time."

He placed his barrel to her lips. "Open your mouth."

Tuesday shook her head. Her eyes stared back at him defiantly.

He punched Tuesday harder than she had ever been hit by a man or woman. Her head rolled to the side, her eyes rolled in their sockets and the room spun faster than before, only this time peppered with flashing white spots. Her body wanted to quit but it took all she had to fight off the pull towards unconsciousness.

"I don't give a fuck what Guapa said. Emilio was my brother." He let out a series of coughs, probably from the smoke, then pushed the gun back to her lips. "Bitch, I said open yo' fuckin'—"

Tuesday didn't hear anything, just saw his body jerk, felt a red mist spray her face and saw him tumble to his side. She looked left and he was face-to-face with her, only with a newly formed hole in his forehead.

When someone helped her to her feet, she knew it was her stepfather. Her eyes were stinging from the smoke, but she was familiar with the feel of Egyptian cotton in Brandon's rare custom shirts as well as the scent of his cologne. He supported her with one arm while his silenced pistol was in the other hand.

"Nisha? Dani?" Tuesday's speech was slurred like a drunk.

He navigated Tuesday over towards the window, fired two muffled shots then cleared out the shattered glass with several kicks. "I got 'em. They're already outside. After last time, I promised nobody would ever take either of my babies again."

Chapter Twenty-four

"You know this is just the beginning."

Brandon was behind the wheel of a faceless white Ford economy van without windows or logos. Tuesday was in the rear cargo space sitting on the floor with Danielle, holding Tanisha who still hadn't stopped crying since being taken from their beds.

Brandon explained that it was only by chance that he was stopping by the house to pick up some company paperwork when he spotted the flames and the van parked by the front gate. Brandon claimed the driver was waiting for his partner when he crept up and got the drop on him. He was able to piece the play together after seeing Danielle and Tanisha zip-tied and blindfolded in the back. The former hit man snatched the driver out, painted the ground with his silenced .32 then went inside for Tuesday.

When the cry of sirens announced it was time to leave, they took the van simply because the girls were already there and it was closer to the street.

Tuesday tried to calm her daughters, convince them that they were safe and the danger was over. Her bruised face only made Tanisha cry harder. Danielle was quiet, only responding to Tuesday's concern with short one-word answers, as if annoyed.

Brandon swerved to go around a slow-moving truck on the highway. "Police and fire crews are on the scene by now, so clean-up is out of the question. The arson and the murders will get press, nothing we can do about that. The one inside the house will be easier to explain than the one by the gate. The home invasion allows us to play the self-defense card if need be, but without Sebastian's influence we've lost a lot of our political leverage. Not gonna be so easy to just make this disappear."

Tuesday only half-listened to him. She respected that he was thinking about damage control; the throbbing in her head made it impossible for her to think at all.

"I didn't anticipate her trying something so bold. I assumed with the trust in place she wouldn't make an attempt on your life."

"I'm not sure she did." Tuesday explained what Red Shirt had said which made her think that La Guapa hadn't ordered him to kill her.

Brandon said, "I can deal with the investigation but first we have to get you and the girls somewhere safe. Lay low for a while until I get things situated. You'll have to leave Abel in my hands for now."

Tuesday put Tanisha in Danielle's arms, then joined Brandon at the front of the van. She took the passenger seat and spoke low so the kids wouldn't overhear.

"She just burned down my house and tried to snatch my girls. It's on now so I don't wanna hear no more of that live-and-let-live shit. How do we kill this bitch?"

He ran a hand through his gray curly hair. It seemed to be a nervous habit. "I've been in this game for a minute, so I know a little something about going to war, and the main thing you need to understand is that there's always collateral damage. Before you start this, defend what you love first."

She nodded. "I didn't start this but I feel what you're saying."

"Reina doesn't just have money: she has men and the backing of the Mexican cartels. You'll need an army."

"I'll get one."

"You'll need allies."

Tuesday didn't have a quick response for that. For her, friends had always been in short supply.

Brandon turned to examine her face. The entire left side was swollen and bruised, the eye half-closed. "You might need a doctor."

"I'm good. Not the first time I caught a fade. Some ice and a couple days, I'll be right back to my fine ass self."

That made the old man chuckle. He couldn't believe that Tuesday was able to make a joke right then.

"Our story is that you and the girls weren't home at the time but the authorities will still want to talk to you. I'll stall that as long as I can but we still got to get you out of sight for now. Nearly all the hotels have cameras and the company jet won't be available for a couple of days."

Tuesday slipped into her own thoughts for a moment then told Brandon to pull off the freeway at the next exit. "I know where me and the girls will be safe, at least for a little while."

An hour later Tuesday was pounding on the door of a low rent bungalow in West Hollywood. Brandon took an unnecessarily long and circuitous route to make sure they weren't followed and still watched the house for a moment first.

Shaun finally answered wearing a robe, head wrapped in a scarf. She blinked sleep from her eyes when she saw Tuesday standing under her porch light at three in the morning. Shaun's expression went from surprised to horrified at the sight of Tuesday's face.

Before Shaun could start in, Tuesday silenced her and pushed her back across the threshold.

"Is anybody here with you?" her voice an urgent whisper.

"No. Nobody's here." Shaun mimicked her tone. She looked nervously at the pistol in Tuesday's hand then past her to the creepy van parked out front. "Bae, what's going on?"

"I know we left things fucked up, but you the only person on this side of the country I can trust right now. I'm in trouble and I'm gone need to stay here for a couple days. Is that cool?"

"Yeah. Of course."

"It's the worst kind of trouble," Tuesday warned. "The kind that might get you into trouble just for being close to me, so think on it and don't just say—"

Shaun was emphatically bobbing her head before Tuesday could finish the statement. She kissed Tuesday several times on the good cheek.

Tuesday gently pushed her back. "My girls in the van: they scared, they confused, they been through some serious shit. Before I bring 'em in, we need to go over some ground rules."

Chapter Twenty-five

Marcus's Gulfstream G-650 officially belonged to Abel Incorporated, but had always been at Tuesday's disposal when not in company use. During the four days she hid out at Shaun's house waiting for the plane to become available, Brandon had come through with the paperwork that declared Marcus dead and transferred the estate and business to Tuesday. This only gave her more right to the jet.

Tuesday looked out the window on their approach and saw the familiar Detroit skyline begin to take shape: the mirrored glass towers of the General Motors building (formerly known as the Renaissance) and the Ambassador Bridge stretching across the river to Windsor. With each thousand feet they descended, more came into focus, and Tuesday bounced her knees with nervous excitement.

By the time they landed at Metro Airport, the excitement was gone, only leaving her the nerves. She was fearful the police would be waiting for her to arrive. She may have spent the last three years as Tabitha King, but Tuesday Knight still had warrants for three homicides and a missing person's case. Despite having all the IDs and certificates to prove she was somebody else, she was still wearing the same face and fingerprints.

Coming back to Detroit had been a big risk because if she were arrested by chance, she might never leave it.

Her heart rate slowed a bit when she, Shaun, Danielle, and Tanisha made it through the airport without incident. She used her Tabitha King info to rent something inconspicuous and they pulled off in a blue Hyundai.

Tuesday had set Shaun and the girls up at Marcus's old house in a suburb of Metro Detroit called Romulus. It was the same low-key house where he had been living with Danielle when Tuesday first met him. She could only hope that La Guapa didn't know about it.

Tuesday never intended to bring Shaun along but the girl had insisted. After saying no a few times, Tuesday agreed for selfish reasons. She would be busy in Detroit and Shaun could help by watching the girls.

Tuesday had appreciated Shaun letting her crash but needed her to understand they were not playing house. The ground rules were simple: no sex, no touching, no calling Tuesday Bae, Boo, or Sweetheart; none of Shaun's loud declarations of her undying love. When Tuesday introduced Shaun to Tanisha and Danielle, Tuesday stressed the word *friend* so that Shaun would not get it twisted.

They had landed late the previous night. Early that morning Tuesday was driving alone.

In her absence, she had watched as her city got reduced to being a punchline in the national news. The proud Motor City, once the world's leader in production and manufacturing, had only become famous for its corrupt officials, bankruptcy, and desperation. Tuesday drove through the streets feeling like a tourist. She saw some improvements made to downtown in the form of new and renovated sports venues, condominiums, and casinos.

She cruised by the building that held her former condo. The Seymour was still well-maintained. Seeing it reminded Tuesday of the life she had there as well as the life she had taken there. She would never forget the day she came home to find two would-be killers waiting in the parking garage. Tuesday had caught her first body, had blown the chick's brains out in the same elevator she once used every day. It was the last time she had ever stepped foot into a home that had been her sanctuary.

She left downtown via I-96 headed for the Westside. The suburbanites didn't shoot craps or watch the Red Wings there so the inner city didn't see the same investment dollars. The malignancy of blight had grown like a cancer as Tuesday bypassed entire city blocks without livable dwellings, just abandoned ruins and trash-strewn fields.

She continued her trip down memory lane by driving past the home where her best friend Tushie once lived. Surprisingly, the house still stood and appeared to have a family living there, although the overgrown lawn and peeling paint suggested the new tenants took far less pride in it than her girl had done.

Some delusional part of Tuesday thought that if she went and knocked on that door, Tushie would answer it and greet her with a big hug. She would be standing there just as dark and pretty as Tuesday remembered her, wearing a pair of leggings that showed off the booty that earned her name and fame. Tuesday pictured them sitting like they used to, blowing blunt after blunt while they grinned and giggled like schoolgirls, putting each other up on everything that had been happening in their lives. Tuesday would show pictures and eventually introduce Tushie to the daughter she named after her. Tuesday could almost hear that sweet Louisiana accent and the thought made her smile to herself.

Tuesday crept down the block and turned off at the corner. She couldn't fool herself like with Marcus—she knew her home-girl was dead. Tuesday had discovered the body right in that very house. That fateful day she had rushed there to warn Tushie of the plot against them only to find her best friend butt-naked with a hole in her head. That image was enough to remove the smile.

She headed for West 7 Mile to The Bounce House. It was the small strip club that Tuesday went from working at in her teens to owning in her thirties. It was also another storehouse of sweet and sour memories. The club had been more of a home to her than the dozens of apartments and multifamily flats she lived in during the same period. A place where desperate girls danced for balled-up dollar bills had been the only permanent thing in her life.

As much as she had come to hate the place, it also saddened her to see what had become of it. She pulled into the parking lot of the strip mall where her club had shared space with four other businesses to find a burned facade with boarded windows. The bricks were seared as black as charcoal briquettes. The plywood slab that covered the entrance had been tagged by the 7 Mile Bloods.

She didn't stop, just drifted past remembering all the faces she had seen come and go in that twenty years. A few girls had used The Bounce House as a spring board to better things; many more had taken losses so huge that it was their rock-bottom. Tuesday stared at the charred remains, silently paying homage to all of those women who had been made and broken there before she pulled out of the lot.

As she drove it occurred to her that Detroit was pretty much the antithesis of Beverly Hills. One place represented abundance; the other, scarcity. One was mansions and movie stars, the other was crack houses and carjackers. Much of her city looked like the setting for an apocalyptic sci-fi thriller. Tuesday had been molested there as a child and raped there as an adult. She had been robbed, shot at, and nearly killed on these streets more times than she cared to count.

When she paused at the red light on 7 Mile and Livernois, an '83 Monte Carlo pulled up next to her, dripping green candy with bass that sounded like a gorilla trying to escape from the trunk. The driver wore a white do-rag, Cartier woods with ice in the frames, and had a three-year-old, red-nosed Pitbull riding shot-gun. He puffed a Backwood, then gave Tuesday a slow nod that said she could get it.

Tuesday returned the nod. He even brought out her smile again.

It was not because she was feeling this nigga. It was because she missed *these* niggas. This was that Detroit shit. This was home.

Chapter Twenty-six

24 Karats was set in an old commercial complex that had once housed a supermarket, an auto parts store, a Foot Locker and a small coffee shop. Detroit's sharp economic decline had claimed three of the five businesses. The community around Joy Road and Greenfield had obviously decided they needed caffeine and strippers to make it through the struggle.

Due to the casualties, the strip club had inherited copious amounts of parking. In the huge lot, a cluster of vehicles fronted 24 Karats. The place was jumping for noon on a weekday. Tuesday left her rented Hyundai several rows behind the other patrons.

Inside, the owner had gone with a cheesy Tibetan theme, played to death by so many Chinese carryout restaurants. The walls were covered with Oriental fret-work and the overuse of Buddha statues, dragons and paper lanterns, and would offend any Asian person who might walk in. Worse, they tried to tie it back to the club's name by coating everything in cheap gold paint that looked closer to bronze.

Tuesday did notice that more care had gone into selecting employees than in selecting decorators. The ladies were top notch at every position, from the dancers to the servers to the ones tending bar. The female deejay was even fine enough to make Tuesday take a second look.

Most impressive was that Tuesday knew this couldn't be their best line-up, not working this early on a weekday. The first string only worked the weekend nights when the real money showed up. Tuesday imagined they had to be goddesses.

She approached one working the floor to inquire about the owner. She had to shout in order to compete with the music.

The dancer responded with a friendly smile. "Big D's office right up the stairs, but between me and you, I wouldn't even do it."

This earned a puzzled look from Tuesday. "You wouldn't do what?"

She leaned into Tuesday's ear as if sharing a secret. "I'm just sayin' Big D is picky as a muthafucka. My li'l cousin's nineteen, and so bad her IG page doin' a hundred k, but the nigga turned her down just cause she got a birthmark on her cheek.

"Now Auntie, I can tell you was a bad bitch back in yo' day but—"

Tuesday erupted. "You silly ass bitch, I ain't trying to work here! Look at my bag, look at these heels! Take in my overall swag. Do I look like a bitch who need this in her life? Every morning I get dressed, I put on ten years' worth of yo' tips!"

The apologetic look on the youngster's face indicated she was only trying to be helpful but Tuesday still mugged her.

Before she hit the stairs, Tuesday went into that huge ostrich bag, blindly tossed a stack of bills at the stage. It took the girls up there a moment to realize hundreds, not singles, had been rained on them. It caused a commotion to break out between the dancers and some of the slimy customers snatching at the bills.

At the top of the steps was a short hall that terminated in a door with a camera mounted above. She put a hand over the lens and pounded on the wood like the police.

After a few seconds of continuous hard knocking, the door was snatched open. The man looked like a grizzly bear standing on its hind legs; he stood six feet nine inches tall and weighed four hundred pounds. Sweat-shine and elaborate tattoos covered nearly every inch of his bare arms, chest, and bloated stomach. He used one hand to keep up his unbuttoned jeans, the other gripped a pistol.

He barked, "What the fuck wrong wit' you?"

She smiled. "What's up, Fatboy. Miss me?"

He looked down on her, confused, and it took his red eyes several seconds before they flashed with recognition. His face morphed from pissed to pleased. "Are you kiddin' me right now? What tha fuck you doin' here?"

DelRay tried to go in for a hug but Tuesday quickly pulled back. "Hell naw, nigga. I already know what you was doin' in that bitch. I can smell weed and unwashed ass halfway down the hall."

Tuesday pushed her way inside and sure enough, found a pretty little mixed girl with blue weave on his sofa, hastily climbing into a fishnet body stocking.

"Oh, so this how you gone play me, DelRay!" Tuesday said, pretending to spazz. "First yo' ass give me herpes and now this!"

Once the girl was presentable, she darted out of his office without comment but did throw DelRay a *what the fuck?* look.

He tried to call out after her, "Aye Niecey, this my homegirl from back in the day. She just playin' bout that herpes shit!"

Tuesday laughed. "You shouldn't be shittin' where you eat, nigga."

He turned to her.

"Just one of the perks of having a club. Like when you got a car dealership and get to drive the new models."

She countered, "But cars don't get in they feelings when you wanna drive one today and a different one tomorrow."

"Damn girl, look at you," he said shifting the focus to her. "Aging like fine wine. Still sexy than a muthafucka. Over forty and killin' every bitch I got downstairs."

She checked him. "Just forty, nigga." Tuesday still blushed like a teenager. She knew he was pouring it on but still sucked it up like a dry sponge. La Guapa had stirred insecurities in Tuesday which was why that 'Auntie' comment made her snap like that.

DelRay dove into a 5x Polo shirt then shelved the Ruger he had carried with him to the door. "But on some real shit, blockin' my camera and beatin' on the door like that almost got you shot. Cain't play like that, cause niggas hungry enough to run up on your business in the middle of the day."

Joking she said, "I know you ain't worried 'bout nobody runnin' up on Big D. Especially not here in the Filipino Palace."

"Big D, that's just what everybody callin' me now." He wore a smug grin.

"Everybody but me."

"And don't be talkin' shit about my spot neither. This bitch fuckin' over The Bounce House."

She shrugged. "I cain't hate, it is popping down there. It's just that when I walked in, I ain't know if I was gone get a lap dance or a pint of almond chicken."

That made the big man double over with laughter. When he was finally able to catch his breath he said, "Damn I missed you, TK. What the fuck brought you back to the city anyway?"

The smile left her face. "The only thing that could: Life-And-Death shit."

Chapter Twenty-seven

Clearly the time for joking and catching up was over. DelRay's demeanor changed to reflect the seriousness Tuesday projected. He pushed the door closed to give them privacy.

His office was large and it broke away from the fake Oriental theme created for the customers downstairs. Tuesday thought it looked like something for the CEO of an investment firm that handled clients with old money. The twenty-five-by-forty-foot space was masculine, with black leather furniture, and walls covered with dark wood paneling. She could tell by how her shoes sank into the padding that the carpet wasn't cheap.

She took one of the seats that fronted a huge mahogany desk, while DelRay wedged his big body behind it and sank into a leather wing chair. It was a boss's chair, and it made Tuesday feel good to see him in it. Her former bouncer had come into his own. She had the pride of a big sister.

"I see you made some moves wit' that li'l paper I left you. Now I gotta call in a favor."

He stared at her from across the desk. His eyes were earnest. "Everything I have is cause of you TK, and I ain't never forgot that or took it for granted. Just tell me what you need and I got you."

"I need an army."

DelRay seemed to be waiting for her to elaborate, but nothing else followed. He wore a low fade that was a week overdue for a touchup; he scratched at the new growth with thick sausage-like fingers.

"I don't even know how to respond to that. When you said *favor*, I was thinkin' a small loan or maybe a place to crash for a few days."

She said, "The night I left I put you up on a lick. What happened to the guns?"

"Oh yeah, I've been waiting to talk to you about that," he said with attitude. "That so-called lick almost got me murdered."

He explained. "Not an hour after you tell me about it, I grab one of my niggas and we shoot over to that junkyard on Grand River. And it's just like you said it was, a little trapdoor in the floor of his office, down those stairs a room full of heat. Everything in that bitch: Uzis, SK's, AR's, AK's, every pistol you can think of, even some explosives and shit. Crates and crates of this shit, military grade."

"Well what the fuck happened to it?" Tuesday asked impatiently. He was only giving her the same information she had given him about the score.

"Because you had me thinkin' it was all good, I had my mans come through with a U-Haul and we cleaned that bitch out. And for a minute I'm in the arms business. But only for a minute though. About a month later, The Bounce get firebombed by some Colombians sayin' they want they shit back."

"Colombians?" Tuesday was baffled by that. "Those guns belonged to a black dude named Face, ugly ass nigga with the acne scars; you met him when we had to get that body out of the club. I used to get all my straps from him when me and the girls did sticks. He the one who owned the junkyard."

"Well I'm sorry TK, but the bean-eatin' muthafuckas who was about to shove a machete up my ass disagreed." DelRay picked up the half a blunt he was smoking with old girl and re-ignited it. "They came for everything we took. Everything! I didn't just have to pay 'em back for the guns I sold, the bitch they work for made me apologize and charged me another hundred bands on top of that to keep my life."

Tuesday had always thought that Face was independent but only then did she realize that her long-time gun connect was just a frontman for somebody much stronger. That explained to her how a back-alley mechanic was able to get hold of grenade launchers.

For a moment they sat in a shared silence. Tuesday had played a long-shot hoping that DelRay was still connected to the guns and then had to contemplate her next move. She was pulled from her thoughts when he tried to pass her the weed.

She frowned. "Fuck is this bullshit?"

He was defensive. "What you mean? This some head-cracker. Ounce of this cost four-fifty."

She shook her head. "You rich now, but still smoke like a broke nigga."

Tuesday dug into her purse until she found a small plastic vial. It only had one light-green cluster of buds inside about the size of a marble.

"They call this Executive Order kush. It's engineered by the government so you won't find it in any legal dispensary or hash shop. This the shit Barack and Michelle smoke when the kids ain't around. It's only sold by the gram."

DelRay put away his low-grade and rolled up Tuesday's. He took the first hit, expecting something so potent to choke him, but it smoked smooth and tasted good.

They again fell into a pensive silence. The blunt floated back and forth across the desk. The music played downstairs, but only the heavy bass lines penetrated the walls and vibrated the floor beneath their feet.

"TK, what the fuck you done got yo'self caught up in?" He asked in between puffs.

Tuesday heard a concern in his voice that extended beyond just her well-being. Without saying the words, DelRay was asking if this was the type of drama that might follow her to his doorstep.

Tuesday answered without the benefit of words. With her eyes, she communicated that she was in serious beef that might've followed her back to Detroit. She also made it known that if he told her to get the fuck out and never come back, she would respect that without holding it against him.

DelRay's beet-red eyes said: *You know that'll never happen. I got yo' back no matter what.*

Message received, Tuesday slowly nodded her appreciation.

Just two-thirds into the blunt and they both reached their tolerance. By the time Tuesday butted the weed she knew what she needed to do but figured DelRay wouldn't like it.

"Aye Fatboy, I need you to take me to meet them Colombians."

Chapter Twenty-eight

DelRay was still muttering doubts while he slipped into a leather coat so large it must've killed three cows. He explained that the Colombians had spared his life and he had thanked them by staying the fuck off their radar.

Tuesday explained more adamantly that this was a different scenario. Then, he had come as a thief; this time they were coming as customers. She had money to spend. The right amount could even buy forgiveness.

She didn't necessarily sway him, but DelRay made the call anyway. He knew Tuesday well enough that she would do this with or without him.

They left 24 Karats with him insisting to drive. Tuesday was fine with that because she knew the Hyundai would be a tight fit for him.

She noticed a cocky little smirk when DelRay hit the alarm and locks on a new pearl Escalade. It was the premium model with the extended frame. The noon-hour sun reflected brilliantly in thirty-inch chrome rims that resembled ninja stars.

He stared at Tuesday as if waiting for a compliment.

She slid into the passenger seat. "Nigga, don't act like you ain't the same muthafucka who had that raggedy ass Monte Carlo, dripping oil in front of my club for all those years."

"As you can see, I don't ride like that no more." He settled himself behind the wheel. "This just my everyday driver—I gotta Benz S550 I pull out when I feel like crackin' they heads. Copped the new 'Vette too, drop-top, but I only hit 'em with that every blue moon."

"I remember you used to have the white CTS-V until you lost your Caddy to pay for Brianna's bullshit. So, what you pushin' these days?" He gave Tuesday side-eye while pulling from the lot.

Tuesday was happy that DelRay was doing better, but warned him that trying to dick-measure against her would leave him feeling short. He foolishly persisted in his game of Who's Got the Bigger Stack? until Tuesday finally had to shut him down.

"Alright Fatboy, I see yo' basic ass S550 and raise you the AMG Benz SLS coupe. That and a limited-edition V-10 Range Rover Autobiography are my everyday drivers. When I feel like crackin' heads, I jump in one of my two Rolls Royces—the Ghost or the Wraith—depending on my mood. When I feel like being eco-friendly, I do my electric joint, the Revero by Karma Automotive, but you probably ain't up on that. Then every blue moon I'll bring out that neon-green Lambo my baby bought me 'cause he said it match my eyes." She playfully batted hers at him in the flirtatious manner of a Southern Belle. "And that ain't even everything in my garage, nigga.

"Do you wanna talk 'bout that Gulfstream being fueled up and waiting for me at Metro? I don't fly it myself so I don't know if you technically consider a private jet something that I'm pushin' though."

DelRay looked tempted to call "bullshit" but then thought better of it. Maybe it was because the night she left she had enough cake to break him off half a million in cash like it was nothing. Maybe it was because she had a piece of ice on her finger so big that it could've sank the Titanic. Maybe it was because in all their years of being cool, he had never known Tuesday to be on no fake shit.

"TK, where the fuck you been and who is this helluva nigga you married to?"

Just the mention of Marcus was enough to sour her mood. Her face grew tight as she turned forward in her seat. "My dude, you wouldn't believe me if I told you."

After that, the conversation was minimal until they reached their destination. Face's Salvage Yard was still open and doing business under the same name, but Tuesday could only guess who the current owner was.

The Escalade pulled through the entrance gate, stirring dust as well as memories in Tuesday of the last time she was there; she almost died that day. They weaved through a maze of junked cars until reaching a two-stall carport and adjoining office. It was a simple structure: a junkyard dwelling made of corrugated sheet metal and the very junk itself.

Tuesday was unfamiliar with the man in the first stall. He was a greasy white dude with long hair, taking a socket wrench to something under the hood of an old Mustang Fastback. Tuesday jumped out to approach him and DelRay followed.

"Twenty minutes," he said, never looking up from his work. He apparently already knew what the business was. "Y'all can either wait here or come back."

"We'll wait." Tuesday quickly spoke over DelRay who she knew was about to announce they were leaving. They were at the meeting place first which offered some, if not much, strategic advantage. Tuesday thought it was better than walking back into a trap, especially in a junkyard where so many places could conceal shooters.

When the mechanic pulled his phone and snapped their picture, DelRay shifted uneasily. "I ain't feelin' this shit, TK."

"It's cool," she whispered calmly. "They got every right to be curious."

She and DelRay went back to lean against his truck while the mechanic returned to his craft.

She spoke low. "You got a heater on you, right?"

He flashed her the butt of the Ruger jammed into the waistband of his jeans.

Brandon had replaced her Heckler in California, and since then it hadn't left Tuesday's side. "Good. We 'bout to be outnumbered and damn sure 'bout to be out-gunned. It won't look good for us if we have to shoot our way out this bitch, but at least we ain't naked."

DelRay grimaced as if that thought made him sick. "I woke up this morning thinkin' my biggest problem of the day would be a long line at the pharmacy. Yo' ass ain't been back a half hour and already got me in a situation where I might get killed."

She smiled at him. "Don't you miss the excitement I bring to your life?"

Chapter Twenty-nine

Tuesday used their wait-time to call Brandon and make some inquiries, but while talking to the old man she watched DelRay. She could sense the mounting anxiety in him with each passing minute. By the time the sellers showed, he was glazed with sweat despite the cool temperature. She knew that big man was no coward as he had already proven himself dependable in a jam, however, that was in the past, and time had a way of changing people. Especially after they gained more than they were willing to lose.

The Colombians arrived at the junkyard in two cars. Tuesday tucked her phone and gave DelRay a look that said "focus up."

Men sprang out each of the four doors on a silver Dodge Charger. All of them youngsters trying their best to look hard. Tuesday guessed the oldest to be twenty-three. Brown but assimilated into black culture: Balmain, Jordan's, Migos exploding out of their speakers. The driver had a chain on with an iced-out Michigan mitten.

Tuesday looked past them, kept her attention on the trailing vehicle. The passengers in the white-on-white BMW 760 chose not to exit right away. Three figures sat silhouetted behind lightly-tinted glass.

The mechanic rushed over to greet the foursome from the Charger. Tuesday waited patiently for them to talk among themselves. She refused to present herself as eager or nervous—even though she was both.

Soon they approached her and DelRay, where they stood against his Escalade. The quartet walked with the cockiness of young dudes getting money for the first time. Tuesday knew the type because she used to rob niggas like them.

"What's good Ma?" This came from the driver whom Tuesday had already peeped as the Alpha. The kinky mohawk warranted Tuesday's closer inspection which revealed predominantly black features mingled within his Colombian ones. She saw the resemblance immediately.

"I heard ya lookin' for something." His eyes lingered long on the Fendi denim hugging her thighs.

She offered a humorless smirk. "Look young dog, you Face's boy right? I'm a long-time customer with deep pockets who lookin' to buy in bulk. I'm here to talk grown-folk's business and I don't do that wit' kids."

One of his boys tried to swell up. "Yo A'Ron, who this li'l bitch thank she is?"

Tuesday said, "This li'l bitch thank she a boss. And bosses only do business with other bosses."

Face's son tapped his bird chest. "I am a boss. Ask anybody in the 313 with a Drecco, bet they copped it from me."

Tuesday waved him off. "This ain't amateur hour. C'mon li'l nigga, them stones cloudy as fuck, and half of 'em moissanite. You ain't even in the Hellcat—you rolled up in the V-6. Quit playin' wit' me and go get whoever really in charge. Run tell yo' people to come holla at me or they gone watch a couple million walk up out this bitch."

The Alpha mugged her for a moment, looking angry and embarrassed. Then he finally turned and walked over to the BMW. He tapped on the window, and this seemed to be enough to let the occupants know the buyer was serious.

All three climbed out in unison. The driver and rear passenger were older than the boys, full-blooded Colombians, with long hair and cowboy boots. Tuesday recognized the quick searching eyes of experienced killers.

The only female came from the passenger seat, barely five-foot-one and dressed in a white linen one-piece with silver heels. Tuesday thought the woman was at least ten years her senior but had aged gracefully. She was also Latina but with black-girl swag. Her hair was done in a short wrap with several gray streaks styled into it as if proud of them.

She approached with the driver of the Charger while the others slipped into the background. Tuesday knew they weren't present just to be spectators. To her, their body language suggested the quiet expectation of drama.

The woman in white stood before Tuesday, barely measuring up to her tits. She recalled Face mentioning a short Colombian dimepiece who drove a triple-white Range Rover, but the two had never met.

"I'm Maria Vega, but everyone calls me Madame."

Tuesday went with her alias: "Tabitha King." She accepted a warm manicured hand that made her feel some type of way that her nail-game currently wasn't on point. Tuesday had been involved in too much shit to even think about the salon.

"I typically prefer not to do business like this, but I was told you and my husband had a long lucrative relationship."

"How long has he been missing?" Tuesday asked innocently.

"Almost three years." She punctuated that with a solemn nod. "We are not optimistic."

Tuesday offered her condolences.

"You told my son that you were interested in a very large order. So what does a pretty girl like you need with so many big guns?"

"I don't just need guns, but men to pull the triggers. I'm thinking 'bout two dozen or so, who know how to handle themselves and are willing to take orders from me. Money is no object."

Her son broke in. "Where's the money? Let's see it?"

Tuesday screwed her face. "Of course I wasn't stupid enough to bring cash here. Trust me though, I'm more than good for it."

Madame Vega said, "You come here with a man who already stole from me, asking for trust."

Tuesday motioned to DelRay. "He brought me to you as an apology—a gift. He knows the ridiculous amount of money I'm about to spend with you people."

The son waved Tuesday off. "Bitch, you talk a damn good game, but until we see some—"

"*Basta!*" Madame Vega's command silenced him mid-sentence. She spoke to Tuesday but never looked away from him. "I'm sorry but ever since he lost his father, my son Aaron *thinks* he runs my business."

Tuesday smiled. "I understand. I'm also a mother dealing with a child with a reckless mouth."

Vega chastised him with a glare for a few seconds longer, then looked back to Tuesday. "Guns I can help you with, but you're on your own for the second part. I don't run a temp service. You'll have to find your own people."

Tuesday took a step towards her. "I didn't come into this meeting without doing my homework. Guns is just one part of how you eat—the other part is human trafficking. Your husband Face was just a front man for you, and for years your family has been making a nice piece of money smuggling illegals up from South America through Mexico. Like these muthafuckas right here." Tuesday nodded to the two with the long hair. "Probably ain't been here long enough to learn English yet."

Madame Vega didn't admit to anything, but the look on her face was enough of a confession. "Even if I could manage that, why would I? You're obviously caught up in something serious. Why would I involve my family in your problem?"

"Because both of our families have the same problem: Reina Rodriguez.

"It was your people she was beefing with over the border

towns. The story about her sending an exploding cake to a little girl's party helped to build her reputation. How many of your relatives died in the blast?"

The sour expression on Madame's face went deeper. "La Guapa sees everything, knows even more. Even the Medellin cartel bosses fear her, and they don't fear shit. They say she is a *bruja*."

Years living in L.A. allowed Tuesday to pick up some Spanish. "She ain't a witch. She's smart and very detailed but not invincible. If we partner up we can chop this bitch down. You got the muscle; I got the mind and the money."

Madame Vega stood there for a moment as if contemplating that. When she whispered something in her son's ear, Tuesday just figured it was her opinion on the deal.

Tuesday didn't notice how during their conversation that one of the long-haired Colombians had inched closer to DelRay.

He didn't notice either until his Ruger was snatched from his hip with an expert hand. Another pistol was in his face before the big fella could respond.

Tuesday didn't even get the opportunity to turn back to Vega and her son. She froze when she felt the familiar touch of cold steel against the back of her skull.

One of the other youngsters from the Charger came over to confiscate her big Birkin bag. He shook everything out onto the ground then fingered through the personal items. He picked up her phone, the Heckler, and two cash knots that contained about seventeen thousand.

Tuesday spat, "So this how y'all do business? Just like petty muthafuckas—gone stick me for crumbs when I was coming to spend real paper wit' y'all."

Aaron turned her to face his mother and the tiny woman in white frowned at Tuesday. "I've been waiting a long time to finally meet you. My husband was the face of my business, which meant he told me everything. Kinda hard to forget a name like Tuesday Knight."

Tuesday had the look of a bitch who was knew she was busted. All she could do was roll her eyes, mutter a few curses.

Vega continued. "The night he disappeared, he was here waiting for you to come and pay off the four hundred thousand you owed him. I never heard from him again after that.

"My husband wasn't perfect. I know all about his whole foot obsession and I'm willing to bet he probably cashed out or gave you a few discounts on some of my merchandise just so he could suck your toes. But in twenty-three years of marriage, there was two things I could count on: One, he would never bring me any disease that anti-fungal powder couldn't cure, and two, he always brought his ass home."

Aaron jammed the muzzle harder into Tuesday's head. "You were one of the last people to see my husband," Vega sneered. "You're gonna tell me what happened that night or my son is gonna blow your brains out right here, right now."

Tuesday met Vega's stare.

"Your husband is dead," she said coldly. "I killed him."

Chapter Thirty

"Tell me why I shouldn't shoot you in the face right now."

"Because I am a very rich bitch and I am about to make you a lot of money." Tuesday tried to keep her voice calm even though her heart was going at a hundred beats per minute. She imagined DelRay's to be doing a hundred-forty which was extremely dangerous for a person his size.

Madame Vega scowled. "You kill my husband and steal his guns then come back here looking to buy more. I only came to see if you were just that arrogant or stupid."

Tuesday explained. "That night I showed up here and paid Face his money just like I promised, but the nigga did some slimeball shit. He tried to rob me for three million dollars.

"Now I was a thief too, and I know what come with the game. Three mil is three mil, so it don't surprise me that even a nigga I been jam with for twenty years would put down a play for it—I could almost forgive that. But somebody snatched my five-year-old stepdaughter and the money was to get her back. Your husband made me miss the ransom drop and damn near got my baby girl killed. I'm sorry Madame Vega, but that's the part I couldn't forgive."

Pain and anger aged Vega, made her look older then her years. "What did you do to my husband?"

Tuesday stared back with defiance. "The same thing he was gonna do to me. Now that you know, can we get back to business?"

The one holding the pistol on DelRay forced him down to his knees. Execution position. DelRay looked at Tuesday, his huge eyes wide as golf balls, searching hers saying, "Bitch, do something."

Aaron snatched Tuesday's head back by a fistful of good weave then slung her to the ground. She went down hard, then rolled onto her back with her hands raised. He stood over her with the gun hovering over her face.

She looked up at Vega. "I get how you feel. I was in yo' same situation 'bout a week ago. I'm not asking you to not pull that trigger, I'm just asking you to wait.

"If you help me move Reina out the way, that's gone clear a lane for you. You stand to make millions fuckin' with me. Millions!"

"You're just an ex-stripper who robs dope boys. Where's all this big money talk comin' from?"

Tuesday stayed cool even from her position in the dirt. She politely asked them to Google Tabitha King. Aaron kept his pistol leveled at her but quickly pulled his phone with his free hand as if eager to call her bluff. A second later he was linked to pictures of Tuesday and Brandon and the glass skyscraper that was Abel's corporate headquarters. When he passed the phone to his mother, they both looked at Tuesday curiously.

"A long time ago my husband bought a small boat just to help move kilos under the radar. That rusted-out, forty-foot pleasure craft is now an entire fleet of international cargo freighters, and a small shipping company that used to launder cocaine profits is now the third largest importing corporation in America."

Tuesday paused. "I'm married to Sebastian Caine."

Everything fell silent. Two of the youngsters abruptly cut short the conversation they were having among themselves. Even the cranking sound from the ratchet quit as the greasy mechanic suddenly stopped tightening a bolt. Everybody froze and just stared at her dumbly, especially DelRay.

Skepticism twisted Vega's face. "And I'm fuckin' the Loch Ness Monster."

Tuesday smirked. "Yeah, I know a lotta niggas been pump-faking and hiding behind that name over the years. My bae's a real private person and he'd be super pissed if he knew I put him out there like this.

"But please believe he'd be more pissed if somebody put a hole in my face. You'll be puttin' somethin' in motion you won't be able to stop."

Aaron spat, "This bitch lying. She ain't been doin' shit but lying the whole time."

Tuesday said, "Li'l nigga, it's a reason yo' Mama ain't told you to pull that trigger yet. It's only two ways a bitch would come here and tell a story like that: one they was crazy, or two if it was true. You just saw what I'm working wit', so you know I ain't crazy."

Madame Vega said, "You might think this strengthens your position but it doesn't. What is the CEO of a large shipping company and Caine's wife doing here in a junkyard trying to buy guns and men? You must be desperate."

"Very," Tuesday admitted. "But desperate doesn't mean weak."

She could tell by the look on Vega's face that her last statement hit home.

She said, "If money truly is no object, I want an upfront payment of twenty million dollars in cash. And I want ten percent of Abel's profits for the rest of my son's life."

Tuesday got back to her feet, gave her a 'bitch, you crazy' stare. "You ain't getting a single percent of my company—not one. But I'm willing to give you a one-time payment of ten million for twenty shooters. That's more than you gone make if you selling an AK to every nigga in Detroit."

Vega agreed. "How soon can I have my money?"

"As soon as I can get my army."

Madame Vega made Aaron put his gun away. DelRay was let up from his knees.

Tuesday's purse and money was returned to her.

"Just because I'm willing to do business doesn't mean it changes anything between us." Vega frowned. "And I have to know what happened to my husband."

Tuesday understood because she was just on the other side of that question. "I put him in the trunk of one of these old cars then put it in that big machine that crush it down to a little cube. He might still be here in the yard somewhere."

Vega gasped. "You psychotic bitch."

Tuesday shrugged. "Like I said, it was the same thing he was gone do to me, but I do understand the need for revenge. So if you still feel some type of way, we can deal with that after this is done."

Madame Vega nodded. "We most certainly will."

Chapter Thirty-one

"My bad 'bout the seat."

Tuesday had dusted her clothes as best she could before climbing back into DelRay's Escalade, but her Fendi fit still stained his leather upholstery with sand and gravel.

"We gone stop somewhere so you can vacuum out my shit. Might as well hit the rims while you at it."

She laughed. "You got that comin'."

"Was that the way you thought that shit was gone go?"

"Naw, I thought we'd get killed."

He said, "And I got the feeling we still might."

For a while that was last thing spoken between them. The radio filled the space but the volume was so low that the deejay whispered. DelRay was in the driver's seat staring ahead as if totally focused on navigating Greenfield Road's southbound traffic. Tuesday felt the weight of his unvoiced questions and concerns.

"I broke the rules when I fell in love with my mark, so the team betrayed me and Tushie when I tried to call off the lick. Brianna, Jaye and Baby Doll snatched his daughter."

DelRay was present that night and had helped Tuesday get

Danielle back, never knowing who the little girl was or her connection to his boss.

"That half a million I gave you was s'posed to be part of the ransom. It belonged to Caine."

He finally turned to her. "The real Sebastian Caine? I didn't even think that nigga existed."

"I didn't either. He was so low-pro wit' his shit that at first I didn't believe it was him. That's how I wound up letting my guard down."

It took DelRay about a quarter mile to absorb that truth. His expression of utter disbelief lasted until they reached the light at the next major cross-street.

"Can I see what he look like?"

Tuesday shook her head. "My bae don't do pictures or social media. But you can see my girls." She used her phone to pull up photos of Tanisha and Danielle.

DelRay studied their faces with a brief smile. "But if you're married to The Man, why are you back here needing help?"

"Because he's gone." It seemed to pain Tuesday to even admit that. "Some shit came up from his past, he tried to get out in front of it, but—it's just me. It's all on me to protect what he built."

DelRay would have liked details but there was enough irritation in her voice for him not to pursue them.

A delay near Chicago Ave. slowed traffic to a crawl. Up ahead, a garbage truck had apparently stalled trying to make a left turn from a side street. It blocked two lanes causing congestion as commuters waited to be funneled into one open stream. The Escalade rode the far right lane, creeping slower than the people who bypassed them on the sidewalk.

Tuesday had run to the woman whose husband she had killed for help against the woman who killed her husband. Tuesday was thinking of Marcus as well as how *Webster's* defined irony when the phone interrupted her musings. She expected a call from Shaun or maybe even Brandon just checking in on her.

"Hello green-eyed girl, what are you up to?"

Her pulse quickened. Tuesday only needed a second to get composed after the initial shock of hearing that scholarly voice.

"Looking for a new place to live. You probably didn't hear, but I lost my house in a fire."

"I'm so sorry. I pray that no harm came to either of those lovely girls." There was no sarcasm in her voice but then there didn't need to be. Tuesday understood the entire call was about mocking her. It started with the fact that she had the connections to get Tuesday's new and unlisted phone number.

Remembering that look of fright on Tanisha's face as they fled in the back of the van burned Tuesday. She bit down on her lip but refused to get emotional like she did at the warehouse.

"Me and my girls are just fine but everybody didn't make it out okay." Tuesday threw a slick jab referring to the two men Brandon killed. "I could halfway buy that shit about Marcus being strictly business but you done really made this personal by sending them clowns after my daughters."

"It sounds like you're making unfounded accusations against me of a criminal nature. I have a very large team of very expensive lawyers who take slander quite seriously."

The bitch was clever. Tuesday understood that she was taking precautions just in case the conversation was being recorded.

The line was quiet for a beat. "Hypothetically speaking, who's to say what your enemies did at the house wasn't a complete success?"

Tuesday said, "Because I'm still alive and I still got my girls."

"Maybe you're the one who never understood what their purpose was. What if your enemies' moves are just that far beyond your comprehension? Just for fun, let's play a game of 'What if.'"

"Marcus was right. You thank everything is a game. And that's where you fuckin' up."

Reina said, "What if your enemies weren't really trying to kidnap your daughters, just wanted to illicit a certain response? And what if the fire was never designed to kill as much as weaken you?"

Tuesday played along. "So you're saying these people, who-ever they are, burned down my house just to weaken me? What does that even mean?"

She explained. "Home provides a sense of comfort and stabil-ity that people desperately need in times of duress. Try to imagine a king with no castle or fortress for where he can retreat.

"The additional benefit would be that it takes away a multi-million dollar asset from you. Tuesday, wars are expensive. Insur-ance companies move incredibly slow on claims that large. Even slower when they suspect arson."

A heavy breath expelled from her nostrils. It was proof of frus-tration that slipped from Tuesday and she could almost hear Reina's smile through the phone.

"I told you, Tuesday, I'm smarter than you." Despite her words, the tone was not condescending. "There's no move you can make that I haven't accounted for.

"I already know you're back home in Detroit. I already know you're looking to spend from that inexhaustible war chest. I al-ready know you have a short list of people who you trust." Then after a pause she added, "Like the fat man sitting next you in the white Escalade."

Tuesday eyes snapped wide enough to startle DelRay. She screamed at him, "We gotta move this bitch now!"

Reina added, "And to finish our game: What if this entire con-versation was just a distraction?"

Tuesday didn't even have time to warn DelRay. She pulled his head down into her lap a split-second before the windows ex-ploded. The automatic gunfire that erupted on the afternoon was like a drum-roll played on a tight snare. Tuesday couldn't tell where the shooters were located. The volume indicated they were close.

The screams of women and children as other drivers fled their cars, the ping of lead striking the metal frame and shattering windows, the chatter of what experienced ears knew to be multiple AR-15's: all those sounds melded to produce a deafening cacophony.

The Escalade rocked from the impact of the bullets. Glass rained on DelRay and Tuesday as they crouched in their seats. They were trapped and didn't know if the shooters were on foot or in the surrounding vehicles. Tuesday squeaked when she felt pain stab her lower right leg.

She snatched the Ruger from DelRay's waist and fired blindly out the missing window. She didn't expect to hit anyone. Tuesday only hoped the return-fire would delay the killers from running up to finish them.

"Nigga, we gone die if you don't get us the fuck outta' here!"

The Cadillac was boxed into the far right lane. With his head still low, DelRay stomped the gas and rammed the car in front of him. He pushed an abandoned Honda Civic several feet until it bumped the car ahead of it then reversed to take advantage of the added space. He cut the wheel sharply to the right and powered over the curb.

It was then that Tuesday got her first glimpse of a shooter. He was crouched between two cars wearing the puke-green coveralls of a city worker. He sprinkled the Escalade as DelRay barreled through the pumps of a Shell station, sideswiped an old Chrysler Lebaron, then bounced over another curb at the far end.

As they sped down a side street, Tuesday twisted in her seat to watch a burgundy Tahoe bend the same corner in pursuit. She recognized the vehicle of choice for La Guapa's henchmen.

"Punch this bitch. They on our ass."

DelRay was hunched over the wheel like an old man, squinting hard through a shattered windshield. He took that residential block doing eighty and hit the corner so hard that they skated on two wheels.

The Tahoe stayed close behind. The tinted glass in DelRay's tailgate window had been blown out, making easy targets of him and Tuesday. They stayed low in their seats. A well-placed bullet through that open sight-line could find a home in the back of one of their skulls.

From that side street, he turned onto another residential block then quickly pulled into the first driveway he saw before the Tahoe could make the corner. He sandwiched the long LSV between two burned houses while their pursuers sped by on the street.

Because the property was without a garage or fenced-in backyard, DelRay continued up the driveway and whipped into the alley at the rear. He navigated around dumpsters and debris like a stunt driver then plowed through a grassy field that was littered with car parts.

They came out on the neighboring block. A left and another quick right sent them in the opposite direction they had last seen the Tahoe headed.

After a few streets when they didn't catch sight of a burgundy SUV, DelRay finally chanced to sit erect. "What the fuck was that?"

Tuesday had dropped her phone when the shooting started. She retrieved it from the floor between her feet and noticed the call was still active.

La Guapa had remained on the line. "Hey hoodrat, are you still with me?"

She screamed, "Bitch, dis how you want it? We can do whatever cause I'm about dat life!"

"Calm down, Tuesday, you're getting emotional again." She spoke with the calm tone of a therapist. "Back when I was playing chess competitively, I could always tell when my opponents were rattled by how they—"

Tuesday hung up on that bitch. She was done talking. She was too angry and embarrassed for their little game.

Half a block later, she flung the phone out into the street just to be safe. Tuesday had used cell phones to track people so she knew Reina could do the same.

"What the fuck was all that?" DelRay repeated since she didn't answer the first time.

"Just drive, nigga." Tuesday's heart was still booming, at first from fright and then fury.

Chapter Thirty-two

She had to convince DelRay to leave his truck. Driving a bullet-riddled Escalade would attract too much attention and Tuesday explained how important it was that she avoid the police. They parked it behind the ruins of a closed-down KFC. She promised to pay for the damages.

DelRay called for an Uber as they started down Schaeffer Road on foot. Tuesday moved awkwardly at his side, wincing with each step.

She rolled her pant leg up to inspect the wound. She was only grazed, but the bullet had cut deep. A gash of seared flesh ran across her right calf. She would need antiseptic and possibly stitches, but luckily not a doctor.

The Uber driver met them in the parking lot of a Comerica bank. DelRay directed him to his house so he could pick up his second car, and once in the Benz, Tuesday directed DelRay to the house in Romulus so she could pick up her family.

Tuesday stressed the need for speed. If La Guapa knew she was in Detroit, Tuesday feared she might also know about Marcus's old place. DelRay wasn't trying to get pulled over but did outpace the freeway traffic by fifteen miles an hour.

On the way, she called Brandon to tell him about Reina's latest move. Tuesday explained how this was not like the other times when she felt La Guapa was just toying with her; this was an actual attempt on her life. Brandon said he couldn't imagine that Reina had found any way to break the trust Marcus set up, but agreed with moving the girls to a hotel just in case they were no longer protected.

Tuesday also told him about the deal she made with Madame Vega. Brandon expressed some dissatisfaction at the price but claimed it would take at least twenty-four hours to put together ten million in cash. He called for the return of the company jet with the promise to deliver the money by it when the funds were ready.

Tuesday had kept Shaun and the girls squatting like vagrants, living out of shopping bags. All of Marcus's old furniture was still there although coated with three years' worth of dust. It surprised Tuesday to find the utilities still active.

The moment she limped through the door in dirty denim and tangled weave, Shaun was all over her playing Momma. "Where you been? What the hell happened to you?"

Tuesday pushed past as Shaun tried to pick tiny glass shards from her hair. "Get the food while I get the girls ready. We gotta leave."

Shaun seemed to be waiting for an explanation about Tuesday's appearance or the six-foot-nine behemoth who accompanied her. She received none.

Tanisha clung to Tuesday's leg, staring up at DelRay like he was some monster that crawled from underneath the bed to devour children.

"Ni Ni, get your coat. We gotta' go, okay?"

When she didn't respond fast enough, Tuesday impatiently snapped her fingers to get her daughter's attention. "Hey, I said get yo' coat." She turned back to Shaun. "Where's Dani?"

Shaun indicated upstairs so Tuesday took the steps gingerly on her bad leg then leaned against the doorway of Danielle's old room.

"Hurry up and grab your stuff. We gotta' go."

Danielle was seated on the bed, her phone the only entertainment. She issued an annoyed grunt but didn't move.

Tuesday frowned at her. "What part of that didn't you understand? Grab yo' stuff. We gotta go. Now."

"Why do we have to keep moving around? Why are we back at the old house and where's my daddy?"

In all the craziness that followed the fire, Tuesday never had the opportunity to explain Marcus to their daughters. In being truthful with herself she had avoided it, and the shuffling from place to place had only helped to distract the girls.

"Look, we ain't got time for that right now." Tuesday moved around the room and began stuffing things into a plastic bag.

Danielle stood defiantly. "I wanna know where my daddy at. I ain't going nowhere else 'til you tell me. I know something bad happened. You think I'm a stupid little kid, but I'm probably smarter than you."

Tuesday paused and drew upon all the strength she had not to put hands on the child. "You think you grown now 'cause you can do big math problems and quote Shakespeare? You don't know shit about the stuff that really matter.

"But if you want the grownup version of the truth, here it is: Daddy gave his life for that stupid company—not for me, not for you or Ni Ni, but that damn company. And now it's up to me to keep y'all, and it, safe, but every day I feel like a bigger fool for not just taking the money."

Danielle shrieked, "I just wanna go home! I wanna go back to school!"

Tuesday shot back. "You think I want this? I never signed up for any of this either. You ain't got no home—all you got is me. People are trying to hurt us, Dani, and I'm all you got protecting you. Not Daddy, me!"

Tuesday immediately felt like shit and expected to see Danielle's eyes tear up. However, the nine-year-old actually demonstrated a lot more maturity than she had.

She said, "My daddy'll come back and he'll fix everything. Just watch."

Tuesday didn't argue with her. She had carried that same denial for weeks and would allow Danielle to come to terms in her own time.

They piled into DelRay's Benz and drove to a Residence Inn three miles away from the house. Tuesday had Shaun check them in under an alias.

DelRay admired her form as Shaun walked to the front desk. He leaned into Tuesday's ear. "What's up with old girl fine ass?"

Tuesday only said, "Long story."

The rooms were designed like small apartments with a living area, two bedrooms and a kitchenette. Tuesday didn't know how long they would be stuck there, so DelRay took her to a nearby store for more food and toiletries.

There was a little drama at the checkout when Tabitha King's American Express was declined but Tuesday decided it might be safer to pay cash anyway just in case La Guapa was somehow tracking her credit.

Next they swung by a Coney Island on the way back to the motel and Tuesday was stuffing chili-fries into her mouth when she noticed DelRay looking at her sideways.

"You done damn near got me killed twice. Don't you think it's time you told me what the fuck up with this Gaucho chick?"

"Guapa!" Tuesday said through a mouth full of potato and cheese. "I guess it mean 'pretty muthafucka' in Spanish."

Tuesday pulled up the Facebook page for Reina Rodriguez using his phone. She passed it back to DelRay and rolled her eyes when the photos contorted his chubby face into a *Damn!* expression.

"If Alicia Keys could get Beyoncé pregnant, their baby wouldn't have shit on her."

Tuesday sucked her teeth.

"Child prodigy; 197 I.Q.; earned two Ph.Ds. before turning twenty-five." DelRay quoted from her profile. "Father was a wealthy immigrant entrepreneur."

"Drug lord," Tuesday corrected. "And now she's running his business." Tuesday explained how her husband left Abel to her and why Reina wanted it.

"How in the fuck did she do that? I didn't even know we'd be on Greenfield and Chicago, so how could she know exactly where we was at?"

Tuesday shrugged nonchalantly while attacking her burger. "She real good at setting traps and shit."

DelRay slumped in his seat, expelled a heavy breath. "Boss Lady, you know I love you to death but the shit you got goin' on is way above my level. I'm a big nigga who can handle myself on these streets—but damn! You fuckin' with evil geniuses and trained killers. You need somebody having you back that's better than me. I'm a bouncer; you need a goon."

"I need two hundred of 'em," she snapped.

DelRay tucked his phone. "That's out of my reach, but I might be able to point you to one helluva hitter. Probably the best. The nigga good with his hands, guns, explosives—they say he like a black Jason Bourne."

They stopped by the hotel room just long enough to drop off the fast food and groceries. After blowing another blunt in the parking lot, they headed back to the city with DelRay promising Tuesday a surprise.

She asked, "We on our way to meet Supernigga?"

"I'm gone get on that for you later, but first I wanna show you something."

Tuesday screwed up her face. "The weed already got me noid, nigga. I don't like this shit."

DelRay drove for half an hour before coming to a large Baptist church on the north end of Detroit. He slipped around to the rear parking lot where volunteer parishioners in matching purple T-shirts loaded donations onto a fleet of cargo vans.

She cut her eyes at DelRay as he threw the car in park. "I don't think Jesus can help with the shit I'm dealing with."

He sent a quick text. "Wait a minute. I wouldn't bring you all this way for nothing. You gone love me for this."

Just then a dark-skinned man about six-foot-three stepped into the afternoon sun wearing a Tiger's hat and carrying a box under each muscular arm. He dropped them into a van then retrieved his phone from his Dickie's cargo pants. He read the message and scanned around curiously until he spotted DelRay's hand waving him over from the open window.

Tuesday recognized that walk, and as he drew near her throat went dry. The Coney Island suddenly felt sour in her stomach and the temperature in the Mercedes seemed to jump thirty degrees.

By the time he reached the car, Tuesday couldn't breathe and thought she was about to faint. He peeked in on her from DelRay's window. Even when he took off his baseball cap to give her a clear view of his face, Tuesday still couldn't believe it was him.

After his initial look of shock, he flashed a smile lined with straight white teeth. "What's up wit' you Bright Eyes?"

Tuesday threw open her car door to vomit on the pavement.

Chapter Thirty-three

Once her stomach settled, Tuesday scrambled around the front of the car and dove into his arms. A.D. wrapped her up tight, lifted her a bit and just smothered her with his chest. It felt surreal; she couldn't believe it was actually him, that he was actually there. She couldn't believe that after all those years, being in his arms still felt like home.

She pulled back, didn't even realize she was crying until he wiped a tear from her cheek. "You?"

He gave a slow nod. Tuesday had to touch his face, needed one of her other senses to confirm the report of her eyes.

"When?"

He said, " 'Bout eight months ago."

"How?" Her mind was so blown that all she could formulate were one-word questions.

"By the grace of God," he said with a slight laugh. "I thought I was done, had exhausted all my remedies. Then out of the blue this lawyer comes to see me who wants to take on my case for free. He specializes in Constitutional violations, says the judge screwed me over when he never instructed the jury on any lesser charges. I got a new trial and Murder in the First Degree got dropped to Manslaughter One.

"I still got found guilty but Man One only carries a fifteen-year maximum sentence and I already had sixteen years in. Since it was past my release date, I didn't even have to go back to prison. I got processed right there and walked out of the county jail a few hours later."

Tuesday was struck dumb. The last time she had seen A.D. was in the visiting room at Ryan Road Correctional. She had rode with him for the first twelve years of a Life bid, but when his final appeal was denied, he broke off their relationship. He explained that it was too hard to do his time trying to hold on to her and asked her not to write or come see him again. They both were resigned to his fate, yet there he stood with no bars or unbreakable glass separating them. Tuesday looked at him mesmerized.

"Damn, you lookin' good."

His voice was a hot whisper that made her blush.

It also made her aware that he was being generous, because Tuesday knew she looked a mess. Her Fendi outfit was still covered in dirt, her hair a bird's nest from being pulled by Vega's son, and she was walking with a limp. Every day of her life she'd been so fresh and so clean, but on this, of all days, she would run into her ex looking like the bitch on WorldStar who lost the fight.

But to Tuesday he looked good enough to eat. His gear was cheap but crisp. Prison had preserved him; A.D. was a few years older than her but could easily pass for twenty-seven. He looked healthy and strong, added close to one hundred pounds of muscle to his lean frame. His hair was a low Caesar with thick waves spiraling in three hundred and sixty degrees. Staring at him made Tuesday's heart hammer in her chest as if eager to escape and return to its original owner.

"Ain't no fuckin' on church grounds!" DelRay interrupted their staring contest. She was so lost in A.D. that she had forgotten Fatboy was sitting in the car three feet from them.

"You knew this nigga was home. I been with you the whole day and you ain't said shit." She reached into the window and pushed his big head.

A.D. asked, "So where ya' been at, stranger? I get out, the club is closed and you in the wind."

"L.A. Things got super-hectic with the last lick. So much that I had to bust up from the D."

"I got bits and pieces of it from the streets but nobody really knew what went down. I was sorry to hear about Tushie, though. I know she was like a sister."

Tuesday shook her head. "Not *like* a sister. A sister."

"So I'm guessing congratulations are in order."

Tuesday didn't understand what he meant until she caught A.D. eyeing her ring. He teased, "Can we go skating on that later?"

Tuesday tucked her hand at her side, suddenly embarrassed by the massive diamond she usually wore so proudly.

"It's clear he's a rich man but is he a good one?"

"He's a complicated man. A man who sometimes does the wrong things for the right reasons." She gave A.D. a knowing look. "I guess I got a type."

He laughed and threw up his hands in surrender. "Okay, shots fired."

She asked, "And what about you? What does your type look like these days?"

He offered a nervous smile, tugged at his left ear. She recalled him always doing that when he was uncomfortable. "I got a little situation that I've been dealing with for a minute. We met right after I came home. She's a good girl—keeps me grounded."

She had married Marcus and had his baby so she had no reason to feel jealous, but part of her still did. Their love had spanned eighteen years, so on some purely selfish level she felt like A.D. would always belong to her.

Tuesday didn't trip though, kept her game-face on and congratulated him on finding somebody.

They spent a few more minutes catching up when DelRay got an important text and A.D. had to return to work. Tuesday took his number, but since she had trashed her phone, she gave him the number to the one she intended to buy. They agreed to get together as friends but shared an embrace that lasted too long to be friendly.

As DelRay pulled off, Tuesday couldn't stop glancing back at the church.

"Didn't I say you was gone love me for this?"

She nodded. "Yeah, that was a helluva surprise. I cain't believe that nigga home."

"Remember that li'l thing we used to do at The Bounce, how when I won a bet or did something good I got to smack dat fat ass?"

She cut her eyes at DelRay who was smiling like a kid.

"I'm just sayin', that's gotta be worth like twenty good ones."

"You got your own club now with a hundred different asses you can slap all you want. How after all this time you still so obsessed with mine?"

DelRay stroked his chin as if giving that serious thought. "I might need to see a therapist.

"On some real shit, Boss Lady." Tuesday no longer heard humor in his voice. "I thought you might need that pick-me-up after everything you been through."

She agreed. "Did help to take my mind off shit. He looked good but he seemed different though. His swag was off, and I don't know what's up with the church thing."

DelRay waved it off. "That's just how niggas be when they first get out. They be a little shook, all on that good-brother shit 'til the streets wash it off. Then they be right back to doing them."

Tuesday nodded, but didn't necessarily agree. It wasn't just that A.D. sounded different, she noticed a different look in his eye. His energy had changed.

DelRay said, "While you was catching up with your boy I was

shooting out texts trying to catch up with the goon. That's who hit me up. He wanna meet and talking 'bout bring cash. You ready to do that?"

Tuesday said, "Let's get it."

As DelRay pushed the Benz back towards the Westside, Tuesday was hopeful that finally something was about to go her way.

Chapter Thirty-four

"They call him Silence and word is he ain't got no gang or crew affiliations," explained DelRay. "He a hired goon, a street mercenary who put in work for whoever holding his lease. It might be red one week, blue the next week—all he care about is the green."

They waited in the stall of a coin car wash on Telegraph Road. DelRay vacuumed the interior of his S550 just so they wouldn't look suspicious.

Tuesday leaned against the hood, staring across the street at a motel that held history for her. She had been raped in one of its rooms but later in that same room had also brutally mutilated the dirty cop who violated her. She revisited those memories, listening absently as DelRay spoke.

He continued. "They say he don't work cheap but he worth the money."

"Well he need to get his ass here. In the corporate world you cain't be showing up twenty minutes late. Shit ain't professional."

DelRay was cleaning the trunk. "You know you sound bougie as hell right now."

While they waited, Tuesday thought back on the conversation with Danielle and wished she had handled that better. Some part of her had always known she would fail at motherhood because she had been failed by her own mother. Between the new job, baby Tanisha, and then creeping with Shaun, Danielle had been getting lost in the shuffle. Tuesday remembered her mother always chasing after the next new boyfriend rather than spending time with her.

She also took a page out of her mother's playbook by going in on Marcus—a bad look to put down a father to his daughter. Tuesday didn't realize until then how much trouble she was having accepting what he had done. Brandon kept trying to convince her that he'd done an honorable thing but she didn't see him as a martyr who gave his life to protect his family. To her, Marcus had basically committed suicide and Tuesday saw no honor in that.

DelRay brought her back to the moment just in time to see an '84 Chevy 2-door Caprice roll into the car wash. The paint looked sticky and wet like a grape Jolly Rancher. It sat high on twenty-eight-inch Giovanni's; purple candy and chrome reflected the late afternoon sun. The motor growled like something primal until he pulled into the next stall. The driver was already out of the car when they came around to greet him.

Tuesday didn't know what to expect but he surely fit the bill of a professional goon. The six-foot-five juggernaut seemed capable of walking through brick walls. She knew men for whom muscles were mostly cosmetic like A.D. and Marcus. His level of swell marked him as somebody who made a living with his might and had the battle scars to prove it. A massive chest and arms bulged under a snug T-shirt that read: 'Built in Detroit.'

Even DelRay seemed diminished by him despite being four inches taller and a hundred pounds heavier. One was sponsored by Hennessey and fast food, the other protein and discipline.

Tuesday asked, "You Silence?"

He nodded then engulfed her whole hand with a callused palm the size of a bear's paw.

DelRay's eyes flashed with recognition. "We did some business a few years ago. I had a spot on the eastside, State Fair off Gratiot.

You and yo' mans in the white Range came through, bought a couple AR's from me."

His face remained expressionless. Tuesday thought he was cute even with the nasty welt parting the hair on his left cheek. Only his complexion was lighter than she preferred.

He extended his new Galaxy S to Tuesday who looked at it skeptically before accepting. A message was written out on the screen. Tuesday read it then handed the phone back to him.

"Ten thousand a week is a lot of money. How do I know you worth all that?"

He gave her a *bitch, please* look.

He typed something into his phone with huge fingers that were lightning quick. He passed it to her and she read the text out loud: YOU KNEW ENOUGH ABOUT MY REPUTATION TO CALL ME SO YOU KNOW I'M WORTH IT.

DelRay said, "I definitely remember you. You ain't never say shit then."

"You don't speak and your name is Silence. That's cute." Tuesday let out a phony laugh. "So you actually cain't talk or is this like some gimmick thing you doing?"

He just stared down on her like a grim statue.

Tuesday looked him up and down. He was built like an action figure but she tried not to look too impressed. "Alright, you cut up, and you probably intimidate all the jack boys and gang banging niggas in the hood. But I got serious beef with professional hitters. I need a real shooter who know how to play wit' them guns—and I ain't talking that fake-thug sidearm shit."

Silence walked away from her while she was still talking. He went to the coin-operated water sprayer, and with one powerful yank, snatched open the locked change drawer causing quarters to spill to the ground. He stooped to pick up a few, walked back to them. He searched his pocket then stood in front of Tuesday with his huge hand cupping what appeared to be about four dollars in quarters, nickels, dimes and pennies.

The message he typed this time was for DelRay to read. "Any number from fifty to two hundred. You want me to pick a number?"

Tuesday wrinkled her nose. "This nigga 'bout to do a magic trick?"

Curiosity made DelRay play along. He didn't think, just randomly blurted, "one forty-one."

Silence stepped from underneath the stall and motioned for them to follow. He stood in the lot behind the car wash and when he pulled a Sig Sauer 9 with an extended clip from his hip, DelRay already knew what he was planning.

"Hell naw Playboy. I got two racks that say you ain't layin' like that."

He tapped his nose to signify they had a bet then screwed a silencer into the muzzle. Tuesday still hadn't caught on yet.

Silence tossed the change high into the air then took aim with the pistol and fired eight shots. A second later when the change struck the ground, he scoured the pavement to collect the coins.

DelRay paid him two thousand dollars right before Tuesday handed over a stack with ten more.

When the man they called Silence opened his palm, he held five quarters, one dime, one nickel and one penny. Each had a bullet hole dead center.

Chapter Thirty-five

Tuesday wanted Silence to start immediately. He revealed that he had offensive or defensive capabilities, which meant he could play the bodyguard or the hitman.

He also confessed that a childhood illness had taken his hearing. He assured her that his handicap in no way diminished his abilities. He claimed to be an expert lip-reader and had no problem communicating as long as she faced him while talking or used texts.

Tuesday almost asked for her money back. She considered all the ways him being deaf and mute might endanger them in a shootout. Even with armor-piercing rounds, she admitted his trick with the coins was impressive, but she wondered what would happen when bullets starting flying instead of change.

Silence texted that he needed to drop off his car so he had them follow him to the hood around 12th Street and Richton, a notoriously cutthroat part of a cutthroat city. From behind the wheel DelRay watched each pair of young, hungry eyes watching him as he cruised by. Dusk had started to descend and the big shiny Benz had nocturnal predators licking their chops.

This was the type of area that had DelRay leery about parking on the street, so he became even more nervous when Silence pulled deep into an alley that ran behind a liquor store. He frowned at Tuesday before his new European followed the old school over rocks and broken glass.

Silence parked somewhere past the midway point, got out, circled around to the rear of the purple Chevy. Tuesday expected him to grab a gym bag or maybe a few guns from the trunk. Her eyes went wide when he snatched out a man.

She and DelRay exchanged looks as Silence picked up and manhandled some scrawny nigga like he were a child. He wore nothing but a wifebeater and boxer shorts. Thick bands of gray duct-tape bound his ashy arms at the wrists and matching legs at the ankles. Dried blood from his nostrils crusted his upper lip. He was gagged by a Gucci head scarf.

Dude shivered like a cold puppy when Silence pulled a big ass hunting knife. His eyes followed the serrated blade as Silence drew near. He began to plead for his life. Tuesday thought dude would shit himself until Silence cut his wrists free.

Silence tossed him a wallet but held on to the driver's license. The mute man gave a serious glare that was clearly understood because the ashy one responded with a vigorous head shake for an emphatic no. Silence then pressed the car keys into his palm along with a few crispy hundred dollar bills. He gave dude a friendly pat on the back then joined Tuesday and DelRay in the Mercedes.

Tuesday turned in her seat. "What the fuck was that?"

He already had an answer waiting on his phone, obviously anticipating the question. The screen read: CAR RENTAL.

The quizzical look on Tuesday's face ran deeper, forcing him to quickly punch out a second message: DON'T KNOW Y'ALL NIGGAS. WASN'T COMIN' TO MEET IN MY OWN SHIT!

After a few seconds of DelRay sitting there watching the trunk-dweller try to peel duct-tape from his ankles, Silence made a motion with his hands that said 'we can go now.'

DelRay drove back to 24 Karats where Tuesday picked up her

car. From there she and Silence left together in the Hyundai with him insisting to drive. He didn't share this but Tuesday guessed it was in case somebody tried to follow them.

On the way back out to Romulus, Tuesday made him stop so she could pick up a new phone. As she walked through the Apple store, Silence lingered a few steps behind her, his eyes clocking everything. Tuesday appreciated DelRay but having Silence watch her back made her feel like a politician with her own secret service agent.

Tuesday returned to the Residence Inn and introduced the new bodyguard to the family. Danielle was her usual sullen self but Tanisha seemed less fearful of Silence than she had been of DelRay. Tuesday smiled when she caught Shaun throwing repeated glances at the brown-skinned mountain of muscle.

Tuesday offered to buy the room next door for him but Silence indicated that he preferred to stay close and agreed to sleep on the couch.

For the next three hours all the women found ways to cope with the boredom of being cooped up while Silence spent the entire time posted like a sentry. He squatted down on powerful haunches staring out the front window, his Sig Sauer hanging from his hip.

Tuesday could sense that Shaun wanted to talk in private for what she assumed was to pump her for a thousand "whats" and "whys" about the situation. Tuesday actively tried to avoid being alone with her.

When Tuesday's phone rang she knew it was only one of three people who had the number. She didn't expect to hear from A.D. that quickly. And when she slipped into the bathroom to take the call, she certainly didn't expect a dinner invitation.

Tuesday could list twenty good reasons why she shouldn't go. She knew the smart thing would be to just lay low and wait for Brandon to send the money. She was facing a deadly foe who always seemed to be a step ahead of her and could possibly be exposing A.D. to that threat. She was still hurting over Marcus and a dinner date seemed a little too intimate, a little too soon at a time when she was a little too vulnerable.

She could have made a rational decision if it were any other man but A.D.

Tuesday got an earful from Shaun and an eye roll from Danielle upon announcing that she was going out with no explanation. Silence only nodded compliantly when she ordered him to stay behind with Shaun and the girls.

Tuesday convinced herself that A.D. coming back into her life just when she lost Marcus was too much like Fate. She couldn't resist the pull to her first true love any more than a falling object could resist the pull of gravity.

Chapter Thirty-six

Earlier, DelRay had surprised her with that reunion but Tuesday refused to let A.D. see her looking bad again. Since her entire wardrobe burned along with her house, she caught an outlet mall minutes before closing and bought a tight off-the-shoulder dress by Julien MacDonald and pair of Louboutins. Another glitch with her credit card forced her to spend from her dwindling reserve. She wore both right out of the store.

Tuesday used to be able to walk into her favorite salons and get straight into a chair regardless of how many pissed off bitches were ahead of her. She'd been gone too long to have that type of juice anymore. She had to pay extra to get squeezed in late without an appointment and still waited an hour and a half to be seated.

After getting worked on by a hair stylist, a makeup artist, and a nail technician, Tuesday checked her reflection and felt more like herself than she had in weeks. Long spiral curls, red bottoms, skimpy black dress. She was a little insecure about the new scar on her leg but would eventually get that tatted over. She was ready to face A.D.

It was twenty minutes after ten when she finally met him in the parking lot of the place where they had their first date. Her club had been in a strip mall that also shared space with a rib joint, a beauty supply store, a clothing boutique and an empty storefront. Luckily the fire that burned The Bounce had not spread to the adjoining units. Bo's BBQ was still doing business.

He drove a modest fifteen-year-old Mercury Mountaineer with a dented quarter panel. A.D. stepped out in a button-up shirt and slacks that were cheap but hung on him well. Despite them both insisting they were only meeting as friends, Tuesday was already thinking of all the ways she could upgrade him.

He held the door for her as they entered an eatery they were overdressed for. Tuesday brushed past him, close enough to inhale his soapy scent. She walked with a wiggle that was supposed to draw his eyes to her ass.

At the counter it pained Tuesday to learn that the owner and namesake passed eighteen months prior. For twenty years, Bo had been more than a neighbor, he'd been a friend.

His eldest daughter ran the establishment, so Tuesday offered her condolences and intended to leave a generous tip out of respect for the old man who had been kind enough to give a starving young stripper a lifetime of free barbeque.

She and A.D. used preliminary chitchat to hold them over until their orders were prepared. Bo's BBQ was primarily a carry-out but offered a small dining area with five tables. Tuesday took a seat that faced the entrance, Heckler in her small clutch. She let A.D. explain how he was adjusting to the free world.

"Things done changed like a mutha in the years since I left the streets. The city looked like somebody dropped a bomb on it. These young dudes crazy off the pills and codeine. All the OG's who had the bag in my era either smoked out, dead or doing Fed time."

Tuesday listened for a while and answered his questions when he inquired about mutual friends he lost touch with, but when A.D. innocently asked to be caught up on her life, he wasn't prepared to have his mind blown.

Tuesday told him everything, even things she had been keeping secret when she was still going to visit him. It was an epic story of shoot-outs, setups, and a kidnapped child. She'd been raped by a dirty cop and nearly crushed to death in a junked car. The L.A. chapters included the fire, the ambush at the restaurant, and the fight for her company.

A.D. sucked it all up, wide-eyed like a kid by a campfire. He didn't butt in and only commented to say "Damn!" at the most unbelievable parts.

It wasn't just for dramatic effect that Tuesday was slow to reveal the biggest plot twists. It was hard to confess that she was a mother, considering they had mutually agreed to abort two pregnancies during their relationship. It was harder to explain who the child's father was.

The second revelation knocked A.D. into a stunned silence that had him unable to formulate words for a full minute. He glanced at the massive diamond on her finger then back to her. She could tell he was recalling the details of her story and could pinpoint by his expression the exact moment skepticism became belief.

Tuesday had never known A.D. to be a coward. She had met and fell in love with him as a thoroughbred street nigga with a slick mouth and a big .40 caliber to back it up. But right then he seemed ready to jump up and run out of the restaurant.

Tuesday tried to calm him. She reached out for his hand but A.D. snatched away from her like she were contagious.

She hid how much that hurt behind a smile. "Come on boy, it ain't that serious."

"Your baby daddy done killed more niggas than cigarettes and you got me in a public place with you. Girl, what the fuck is you thinking?"

"All the rumors we heard 'bout him being a monster is bullshit. He's a regular guy. Look and act a lot like you. I told you I had a type."

A.D. wasn't feeling her attempt to be funny. "Well if he anything like me, I know he won't be cool with his wife being on a date with her ex. It didn't end too well for the last dude who got caught messing with Caine's woman. I like my head being attached to my neck."

"That story about him cutting those people heads off ain't never happen." Tuesday hoped that lie would ease his tension.

A.D. was still looking sick when their plates arrived: two half-slabs of beef ribs, two small salads, and one platter of large-cut steak fries to share. They both chose pink lemonade to wash it down.

Tuesday pulled a bone from the slab and eagerly tore into it, but the first two bites revealed that these were no longer Bo's ribs. The taste wasn't bad, just unfamiliar. Either the daughter didn't inherit the old man's recipe for his amazing barbeque sauce or she didn't inherit his culinary talent.

For a while, Tuesday watched A.D. pick at his food with low enthusiasm. She could tell that it wasn't the flavor that had him put off.

"So what, you scared of me now?" she said irritated. "Adrian, you was the first nigga to put a dick in my mouth, and my ass! Don't sit here and act all weird like you don't know me."

He shook his head. "I'm not scared of you—I'm scared of your husband. I'm intimidated by you."

Arms crossed beneath her bosom. "What's the difference?"

"When I met you, you was just this fine little green-eyed girl with a cute smile, dancing at a rinky-dink club and surviving off Top Ramen. Only beef you had was with the next chick trying to steal your tips.

"Now you bossed up to Beverly Hills mansions, private jets and hundred-million-dollar corporations. You're married to a real-life kingpin and beefing with the cartels."

Tuesday asked, "Would you be happier if I was just another bridge-card bitch out here waiting on the first and chasing every nigga wit' a Rolex?"

A.D. dragged a hand over his face. "You know that ain't what

I mean. It's just that I'm the one who started you out helping me stick guys for thousand-dollar sacks. Part of me is happy that you doin' big things but another part of me feel responsible for introducing you to this life."

Tuesday had seen him like this before during their visits at the prison and had no interest in watching him guilt trip.

"I went through hell to get my hair done and stuff myself in a dress two sizes too small. Can a bitch get complimented on her sexy? Damn nigga, at least sneak a peek at my cleavage or something."

"I see you still use dick-teasing to throw niggas off balance. I got a situation, you got a situation. And your situation is complicated."

"It's not like I'm asking you to get a room. I just wanna hear that I'm looking good after all these years. Just cause you on a diet don't mean you can't scope the menu."

A.D. laughed. "You still crazy as hell. And you still lookin' good."

That seemed to make A.D. comfortable again so the two of them reminisced while the ribs cooled on their plates. After another forty-five minutes, they got the leftovers bagged up and Tuesday still left that generous tip despite the subpar sauce.

She felt A.D. tense up a bit when she linked her arm into his on the way out.

"He's not in the picture," she said eyeing him seriously. "I wouldn't play a game like that with him, or you."

It was close to midnight and the strip mall's parking lot had emptied except for their vehicles slotted side by side right out front. Bo's was the only business with its sign still glowing. They stood in the space between their cars bathed in the orange light of a cartoon pig.

"I didn't just come here to catch up," Tuesday confessed. "I need you, Adrian. I'm at war and I'm losing. If everything plays out the way it should, I'll have soldiers in a minute. But I need a general, somebody to help me direct. I'm not trying to mess up your situation but I could really use you on my team. Won't have to worry 'bout money or anything."

He leaned against his SUV. "I just spent sixteen years on my bunk thinking about what I would do if I ever got the chance to get out here again. At first you miss the cars, the money, the life, but after a while you start missing the small things. The simple freedom to come and go as you please, the comfort and privacy of sleeping on your own bed in your own home.

"I thought I was gonna die in that place and then a miracle happened. Tuesday, you know I ain't never been on that religious trip, but when that lawyer came out of nowhere, I knew God was real. I promised myself and the Man upstairs that if He got me out, I would do the right thing from then on out."

That suddenly made sense of why one of the most thuggish niggas she had ever known was volunteering at a church.

A.D. read the look on her face. "Naw, I ain't one of them types. I ain't the dude who gone bring up Jesus every two minutes or quote scriptures at you all day. I'm just trying to live right. You said your husband changed his ways so you can relate to where I'm coming from."

Tuesday understood but really didn't want to.

"Well at least let me help you out with some cash. Maybe get you a new car. I ain't surviving off Ramen noodles no more."

He shook his head. "You held me down for twelve years inside. I appreciate it but you don't owe me nothing else."

She smiled. "It would be sort of a welcome-home gift. Friends buy gifts for friends, Adrian."

He gave her a *bitch, please* look. "Tuesday, let's quit playing. There ain't no world we could be in together as just friends. We both know what would end up happening. It's all in our eyes when we look at each other."

Tuesday couldn't deny that she wanted him. She felt like shit for thinking it, but if A.D. said the word, she would be in the back of his raggedy Mountaineer with that two-thousand-dollar Julien MacDonald piece balled up on the floor right next to her thong.

He continued, "Like I said, she's a good girl and I ain't trying to be that dude."

Tuesday forced herself to respect that. She knew it wasn't smart or even safe to bring A.D. into her life. Just meeting him for dinner might have put a target on his back.

It had been a rough couple of weeks and Marcus was still a fresh wound. She didn't go there looking to replace him. Tuesday had just needed a distraction, and maybe a little validation which was why she bought that tiny dress.

They reached that awkward moment during the date when there was nothing left to say, when it was time to leave but neither person seemed ready.

Neon light shimmered across his wavy hair like the moon on a dark ocean. His brown eyes held her captive. "Take care of yourself Bright Eyes."

She implored him to do the same.

Tuesday didn't know who initiated the kiss, only that they both surrendered instantly. He pressed her against the Hyundai, his tongue danced in her mouth. As some point she didn't remember, she leaped into his arms and wrapped his waist with her thighs. The motion hiked her minidress so high that anybody who pulled into the lot would get mooned. Tuesday was too lost in the kiss to either notice or care.

It wasn't long before she felt that warm wood growing and pulsing through his slacks. She moaned in anticipation. The length of him excited her. It was like the years in prison had made his dick a bigger, hungrier beast.

They attacked each other for a full minute until the flashing lights and annoying screech broke their trance. She and A.D. didn't realize that they had grinded each other so hard they set off the Hyundai's alarm. She silenced it with the remote.

"Lord forgive me, but I been wanting to do that since the church." A.D. puffed the words through heavy breaths. "I think I overstepped the line?"

Tuesday's head was still spinning as she adjusted her dress. "I don't know. The line kinda' blurry right now."

They stared into each other's eyes and said what needed to be said without words. No tears, no goodbyes. They shared one final hug.

Then they shared one final laugh when Tuesday showed him her huge butt-print steaming the glass of her driver's window.

Chapter Thirty-seven

Villa Bella was a massive ranch sitting on three hundred and ninety-five prime Texas acres just outside of San Antonio. The wooded areas offered good hunting for deer, wild hogs, and geese during the migratory seasons. The stable housed twenty-four well-bred Spanish stallions, including the descendants of two Derby winners. The main house was a twenty-thousand-square-foot masterpiece done in the classic Mediterranean style.

Reina padded the glazed hardwood of the great hall in bare feet. Aztec-inspired ceramics and pottery were on display on every table and shelf. The walls were adorned with black-and-white photos of Vaqueros along with oil portraits of heroes who fought for Mexican independence. The decor was intended to prove that, despite their incredible wealth, the Rodriguez family had not forgotten their proud heritage.

Reina slipped into the main kitchen where the staff was cleaning up after dinner. She stood in the doorway, quietly overlooking them for a minute before someone noticed her and whispered to the others.

"Doña Rodriguez, can I help you?" The head chef had been

lured away from a four-star restaurant in Fort Worth. Protocol dictated that as the senior member of the kitchen staff, he should be the only one to address her. "Is there something more we can do for you?"

She asked, "Which of you were responsible for preparing the *antojitos?*"

He asked, "Was something not to your liking, Miss?"

Reina threatened him with a frown. "I asked who was responsible for the appetizers served with dinner?"

Fear made his brown face turn pale. The elderly chef looked to be on the verge of a panic attack.

"The food didn't just appear on my table by magic."

She stepped into the kitchen and coldly scanned all six of their faces. The tension grew heavy enough to crush a walnut.

"I prepared the first course, Doña Rodriguez." The young assistant chef stepped forward who was scrubbing the industrial sized broiler. "If something was not satisfactory, please do not blame Chef Lawrence. I take full responsibility for—"

Reina cut him off. "I thought the apple and sweet pepper slaw was the most delightful thing I've ever tasted. I only wanted to come offer my compliments in person."

She watched the entire staff collectively exhale in relief.

"Thank you, Doña Rodriguez. I'm happy you enjoyed it."

She approached the young cook. "It was so delicious that I had a second and a third helping. I'll have to spend an extra hour on the treadmill because of you."

She got close to him, close enough to invade his personal space. She watched him get nervous again as he tried to decide whether it would be more insulting to stay close or pull away.

This was a different type of fear because the mistress of the house was dressed in a black satin gown by La Perla that was totally see-through. She wore nothing underneath.

Reina asked, "What is your name?"

He stammered, "M-Marco, Doña Rodriguez."

She pressed even closer to him, made him squirm. His eyes ricocheted from her eyes, down between her legs to some empty spot on the floor.

She smiled amused, "You're not trying to get me fat, are you? Marco, *me prefieras gordita?*"

He shifted uncomfortably. "No, ma'am."

"Well I was extremely pleased by the slaw." La Guapa thrust her chest out, dared him to notice the erect nipples of her perfectly-doctored 34Cs poking through the fabric. "I look forward to seeing how you will please me in the future."

He nodded shakily, swallowed hard as if a golf ball were lodged in his throat.

She sashayed out of the kitchen knowing full well that rumors of this latest antic would circulate among the house staff and give them something to whisper about for the next couple of weeks.

Reina was on the way back to her bedroom when she spotted something that was never supposed to be. Someone was in her father's office.

Rene Rodriguez had constructed a secret room deep within the interior of the house for conducting his most sensitive business. It was a closed-in space with no windows from which he could be spied upon. Her father was a disciplined man who discussed no aspect of the criminal side of his empire outside its walls, walls that were stuffed with a foot of expensive soundproof material.

The hidden door was camouflaged into the wall paneling. This was wide open, throwing a shaft of yellow light across the hall.

Reina stood at the entrance of her father's former sanctum, a masculine space with plenty of wood, stuffed leather furniture and hunting trophies. She saw her sister seated behind the desk.

Reina hissed at the trespass. "What are you doing?"

"Just drinking." Roselyn sipped from a glass next to a crystal decanter half-filled with pale liquor. "I'm having some of his ten-thousand-dollar tequila and thinking about smoking one of his Cubans."

"You shouldn't be in here, Rose."

She took a swallow. "Papa is dead and we're not five years old anymore. The ghost of Rene Rodriguez isn't going to rise up and spank us for playing with our Barbie dolls in here."

Reina stepped inside. "Let's give the man's body a chance to cool before we start helping ourselves to his things."

"These are your things now, along with the house, the business, and all the properties. I got a sneak peek at the will and—spoiler alert—he left it all to you. I suspect they'll probably even offer you his seat at The Table."

"Oh, I see. I crashed another one of your pity parties." Reina frowned, disgusted. "Papa did it this way because he knew I would take care of you. When have I not taken care of you, Rose?"

Roselyn jumped to her feet. "When have I ever needed you to, Reina?"

She walked over to a mahogany and glass display case that was adjacent to the matching desk. The shelves were filled with trophies from chess tournaments, academic awards and certificates. In the center was a huge photo of a young Reina being crowned Miss Teen Texas with the tiara and sash hanging next to it.

"Most parents at least pretend to love their children equally. Papa was surprisingly genuine in that respect."

"Knock it over," Reina urged her. "Take a bat, go crazy until it's just a pile of trash. You've been wanting to since you could remember."

Roselyn snorted when she noticed the negligee. "Still playing peekaboo with the house help? It was kinda funny when you were sixteen but now it's just sad."

Reina fired back. "And this whole Daddy-loved-you-more-than-me thing was sad back when we were sixteen but now it's just pathetic. Especially because we both know you could've filled ten of these trophy cases all over the house if you wanted."

Roselyn reclaimed her drink. "The part you never understood was that I shouldn't have had to."

"Rose, I can tell by the slur in your speech that's not your first glass of tequila. And since it's obvious you're not drinking to our father's memory, who exactly are you mourning?"

Roselyn's eyes briefly flashed anger. "Who's to say I'm mourning anyone?"

Reina gave her a knowing look. "I remember when Rico first brought him here to live with us. We were nineteen and it was the summer that Papa first installed all the security cameras. I checked the footage and who do I see sneaking into my man's room at three in the morning? It's me, except I had a FIDE tournament in New York that weekend. Mysteries abound. How can a person be in two places at one time?"

Roselyn shied away from her gaze embarrassed.

"You put on some makeup, styled your hair like mine and slipped on one of my gowns. Sebastian was probably half-asleep and too drunk from partying with Rico to even notice the difference. Hell, maybe he did know after the first few strokes and just didn't care."

"Trust me, he noticed." Roselyn sneered at her. "He just couldn't stop talking about how much tighter I was."

Reina marched toward her. "That would depend on which hole he used."

The twins stared long and hard at each other, their faces matching masks of hatred. Then they simultaneously broke into a smile and then laughter.

Reina said, "In one way or another, he fucked everybody in our family."

Roselyn nodded. "Did you get the feeling that Papa was hanging on just long enough to see him again? They were alone together talking for a long time. What do you think they discussed?"

"What difference does it make what a dying man said to one who would follow him in death shortly after?" Reina clucked her tongue. "Whatever Sebastian and Papa talked about, they both took it to their graves."

"What happened in Detroit?"

Reina was speechless for a moment. "The rat slipped through a crack in the wall. She'll look to build an alliance but it won't matter. The second she sticks her head out, I'll stomp on it."

"But why even bother? You've already taken everything. She's already lost and doesn't know it. In a few days the company will be ours. Why are you wasting men and money, at a time when we are short on both, just to torment this woman?"

Reina stared at the oil painting the hung over the fireplace. It was an elaborate rendering of a proud matador standing victorious over a vanquished bull with spears in its bloody hide. Roses fell into the ring from the raucous spectators.

She finally said, "We split from the same ovum and shared a womb. Don't act like you can't understand my motivations."

Roselyn held out her hands. "Come here. Come to me, Pretty Girl."

Reina was hesitant at first but then surrendered to her sister's embrace.

Roselyn stroked her hair and whispered, "After all this time, it's still hurting."

"I didn't think it did. Not until I saw him at the restaurant. I could've forgiven him for Rico, but he married this low-brow bitch, put his seed in her." She wept on her shoulder. "Her every breath disrespects me, Rose."

Roselyn rubbed her back and made soothing sounds. "If it's that important then we'll end her. Will that make the Pretty Girl feel better?"

Reina nodded.

Chapter Thirty-eight

The next morning Tuesday called Brandon to learn that he had already put the money together. The delivery would take place within a few hours. He was supposed to call as soon as the jet landed in Detroit.

Brandon also told her that the investigation out in L.A. had intensified. The police had upgraded her status to "Person of Interest" concerning the two bodies at the house and the boy she had killed at the industrial complex. He advised that the best thing for her was to keep off-the-radar while his lawyers did what they could to delay the inevitable arrest warrant.

He could offer no explanation for her problems with the credit cards. She complained that all of Tabitha King's plastic was being spat back in her face, from the no-limit American Express down to the simple gas cards. Brandon hung up after promising to get that straightened out.

Shaun used the groceries from the night before to cook breakfast for everyone. She served Tanisha and Danielle cheese omelets in the kitchenette while Tuesday took hers next to Silence on the sofa that he slept on.

Tuesday glanced at him a few times while he quietly shoveled forkfuls of eggs into his mouth. She had come in late the previous night with her mind and hormones still in a twist from seeing A.D. Silence was built like a stud which made it easy to fantasize about what he might be working with or what type of damage he could do. Her big quiet bodyguard had no idea of how close Tuesday had come to trying to fuck him.

She asked how he got into that line of work and got an interesting story about black nationalist extremists. Via text he told her that he grew up on a compound where he and other kids had been trained by militants to be soldiers in the oncoming race war. After he broke away at sixteen, he had been living in Detroit freelancing with the skills he learned in his father's strange cult.

He didn't go into how he lost his hearing and Tuesday didn't press for it.

A while later DelRay showed up in his S550 Benz. Tuesday took Silence and started to leave Shaun behind watching the girls again. This was a habit that Shaun raised issues with.

She grabbed Tuesday by the arm and pulled her into the bedroom. "You leave me here all day watching your kids; you run in and out without telling me nothing; you leave us alone with this stranger last night then come back late wearing a freak'um dress. Could you stop and talk to me for like five minutes before you go running off again?"

Tuesday snatched out of the girl's grip. "Bitch, you ain't got no idea of what's going on wit' me right now—the type of stuff I'm facing. I don't owe you shit. I told you what time it was when I came to your door. Now if you wanna go back home, let me know and I can have your ass on a plane in an hour. Do you wanna leave?"

Shaun looked ready to battle back but something made her swallow the words along with a portion of her pride.

"Well, let me handle my business then," Tuesday barked. "And stop stressin' me by actin' like some over-sensitive side-piece who don't know her muthafuckin' place."

When Tuesday stormed out of the room, she wished they had

closed the door. Danielle stood there watching her with something that looked like disappointment.

"Keep an eye on yo' sister until I get back," was all Tuesday could think to say to her.

With nothing else to do but wait for the pick-up, she, DelRay and Silence returned to 24 Karats which had yet to open. They smoked in DelRay's office while Tuesday explained that private flights typically didn't see the level of scrutiny as the people flying commercial airlines. So once the Abel jet pulled into the secure hangar, she said they would carry off two large travel bags, conveniently omitting what would be in them.

Tuesday trusted DelRay, but didn't know Silence well enough to tell him that he would be helping her walk ten million dollars in undeclared cash through Metro Airport. He might try to jack her for it; after all, before she fell for Marcus, she had done the same thing to him for only three.

DelRay looked skeptical. He voiced that with all the recent terror attacks, it shouldn't be that easy for them to get out of the airport with two large bags and no one searching them.

Tuesday didn't blame him, because she had been nervous the first time she did it with Marcus. She again stressed that the rules were different for rich people and promised him it would be easy.

Silence didn't use his phone to express any questions or concerns. Tuesday loved that he just seemed to be down for whatever.

They smoked some more and waited for Brandon's call. DelRay ran downstairs for a bottle of Patron even though she and Silence felt it was too early to drink.

An hour later a buzzed DelRay was reclined across the loveseat resting his eyes. Silence sat in one of the chairs that fronted the desk, consumed by some e-book he read on his phone. Tuesday slouched in the big chair behind the desk staring at the monitors out of boredom.

Then something made her sit erect. She called to DelRay: "Aye nigga, please tell me you got somethin' big and fully automatic stashed somewhere in this bitch."

DelRay lifted his head and Silence focused up when they saw the *Oh Shit!* look on her face.

The outside cameras gave a wide view of the parking lot. On screen, three SUVs stopped in front of the club.

All three vehicles were burgundy.

Chapter Thirty-nine

DelRay claimed not to keep any illegal guns at the club because he wasn't trying to lose his business. All he had for security was a pistol-grip .12 gauge pump he bought at a trade show.

On screen, Tuesday watched eleven heavily-armed men spring from three vehicles and start to surround the building. The doors were locked but they had come for murder and wouldn't stop at breaking and entering.

Tuesday didn't know how they kept finding her; for all she knew she might have led them there. Calling the police wasn't an option because of the heat she already had on her.

Through a series of hand gestures, Silence signaled that he would go down and for them to stay in the office. Tuesday couldn't believe he was indicating that he could handle this alone, but he made a 'gimme' motion for the shotgun. DelRay turned it over without an argument or offer to assist.

Tuesday thought her Heckler also might be better served in his hands, but Silence motioned to say the gauge and his Sig Sauer would be enough. He checked the weapon, racked a shell into the barrel.

Tuesday didn't know if he was trying to play hero or just

wanted to live up to his reputation; either way, she didn't want to see him get killed for the sake of his pride. But to her, Silence didn't project the arrogance of someone desperate to prove himself. He left the office with the calm demeanor of a man simply going to work.

DelRay's conscience seemed clear as he hurried behind him to lock the door. He pulled his Ruger and kept it trained on the wood.

Tuesday used the cameras to keep track of Silence and the enemy. She saw him slip down the hall then leap down the stairs like a jungle cat. On another monitor, four men gathered at the entrance preparing to burst in with no idea he was waiting on the other side.

The instant one used a swift kick to send the doors swinging in, the .12 gauge roared and kicked him twelve feet back into the parking lot. That moment of shock and indecision offered enough time for Silence to mow down another before the other two could respond.

The first tried to turn his weapon on Silence, but his size hid incredible speed. Silence closed the distance between them, blocked down his AR-15 with the shotgun like a swordsman, flipped it like a baton, then blew off his leg at the knee. The gunman wailed in agony at the sight of his severed limb before a shot to the face ended his misery.

The fourth spat machine gun fire in his direction but Silence moved so quickly that Tuesday lost sight of her goon. She did see the rest of the shooters on the other sides of the building flock to the front to press their way inside.

Tuesday manipulated the camera angles and zoom until she found Silence crouched on the floor behind the bar. She called his phone, which she knew had to be on vibrate due to his disability, sent a quick text telling him the number and position of the men. He looked around until he found the camera she had on him then gave a salute that said "Good lookin'."

Tuesday wasn't sure what he was doing when he pulled the

vodka from the bar and twisted the cap. She thought he might need a swallow but figured it out when he tore the sleeve from his shirt and stuffed the cloth in the top of the bottle. Reina's men moved cautiously through the tables and chairs with their assault rifles raised. Silence used the mirrors to target them, lit the wick, tossed the cocktail.

Burning alcohol splashed the one closest to the stage. He flailed and danced, and while his partners watched him thrash, Silence popped into view with the .12 gauge. His aim was surgically accurate and made two more of their heads explode like balloons filled with Kool-Aid.

Tuesday watched the monitor with her mouth hanging open. Ten thousand a week started to seem like a discount.

The few that remained opened fire on the bar forcing Silence to dive for cover. Fear made them spray bullets in wide reckless arcs that chewed up the paper lanterns and fake gold dragons used for 24 Karat's oriental theme.

Tuesday could see that they had Silence pinned down in a tight spot. Shooters were moving in on both sides of the bar to flank him.

She ran to DelRay. "We gotta help him."

"Naw, we gotta get the fuck on." He snatched open a door at the rear of his office that Tuesday had assumed was a closet. Behind it was a narrow stairway that led down to a fire exit. "He done pulled them muthafuckas away from the back door. Let him handle that. We can get clear."

Tuesday had never been the type of chick to leave somebody hanging that was on her team. She gave DelRay a look that called him a 'hoe ass nigga.' She pulled up her Heckler then ran out his office through the other door with him trying to call her back.

Tuesday crouched at the top of the stairs, and while the shooters were faced away from her, she took aim. She fired three times; the second struck one of them in the back of the thigh. The blow wasn't lethal but he buckled to the floor clutching his wound.

That was enough to get their attention. They split up, concealed themselves behind the plush chairs where customers enjoyed twenty-dollar lap dances. Tuesday punched a few holes in the imitation silk upholstery before two of them returned fire. She scrambled backward up the steps, stumbled and fell out of sight just ahead of the rat-a-tat of their AR-15's.

She landed on her ass in the upstairs hall. Tuesday heard two more shotgun blasts, but her angle didn't allow her to see if Silence hit anyone. He must have run out of shells because a second later she heard the Sig Sauer.

Next was the sound of breaking glass followed by a loud *whoosh*. Tuesday guessed he threw another cocktail and somebody's panicked screams seemed to confirm it.

Then she heard heavy footsteps rushing up the stairs but couldn't tell who was coming her way. She raised the Heckler, still seated on the floor. Willpower couldn't make her hands stop shaking.

The man came charging into view, flailing and screaming like a maniac. Bluish flames consumed his clothes. He scrambled blindly, but Tuesday put him down with three shots before he could trample on her.

Seconds later, the gun shots ceased below, coaxing Tuesday to ease down the stairs. La Guapa's men littered the floor and Silence stood in the middle of them holding up one in the air with his hulking arms. Silence strangled him with the strap of his own machine gun; his body wriggled like a fish on a line.

Silence dropped him, then indicated to Tuesday with a series of hand movements that the last two had ran like bitches. He tapped his chest to suggest it was because he was such a bad muthafucka and Tuesday smiled to agree.

That was until a van pulled directly in front of the entrance. The side door slid open to reveal the same two men in the rear. Mounted on a tripod was a huge M-50 chain gun.

Silence snatched her out of the way as the machine started its death melody. He pulled her to the floor and pinned her under his body. The military used .50 caliber rounds to shoot down planes and crack open tanks so the barrage tore through the walls like wet paper. Wood and glass rained on them.

Silence covered her like a human shield, but Tuesday knew that even his stout body wouldn't stop a slug from that beast. Bullets whizzed over their heads coupled with shrapnel just as lethal. It wasn't safe to move but wasn't safe to simply lay there and hope they didn't aim lower. From on top of her Silence communicated their situation with his eyes.

Tuesday covered her ears, fearing the loud metallic clatter would have them both deaf in a minute. She could only pray they didn't catch a hot one before the shooters stopped to reload, but they seemed to have a chain of bullets that stretched on forever.

It was like they were trying to saw the building in half.

Then a louder explosion came from outside, and the shooting stopped right after. She and Silence waited a few seconds to make sure it was safe before he climbed off her and helped Tuesday to her feet. He grabbed a chopper from one of the dead and she followed with the Heckler. They crept slowly to the front of the club and peeked out the gaping hole of brick and metal that had once been the entrance.

The van had been knocked thirty feet. The whole back half was crushed like an aluminum can, frame lifted and pushed off the rear axle. The driver hung halfway through the windshield. The two in back had been thrown clear, their bodies twisted and bloodied on the asphalt.

DelRay's S550 was crumpled and wedged under the back of the van. He was still behind the wheel when Tuesday and Silence ran up on the car. She figured he had to be going about seventy miles per hour when he slammed into them.

The airbag had deployed, but the big man was slumped in his seat, eyes closed. He wasn't moving.

Chapter Forty

"Now you owe me a E-lade and a Benz."

This was the first thing DelRay said to Tuesday after she slapped him awake. His speech was slurred and he looked glassy eyed from the collision. He stumbled a bit when Silence pulled him out of the car.

I owe you another club too. But Tuesday kept the thought to herself. 24 Karats was beyond any hope of renovation. In some places, the M-50 had left holes in the walls as big as soccer balls. The structure looked too weak for safe habitation. A group of kids could probably knock the whole building down with a few good kicks.

Tuesday said, "I thought you—"

"I know what the fuck you thought," DelRay cut her off. "From the jump I told you I had you, no matter what, and I meant it. Even though it's probably gone get me killed."

Tuesday felt like shit. She had been back in his life just over a day and already had cost him so much.

Sirens swelled in the distance. They had to get away from the scene, but Tuesday hadn't driven and DelRay had just totaled his second car. She hated to do it, but had to search the pockets of the dead until she found keys to one of the SUVs. Luckily they weren't with one of the men Silence torched.

Tuesday climbed behind the wheel of the Tahoe while Silence helped DelRay into the rear. Tires squeaked as they left the parking lot on one side of the complex a second before police cruisers pulled into the other side.

Tuesday was only a block away from the club when she got the text. "The package is here. It's time for the pickup."

Silence was in the passenger seat with DelRay seated behind him. He still looked like he had a concussion.

"You talking 'bout going right now? In a stolen ride right after we just shot it out with a dozen niggas?"

"Hell yeah," she confirmed. "That's why I wanna go right now. Before anything else can happen.

"Plus, we in and out. Gone take less than ten minutes. Same way you be in the pussy." She tried but that didn't get a laugh out of him.

When they reached Metro Airport, she let DelRay circle the Tahoe while she and Silence went inside. Because they weren't waiting on a commercial flight, they walked right past all the long lines and security checkpoints. She led him to the private hangar where the Abel jet was being refueled. Tuesday had grown accustomed to the stench of the fumes.

Tuesday met Brandon on board and introduced him to Silence. The two killers knew of each other's reputations and seemed to her they seemed to be sizing each other to see if the old school could hang with the new.

Brandon warned Tuesday that his lawyers had been unable to stall the investigation. Los Angeles police would issue warrants within forty-eight hours. She explained that after what just happened, she would be just as hot in Detroit.

Brandon updated her on a few things about the company then presented her with two large leather travel totes that weighed about one hundred pounds each. After parting words, he pecked Tuesday on the cheek and wished her good luck.

On the way back through the airport, Silence dragged both wheeled cases behind him making her wonder if he had any idea of what was in his grasp. What would he do if she told him? He came off as a principled man, so did ten thousand dollars purchase his absolute loyalty for the week? Or would he put a bullet in DelRay's head and snap her neck like a twig for the chance of coming up on ten million? Tuesday stared at his bulging biceps and decided not to find out.

She threw a nervous glance at the airport rent-a-cops pawing through people's luggage and tagging them for random strip searches. The FAA was concerned about commercial passengers having sharp objects and liquid containers holding more than four ounces; the privilege of money allowed private passengers to breeze right pass them with whatever they wanted.

They were about fifty feet from the exit and Tuesday felt the tension ease with each step that brought her closer to it. Through the sliding glass doors, she could see the burgundy Chevy idling and DelRay in the driver's seat looking anxious.

They were about ten feet from freedom when the commotion erupted. Two dozen people appeared from nowhere, surrounded them all shouting at the same time. Tuesday knew what time it was. She cursed out loud and threw up her hands before they even ordered it. They moved in, Glock pistols raised. They had on body armor with the letters F, B, and I blazed across their chests in bright yellow.

They barked for Silence to release the bags and raise his hands, but he was hesitant. Tuesday begged them not to shoot, screamed that he was deaf and might not understand them.

But she knew that he did understand. They had left their pistols outside; however, she could tell by the movement of his eyes that Silence was trying to decide if he could kill his way out of the situation even with no gun.

He must've concluded that the odds were even too great for him because he finally complied. Agents swarmed and forced them both to the ground with airport customers and employees gawking. Tuesday couldn't get mad when from beneath the pile she watched DelRay speed off.

They pinned her arms behind her back and Tuesday felt something she had sworn she would never know again. The cold touch of steel handcuffs being placed on her wrists.

Chapter Forty-one

Tuesday didn't know what happened to Silence or the money because they were immediately separated. The feds didn't bother taking her to one of the detention rooms at the airport. She was placed in the back of a car and driven straight to downtown's First Precinct.

During the ride she heard something come over their radios about Silence. It was distorted by static and hidden in cop-code, but it sounded like the big man was being a problem.

She wasn't booked or processed, and all the local police looked at her like she was a terrorist when eight federal agents walked her into the station. The inmates did too when an entire bullpen was cleared out so she could be isolated.

Tuesday sat on a hard metal bench with her head down until a few dudes from across the hall called to her through the bars. "Aye, baby. Damn girl, what they got yo' sexy ass in here for?"

She looked up and didn't see a real money-getter among them. They had the look of bum niggas caught up on petty possession cases and child-support warrants.

She said, "I'm in here for some real shit. I'm allergic to broke and y'all niggas fuckin' with my sinuses."

Tuesday tuned them out as they called her a couple of bitches. She tried to figure out what the hell happened at the airport. Back when she and Marcus had to pick up the three million for Danielle's ransom, it had been as simple as walking in and out. She wondered if the situation in L.A. had been the difference. Had the feds followed Brandon and flagged Abel's jet because she was hot?

She expected to sit there for hours, but it was hardly forty minutes when they came for her. Two officers escorted her to a small dank room on the fourth floor. Tuesday was seated and left cuffed to a table, but wasn't alone a minute before the woman walked in. Tuesday rolled her eyes, cursed under her breath.

The black lady was in her mid-forties, wearing dark pants, a white top, and cheap heels. She looked over Tuesday and beamed a smile. "Hey Ms. Knight, remember me? It's been a few years."

"Fraid not," Tuesday lied. The same woman had been part of the team that arrested Tuesday the night she left Detroit for California. The female fed still had a poor fashion sense, and looked about the same, other than wearing her hair natural in a short afro instead of a weak lace front.

"I think you do remember me Ms. Knight. We had a nice long conversation in a room just like this, except out in Romulus."

Tuesday stopped faking. "Love the new 'do, Agent Jackson. It's a better look."

She shrugged. "Had a cancer scare two years ago—my hair always grew slowly. And by the way, it's Assistant District Director Jackson now."

Tuesday offered congratulations that sounded genuine.

Ms. Jackson took the seat across from her. "I guess congratulations are due to us both. It's not Ms. Knight anymore; you're Mrs. King now." She studied Tuesday's massive diamond. "Or is it Mrs. Caine? Which do you prefer?"

"I prefer King because it's my name. I thought we cleared that up before. I don't know anything about a person named Silas Caine, Samson, or whatever."

The agent waved her off like 'bitch, stop.' "You'll notice I'm smiling a lot more this time because I know so much more. I'm not gonna lie, Tuesday, after the last time we met, I kinda made your husband a personal project of mine. Even became a little obsessed: Sebastian Caine, the myth, The Invisible Man. I've read every case file ten times where his name was even mentioned. I'm a bit of an expert now. Probably know him better than you."

"Well I can believe that, cause I ain't never met Sebastian Caine."

She gave a knowing look. "We can just drop that for right now."

It was then that Tuesday noticed she wasn't the only one wearing a new ring. Ms. Jackson had a silver piece on the middle finger of her right hand: triangle-shaped with markings that Tuesday had seen somewhere else.

"Who was the friend you were with at the airport—The Hulk's little brother? The man had no driver's license, credit cards, or identification on him whatsoever."

Tuesday shrugged. "If you have any questions about him, you gotta ask him yourself."

"I would if I could, but he never made it back here. He resisted in the car, caused an incident."

Was Silence dead? Tuesday had heard the commotion over the radio and knew something had popped off. She was worried but could tell Jackson was reading her for a reaction.

"Whoever he was, he had the skills to get out his cuffs and beat the shit outta two armed federal agents. Took their guns, left them on the side of the road, and escaped in their cruiser. But let me guess, you wouldn't know anything about him either?"

Tuesday bit back her smile. She had seen enough to know that Silence would never go out that easily.

"I was here enjoying the comforts of the DPD's finest cage."

Ms. Jackson measured her with a stare. "Why did you come back to Detroit?"

"To visit family."

"You sure it didn't have anything to do with La Guapa?"

That almost knocked Tuesday out her chair but she managed to keep her poker face. "La what?"

"You are good!" Jackson laughed. "Didn't even blink."

Another agent came in just long enough to wheel in one of the travel bags. He strained with the effort it took to hoist it up on the table.

Jackson said, "I know about Reina, about the fight over Abel. I know about everything except this." She unzipped the bag and revealed the green stacks inside.

"You're at war, so it makes sense that you would need money. But this is the part that confuses me." Ms. Jackson pulled up the bills on top and Tuesday was stunned that under a thin layer of cash was bundled wads of grocery store circulars and flyers.

"Why would you go through the trouble of trying to smuggle two hundred pounds of worthless paper through Metro. You had plans on playing somebody." Then she looked at Tuesday thoughtfully. "Or maybe you were the one getting played."

Tuesday sat across from her feeling nauseous because what took shape in her imagination hit her like a gut punch.

But she maintained her fronts. "And since when is it a crime to carry two hundred pounds of worthless paper through the airport?"

"But murder is a crime," Jackson said calmly. She produced a file folder and opened to several photos: the burned ruins of Tuesday's Grecian mansion, autopsy photos of the two men killed there, the young man she stabbed in the throat.

"And not an hour ago a call came in—multiple shots fired. Twelve bodies at a gentlemen's club on Joy Road. Owned by Del-Ray Royce, an old associate of yours. Funny how everywhere you go dead bodies pop up."

Tuesday said, "A terrible coincidence."

"I've got you linked to about fifteen open homicides, and that's just in the last week or so. Not to mention the bodies you left all over the city four years ago."

Tuesday sucked her teeth. "Let's skip the part where you come with all that corny shit 'bout how I'll never see the light of day. You the feds—we both know when y'all really got somebody it ain't nothing else to talk about."

"I get it," said Ms. Jackson with a chuckle. "You've got every right to still be acting cute. The last time I had you in a room like this I was talking big and you made me look stupid.

"Only this isn't anything like the last time Tuesday. The CSU unit in Los Angeles found the weapon at what was left of your house. The gun that murdered the two men was recovered at the scene. It was registered to you and had your prints on it."

"Bullshit. Ain't no way in hell."

"I also have a witness who's willing to testify that you killed those men then burned down your house hoping the fire would destroy the evidence."

She sputtered. "Trick no good. A bitch done watched too much *Law & Order* to fall for that one. You ain't finna get me to confess to some shit I didn't do on a bluff. You got me fucked up."

"Naw, babygirl, I just got you FUCKED!" Ms. Jackson pulled a document from the folder and slammed it down on the table like it was the last trump. The set book.

Tuesday looked it over. At first she read thinking there was no way this could be real. When the truth sank in, Tuesday felt like all the air had been sucked from the room.

Ms. Jackson's smile grew wider when she finally saw something like defeat in Tuesday's green eyes. "I told you this wasn't like last time. My boss isn't going to walk in that door and make me let you go because I'm his boss now. And your husband's not gonna come riding in on his white horse, call in one of his favors and save you like before."

Tuesday ignored her. She was still staring down at and trying to process the paper in her trembling hands.

A sworn police statement signed by Brandon King.

Chapter Forty-two

The First Precinct was an old building with nine stories, and Tuesday was moved to a smaller, more secure, cell up on the top floor. The city's financial crisis kept the higher floors from receiving the modern renovations that had begun downstairs. Light was scarce, moldy brick walls, rusted iron bars; Tuesday felt like she was in a medieval dungeon. She sat on a bunk made of wood pleats next to a filthy sink and toilet combo she prayed she wouldn't have to use.

Tuesday didn't want to believe Brandon had betrayed her, but had seen his signature too many times to doubt it was real.

He painted a hell of a story, putting everything squarely on her. Not only did he tell about the man she killed in the maze, but he framed her with the two he had killed at the house. His statement even hinted that she might have had a hand in her husband's death.

He also claimed to have evidence that proved Tuesday had been stealing from Abel. The ten million was supposed to be embezzled company funds and he had planned a phony drop as part of a sting with the FBI. Brandon had been feeding her false information while cooperating with their investigation on the other side.

For Tuesday all the blocks fell into place like a game of Tetris. The old man had been working with Reina the whole time. It explained how she always seemed to know where she was, from the trap at the restaurant to finding her in Detroit. It was Brandon who had hired her driver. Then the deeper realization sank in that made her furious: Brandon hadn't just betrayed her, the sonofabitch had betrayed Marcus.

Ms. Jackson made it clear that the feds could detain her for as long as they wanted. They still hadn't booked Tuesday or permitted her any of the rights granted by the 14th Amendment. She had no way to warn Shaun, and it was Tuesday's own fault that Brandon knew exactly where the girls were. She couldn't do anything to protect them stuck in a cell. Frustration caused her to slam her fist into her palm and curse out loud.

Tuesday sat there steaming for a while until a uniformed officer stopped by to drop off a cold bologna sandwich along with a small carton of generic fruit punch. Tuesday asked about a phone call only to get laughed at.

She didn't touch the food or drink. She avoided anything that might hasten her need to use that disgusting toilet.

Tuesday paced her small, six-by-nine space like a caged tiger. She was going stir-crazy. The ninth floor was too dark and dank for her liking and offered no view of a window. She paced until she couldn't do that anymore, sat, and anxiously bounced her knees until she couldn't do that anymore, then started pacing again.

A ladies' Patek Philippe with an icy bezel was all she had for keeping time. She walked in tiny circles, throwing repeated glances to her wrist. Each time she expected to see hours had passed but only minutes had ticked off her watch.

She sat again and let out another frustrated grunt when her neighbor started pounding on the wall.

204 • Zaire Crown

"Aye, sixteen, I got somethin' you can read over here." A deep voice came through the brick before a black arm slid a few raggedy books and magazines in front of her cell.

Tuesday called back, "Naw, I'm straight."

The voice became aggressive: "I ain't askin' you if you want somethin' to read, I'm telling you, sit yo' ass still and read something cause you ain't goin' nowhere 'til tomorrow. Our bunks connect through this wall and every time you jump up or flop down, I feel it over here.

"I just did twenty-six muthafuckin' years in the joint—most of 'em in level five; I got court first thing in the morning 'cause I'm lookin' at twenty-six more. Bitch, you shake this bunk one more goddamn time, I'm gone shit in a cup and dress yo' muthafuckin' ass out. Now play wit' me if you want to!"

Tuesday usually didn't let herself get checked like that but then, people usually weren't threatening to throw their feces on her. The nigga sounded way too gangster to call his bluff. She humbly apologized in her sweetest tone.

Tuesday reclined on her back, moved as little as possible, and beat herself up over every mistake. She should've known that Brandon just happening to be at the house to stop the kidnapping was too coincidental. La Guapa had given her a clue when she said the fire had done everything it was supposed to. Not only had it allowed him to set her up, his heroic act made her trust him more.

She signed the company over without blinking.

She spent an hour staring up at a paint-chipped ceiling growing green mold. Boredom finally made her reach through the rusted bars for the reading material.

Tuesday had no interest in a Louis L'Amour western or two issues of *People Magazine* from ten years ago. She perused a small pamphlet titled *As a Man Thinketh* by James Allen but it was the final book that kept her occupied until they turned off the lights at midnight.

A worn and faded copy of *The Art of War* by Sun Tzu.

Chapter Forty-three

Early the next morning she woke up achy and stiff from sleeping on the wooden slab. She obviously hadn't tossed and turned too much because her neighbor hadn't doused her in shit.

She hovered over the toilet to take a piss and finished just as an officer came around with breakfast. Tuesday accepted a dry sausage and biscuit sandwich, a tiny carton of orange juice.

Before leaving, he informed Tuesday that she would be getting transferred to a federal detention center within the hour. Tuesday's stomach sank when she remembered Ms. Jackson's comment about not having Marcus to save her this time.

She drank her tiny four-ounce juice in one swallow then sat on her bunk to think. She worried over Danielle and Tanisha. Tuesday had been gone the entire night without calling and figured Shaun was panicked.

Tuesday only had enough time to absorb a few more pages of Sun Tzu before being taken downstairs. She was placed in another holding pen on the first floor, only this one was filled with fifteen other women. Most of them looked like dope fiends, streetwalkers, or a combination of the two. Tuesday found a spot on the bench and wedged herself between a pair that smelled like musty underarms and fishy pussy.

Every few minutes the same officer opened the pen to call a girl's name. When she reported to the front, he checked her wristband and she was pulled out.

The woman seated next to Tuesday had over three hundred pounds poured into a rhinestone catsuit. Tuesday politely nudged her arm. "They going to court?" She didn't think all of them were waiting on the feds like her.

Big Girl looked at Tuesday like she was stupid. "We already been to court. We waiting to go home. This is outtake."

She explained that they had already been arraigned and received personal bonds or had loved ones paying at the front desk. They all were just waiting to be processed out.

The woman looked over Tuesday curiously. "You ain't been to court yet? Where yo' armband?"

Tuesday was never properly processed in, which meant she was the only one not wearing the white plastic tag with her name and mugshot. While murder charges loomed over her, the women surrounding her were about to be released after wrist slaps. She didn't know if they placed her in there by mistake or simply because it was the only pen available for females. Either way, a plan was already taking shape.

Tuesday stood and scanned the cage but only saw two girls that met her needs.

Tuesday approached the first who was a Latina with the right skin tone but a few inches short. Tuesday stood close and tried to speak so no one would overhear: "Aye, you waiting to get yo' bond paid?"

She looked at Tuesday skeptically. "It's already paid, my nigga was in the courtroom. And why you in my business anyway?"

"Business is what I'm trying to talk to you," said Tuesday. "I got a offer for you. Something that I think gone benefit us both. I just need you to hear me out."

Her face revealed that she was intrigued by Tuesday in more than one way. "What's up, mami. What'cho talkin' 'bout?"

Just as Tuesday went into her pitch, an officer called the name Vasquez and immediately killed their conversation. She turned away from Tuesday like she suddenly wasn't there and pushed through the crowd. The officer opened the pen for her after checking her wristband against his clipboard. Once on the other side of the glass, she threw Tuesday a quick peace-sign.

Tuesday had to act quickly. She had been told she would be picked up within the hour and that was forty minutes ago.

The second woman was a light-skinned black girl, but a shade too dark. She was the perfect height, slender-built, wearing a tight elastic minidress that advertised her crime and profession.

Tuesday's gut warned that her name would be called next so she didn't waste time. Her pitch was straightforward: "Aye bitch, you can make enough money right now to where you ain't never gotta suck dick in an alley again. What's up?"

Under a synthetic green wig was a cute face even with a large hooked nose. She looked at Tuesday like she was crazy but didn't reject her.

"I wanna trade what's on my wrist for what you got on yours?" Tuesday showed off her diamond-studded watch. "This a Philippe— four hundred bands without the stones. A neighborhood pawn shop will stick dick to you so take it to an actual jeweler. Don't accept nothing less than a hundred and fifty K."

The girl stared at the watch skeptically.

"It's real," Tuesday assured her. "Just like these red bottoms and the rock on my finger. Look at me, and look at the rest of the bitches in here. Don't act like you don't see the difference in my pedigree."

When another girl was called, Tuesday pressed the bird-faced chick. "I'm trying to change yo' life bitch. Shit like this don't come along every day."

The few seconds it took her to decide felt like hours to Tuesday. She worked the band off her wrist then traded it for the watch. Then Tuesday got some of the other women to stand and provide cover while they exchanged clothes. Tuesday gave up her Balmain outfit she'd just bought for the cheap minidress. It was tight on the woman who was maybe forty pounds lighter, so Tuesday had to squeeze into it.

Tuesday explained to the skinny hooker that her face and fingerprints would eventually get her released even without a wristband. Tuesday asked that she only give her an hour head start before she reported the mix-up.

The name on her wrist was Sha'Quarla Ruffan and she sat nervously, hoping that name was called before Tuesday Knight or Tabitha King. Ten minutes later, she got her wish.

Tuesday approached the officer a little too slowly for somebody getting out of jail. Doubt made her stomach bubble. Outside of the green wig, she knew her face and Sha'Quarla's mugshot looked nothing alike. She didn't think there was any way this could work.

The man at the bars hardly gave Tuesday a glance before he snatched open the cell. He walked her to a booth to be processed out, then to another where she received a small clutch purse that belonged to the other girl.

After being escorted through several security doors, she was led into the lobby. The young lanky dude stood at the front desk who paid the bond. Tuesday didn't know if he was Sha'Quarla's man or pimp, but read the confused look on his face when she approached him wearing his girl's pink dress and green wig.

Before he could say anything, Tuesday ran to him, threw her arms around his neck and stuck her tongue down his throat in front of everybody in the lobby. She kissed him long and hard like she knew him and missed him.

Once all the cops and civilians turned away from their inappropriate display, she whispered in his ear: "Shut the fuck up and walk me outta here nigga, and I'll make you rich!"

Chapter Forty-four

They walked out the front doors of the precinct just as a black van pulled up with three men wearing FBI jackets. Tuesday passed them on the steps, head down, eyes averted. She followed the lanky dude down the block to his car. As they turned off Beaubien Street, Tuesday said she didn't care where he dropped her off, she just wanted to get away from downtown. She didn't relax until they were on the freeway.

He called himself Aston Martin Meech, even though he drove a busted 2005 Dodge Magnum on a donut. He was about twenty-seven, a light-skinned nigga with long braids who she didn't think was bad-looking, until his smile revealed two missing front teeth.

When he asked about money, she told him that his chick was wearing it. Tuesday also suggested that he be back at the precinct in an hour to pick her up before she could trade the watch for fifty dollars in crack.

He believed Tuesday, but also stared at her DSLs and the way she filled out that dress in a way his regular chick never could. The young pimp spent the first part of the drive trying to recruit Tuesday into his stable.

She asked to borrow his phone and the first call she made was to Shaun. She tried three times but only got her voice mail. Tuesday thought she might be avoiding the unfamiliar number.

Next, she called DelRay who tried to ask her a thousand questions about what happened at the airport. Tuesday was too smart to go into all that on the phone. She dodged his whats and whys, then arranged for him to meet her. They agreed on a gas station on the Westside that was close to his hood but far enough from the club.

The last person she called was Brandon. Even though it was a strange number, he answered on the second ring.

"You're a dead bitch!" Tuesday didn't bother with an introduction. Rage made her hands and voice shaky.

He was probably surprised to hear Tuesday's voice. There was a brief pause on the line before he responded. "This doesn't sound like a jail call. Should've known you'd find some way to wiggle out of that."

"He trusted you. The girls love you. We're supposed to be family. How did La Guapa get you to sell out everybody you love, Brandon?"

"My name isn't Brandon just like your name isn't Tabitha. You see what he does, makes everybody around him play these roles. First, he found a father, then a daughter, and finally brought you in to play the wife. None of this was ever real; we were just actors he hired for The Marcus King Show.

"Well, I never wanted to change my image, and never felt guilty about who I was. Tuesday, if I really wanted a family, I could've settled down with some fat bitch forty years ago, got some job at a plant, and pumped out ten kids."

"If he was here, you already know what he'd do to you."

"In this game, people either die loyal or live long enough to see themselves betrayed." Brandon thundered that statement back at her. "And it's his own fault. Playing this stupid ass game of pretend allowed him to get weak while his enemies got strong. And I warned him a thousand times."

Tuesday said, "He was trying to be a better person."

"He was at his best as Sebastian Caine. If he had stayed the course he could've been a Master by now."

Aston Martin Meech was ignoring the road to be all in her conversation. Tuesday gave him a *mind your business* glare.

To Brandon she said, "You still cain't do nothing with Abel. I left you as CEO but I'm still the majority shareholder."

"You were never the majority shareholder—the girls are. As their legal guardian, you were just the trustor over what belongs to them and that gave you control. You relinquished your status as trustor when you turned over your parental rights to me."

It was as if he could hear Tuesday's confusion in her silence. He mocked her with a *tsk-tsk*. "You really aren't supposed to sign things without reading it first."

She thought back on those endless stacks of paperwork he had brought to Shaun's house. At the time, she trusted him like a father, never thinking he would slip some bullshit in on her.

She sneered into the phone. "There ain't no place you can hide or enough men you can hire to keep me off yo' ass. Before this is over I'm gonna hear the sound of your death screams."

"There's nothing you can do, Tuesday. The legal guardian controls Abel and I already agreed to the sell. You no longer have access to any of the company's assets and all of Tabitha King's personal accounts are frozen. Without the money you're just another broke bitch from the hood with two kids and no man. So you should feel right at home in Detroit."

Tuesday hung up, couldn't stand to hear his voice anymore. She couldn't reconcile the same man who had smiled and played with her daughters for every day of their lives with the asshole on the phone. It was hard for her to believe that someone could be so close for so long while only pretending to love so convincingly. She hated herself when she remembered that she had played the same game for so many years before meeting Marcus.

She had Meech drop her off at a gas station on Wyoming and Schoolcraft. She thanked the snaggle-toothed pimp then joined DelRay who waited in a mid-90s Bonneville that he claimed was his shooter. When Tuesday jumped in, he scanned the pink dress and green hair with amusement. "If a clown could be a thot, that's what it would look like."

"Fuck you Fatboy!" She slammed the door and snatched off the wig. "It's been a helluva day."

She gave him the quick version of everything that happened since the airport: Ms. Jackson, the fake money, backstabbing Brandon, and the armband switch-up.

When she asked if Silence got in touch, DelRay shook his head. "That nigga already move like a ghost: no address, no social media. I guarantee he in the wind, just like you need to be."

Tuesday agreed but didn't know how she could. Brandon left her in a serious bind. She was on the run with two children, a mistress, and no money. Vega was waiting on ten million that wasn't coming. The last of her petty cash was in the purse at the First Precinct. She quietly contemplated her few options as DelRay drove her out to the Residence Inn in Romulus.

When they pulled into the parking lot, Tuesday nearly jumped from the car before DelRay could bring it to a complete stop. The door to their room was kicked in and hung half off its hinges.

Tuesday rushed inside to find the space violated. Food and clothes littered the floor.

Shaun and her girls were gone.

Chapter Forty-five

At the reception office, Tuesday asked about the break-in at Room 115, and it may have been her hot-pink hooker attire that made the clerk on duty so dismissive. Tuesday was treated like a disgruntled customer whining about a faulty air conditioner. The white lady barely listened as Tuesday explained that her nine and three-year-old daughters were missing. When she offered Tuesday a form to file a complaint, DelRay had to stop her from climbing over the desk.

Tuesday started pounding on doors like the police, asking tenants in the neighboring units if they saw or heard anything. Most were still in fuck-sleep from the night before and many creeping on spouses or main partners, so nobody was in the mood to be interviewed. The few who answered their doors slammed them in her face after one or two quick one-word denials. Eventually, enough of them complained to the receptionist who threatened to call the actual police.

This forced Tuesday and DelRay to bail, but not before they ran back to check the room for a clue. On impulse Tuesday snatched Shaun's laptop off the floor.

It was upon leaving that Tuesday noticed the rental car was

nowhere in the parking lot. Her hope was that Shaun had taken the girls before whoever kicked in the door.

Tuesday blew up Shaun and Danielle's phones but hope faded each time she was sent to voice mail. She figured Brandon would have told her if he had the girls; she tried his number again, but this time he didn't pick up.

"We're gonna find 'em." DelRay offered that confidently, with a nudge from his elbow.

Tuesday sank deeper into her seat. "This all on me. I could've just took the money and avoided these problems. I thought I could handle this."

DelRay said, "We are gone handle this. We gone find yo' girls and handle this. We just need to go to my crib and lay low for a while."

Tuesday was dejected. "Agent Jackson know about you and they gone be looking to question you about the shit that popped at 24 Karats. I bet the feds watching your crib already."

DelRay wasn't fazed. "Then we go somewhere else to lay down for a minute."

"Where?" she spat, exasperated. "Nigga I'm broke. The last couple of bands I had was in my purse—I ain't even got enough to get another room. And in case you didn't notice, I ain't gotta bunch of people I can count on.

"You done already lost two cars, your club, and probably getting indicted. You might wanna step away from me."

He looked at her like she was crazy. "Tuesday, you the reason I had all that shit in the first place. And it ain't like you don't got nobody in your corner."

Tuesday lowered her head, covered her face with her hands. DelRay looked over to see she was wrapped in a cocoon of her own pity. He wanted to continue the pep-talk, but knew it wasn't the time. Clearly none of his empty platitudes could ease the concern for her daughters.

A blanket of clouds cloaked the city, producing a gray day. The weather reflected Tuesday's eye color and mood.

She didn't pay attention to the roads and turns that DelRay took. At some point she glanced up to realize they were in an area of Detroit's Westside called Brightmoor. What had once been an affluent neighborhood filled with auto-workers during the '70s and '80s had been in constant freefall since the decline of the industry. Since the '90s, it had been referred to as "Blight-more." Closed liquor stores and gas stations anchored every corner. Residential blocks had ten empty lots for each house. Some of the streets were so unused that weeds had started to grow right up through the asphalt.

DelRay pulled into the driveway of a small wooden house that surprisingly still had all its windows and doors. The front porch sagged on the verge of collapse, and fiends had stolen much of the aluminum siding. On either side of the dwellings were firebombed shells.

Tuesday frowned. "Who live in this raggedy muthafucka?"

DelRay threw the transmission in park. "Probably the one person in the world who would fuck wit' either of us right now."

They left the Bonneville and he led her to the side entrance. As they approached she heard the sound of multiple locks being undone.

When the door opened, A.D. was quick to usher them inside.

Seeing him broke Tuesday's emotional dam. She latched on to him and immediately began to cry into his chest.

Chapter Forty-six

A.D. told DelRay to hide the car in the garage while he took Tuesday into a modest but neat home. Through a clean kitchen with rusted antique appliances, he led Tuesday to the living room where the fake-leather sofa set and smoked glass coffee table were about twenty years out of date. He sat Tuesday on the couch, tried to console her.

Through sobs and sniffs, she caught A.D. up on everything that happened since their dinner. By the time she recounted the shootout, the arrest and the Residence Inn, DelRay was seated across from them on a matching loveseat.

Tuesday wiped her eyes. "I don't know who has my girls or what's happening to them. I'm caught in between a fed bitch who wants me in a cell and a cartel bitch who wants me in a grave. Either one would try to use them for leverage."

A.D. offered his hand to hold. "So what's your plan?"

She shook her head. "Ain't nothing I can do. Brandon worked me out of the company and the deal happens in two days. No money means no help from Vega. And La Guapa was kickin' my ass when I had access to unlimited bank, so what the fuck can I do against her now?"

"You were always the mastermind," A.D. reminded her. "It was your planning, your leadership that allowed your crew to do so well in the stick-up game."

"I used to be that bitch who could peep all the angles. I used to be able to see a mark and know exactly what type of woman it took to put a hook in him, then be that woman. I played the game like I had nothing to lose 'cause I didn't.

"I'm not that bitch anymore. Me and my family was just at Disneyland taking pictures with mouse ears on. I'm used to walk-in' barefoot over seventeen thousand square feet of Italian marble with a personal chef feedin' me gluten-free waffles and avocado toast. I had an office seventy floors up, where bitches with Masters degrees fetched me low-fat lattes."

A.D. shrugged. "You sayin' that to say what?"

Tuesday got to her feet as if suddenly needing to move. "I'm a square now. My mind don't even work the same way no more. When I see a handsome man who look like he got paper, I don't see a mark. I just think about how nice his suit is and wonder if my husband has the same tailor."

DelRay voiced his disagreement: "You makin' it seem like being up made you lose some part of yourself. You still got all that gangsta in you, Boss Lady. I saw it at the junkyard."

A.D. said, "You in a situation where you need to be that chick again. The money didn't make or break you, Tuesday."

Frustration made Tuesday explode. "It's easy for y'all to say that. Y'all used to being broke, used to living fucked up—like this!" She threw her hands out at her side. "I'm used to havin' it. Y'all don't know what it's like to lose it 'cause y'all ain't never seen it."

A.D. stood with her. "I don't wanna sound cold but you fucked up too now. Where's your house? Where's your personal chef and your company? Where's your family, Tuesday?"

That made her look down to her shoes.

A.D. continued. "You can play the game like you ain't got nothing to lose again because you done lost it all."

Tuesday waved them off. "I need a shower. Feel like I got something growing up under my arms."

A.D. saw in her face that she was too exhausted to keep fighting about it so he let it go. He walked her upstairs into a short hall that terminated in a small master bedroom. The bathroom was the first open door to the right.

A.D. motioned toward a linen closet built next to the tub. "There's clean towels and rags in the top drawer. I'll find you something to change into."

Tuesday stopped him before he could leave. "I'm sorry 'bout what I said downstairs. I wasn't trying to take shots. You gotta nice home."

A.D. glared at her. "Tuesday, I ain't your husband. I'm not some kingpin with private jets and Rolls Royces. Even without prison I probably wasn't gone ever be that guy.

"I ain't got much but I'm proud of what I got. I bought this house outright for just under three G's; my car a piece of shit but it run like a champ. I'm free and didn't have to rat on nobody and don't owe nobody shit. Baby, I'm winning."

She nodded. "Plus you could get in a lot of trouble for having us here. And I show my appreciation by disrespecting your spot."

"Don't worry about it. You dealing with a lot right now. I can give you a pass for actin' bougie on me."

A.D. held his fist to dap her up but Tuesday pressed into him and pushed her tongue into his mouth. She kicked the door shut then attacked him like she was trying to steal the air from his lungs.

She tried to pull A.D. towards the shower. He followed her a step then broke away from the kiss.

"This thing with yo' girls got you twisted and I get wanting to take you mind off of it. But this ain't a good look Tuesday. Remember, I got a situation."

She scanned the bathroom and saw evidence of his woman. If she didn't live there, she was putting other bitches on notice like a dog pissing on a tree. Flat irons and hot curlers were purposely left on a shelf above the toilet.

Tuesday didn't care. While he was still talking she peeled off Sha'Quarla's elastic minidress along with her panties and bra. She stepped into the shower and let hot water rain on her naked body.

He stared at her in awe. Brown quarter-sized aureoles crowned her plump titties; her stomach was flat and the waist hardly measured twenty-five inches; her hips and thighs looked too voluptuous to belong on her frame; even two weeks overdue for a wax, her fat pussy looked sweet enough to eat. It was all wrapped in glistening flesh that reminded him of butter pecan ice cream.

A.D. watched her mesmerized. Tuesday saw him chew his bottom lip the way he used to do when he was super-horny.

She put her head under the nozzle then let the wet curls spill down her neck. Her eyes were some indescribable shade of green. "Come here."

He shook his head but Tuesday noticed A.D. stroking himself through his pants.

"It's not just 'bout my relationship with my girl," he explained. "I also gotta relationship with the Man upstairs. Am I supposed to ignore that you wearing somebody else's ring?"

"Don't think about what's on my finger." She poured liquid soap into her palms and lathered her breasts in slow circles. "Just focus on all the soft, fun parts." She turned around and wagged her enormous ass at him.

When a moment passed and she saw that A.D. was still hesitant, Tuesday became serious. "Adrian, we was together for twenty years. Wouldn't you consider me a loyal woman while I was with you?"

He looked her off. "C'mon Tuesday, don't do that. You held me down for twelve in the joint. You paid for my attorneys, kept my books straight. You the downest chick I know. Loyal don't do you justice—Webster's ain't got a word."

"Well I'm broke and homeless. My husband is dead, my

daughters might be too. And in the next day or so I could be joining them, or be cuffed up about to spend the rest of my life in
prison. I ain't never been this scared."

A.D. felt more fear than he saw in her eyes, which changed
color from green to gray as she spoke. To him Tuesday looked like
a wolf stalking prey. Her nakedness primal, hands fisted at her
side.

"Now I hate to call in favors or play the you-owe-me game,
but I need you to bring that big dick over here and pound all
those bad thoughts outta my head. For the next hour I don't
wanna think about nothing but how good you taste and feel inside me. So call it charity or helping out a friend; do whatever you
gotta do to make it right with your God Adrian.

"Now drop them pants, get in this shower and fuck me like
the world about to end! 'Cause for me it might have already."

Chapter Forty-seven

Tuesday watched him strip off his shirt, studied a physique eerily similar to her husband's. The rewards of sixteen years of weight-training were covered in prison ink done by semiskilled artists. The most prominent being 313 decorating his chiseled ab muscles in huge Gothic numerals.

Before he could undo his pants, Tuesday's knees were already on the bathroom floor. She pulled his belt loose, yanked down his zipper, pulled him free.

She devoured his dick like something hungry and wild.

Whatever conflict A.D. might have felt got pulled from him with each smooth inhalation. Her wet mouth quickly inflated his semi-hard piece to its full extension. Tuesday took the length of him with the corkscrew technique she'd perfected, tongue dancing from side-to-side across that sensitive under area, moaning as if he tasted delicious. The pleasure buckled A.D.'s legs and made him lean against the sink for support.

He looked down at her face to find Tuesday's intense eyes waiting for his. She sucked harder, head bobbed faster. She dared him not to look away, challenged him to an erotic staring match.

She had been A.D.'s girl at eighteen but at forty she was a totally different animal. This was a grown ass woman with not just experience, but expertise. She sucked his dick with the type of confidence that came from mastery of her craft. All neck, didn't cheat by using her hands, even relaxed her gag reflex so she could take all of him to the throat without choking. Tuesday grabbed him by the back of his powerful thighs and rammed him into her mouth with force.

It wasn't long before A.D. was grumbling curses under his breath. He lost the staring contest when he closed his eyes and starting rolling his head around in ecstasy.

Tuesday spat him out when she felt his orgasm climbing, didn't want him to bust yet. She snatched down his pants and boxers at the same time. Let him step out of them then led him to the shower.

A.D. offered to reciprocate but he, like most men, didn't understand that giving head was more for her than for them. Nothing turned her on more than watching a man squirm and groan from the pleasure she provided. It was the ultimate exercise of power and control; for Tuesday, the highest form of foreplay.

A.D. bore witness to this when she grabbed his throbbing dick to guide him to her gates. He pinned her against the shower wall and pushed inside. Her sex was hot and ready, so wet she received his ten inches easily.

At first he slow-stroked her, stirred her Kool-Aid in lazy circles. He would suck and pull on her bottom lip to cap each kiss. His fingers traced her hips and the curvature of her spine. He teased her nipples with his thumbs. After licking her earlobe he whispered that her pussy had only gotten better with time. The words excited Tuesday and made her get wetter only to prove it.

Making love may have been what A.D. wanted but wasn't what Tuesday needed. She propped her foot on the tub's faucet and set a faster pace.

"Get off the church boy shit. Thug it out nigga!"

The sex became aggressive just the way Tuesday liked it. A.D.

held her hundred and eighty pounds up against the wall with one muscular arm while the other hand clamped her neck: squeezing not choking. He started digging hard like he was trying to find treasure in her.

She held the back of his head and chanted "Don't stop" when she felt her orgasm building. A.D. obliged her by putting a wicked angle on his stroke that caught her G-spot dead center. Tuesday grabbed hold of the rod that suspended the shower curtains and sang his name in a high falsetto. He manhandled her plump cheeks, pulled them apart and went deep until she came like a tsunami. The wave was so fierce it almost pushed him back out of her vagina.

They washed themselves then left the shower but A.D. was still rock-hard. Tuesday demanded more foreplay before they continued, so he picked her up and flipped her upside down. A.D. held her in the air while they sixty-nined. He carried her from the bathroom as they pleasured each other. Her damp hair swept his legs when he walked her through the hall. He showed her the entire upstairs by going room to room.

A.D. sucked her clit with enthusiasm, and while his tongue-game was only decent, it was the way he carried her that turned Tuesday on the most. With two daughters and a fully-staffed house, she and Marcus had never been able to pull that stunt.

The tour ended in his bedroom. A.D. licked her to a second orgasm but she stopped short before he reached his own.

"You don't get to cum yet nigga. You ain't put in enough work."

She pushed him down on the bed and straddled him. The ride was violent. There were no slow gyrations or smooth body rolls; she didn't entertain like she typically did for her husband. Tuesday bounced on him so fast and hard that A.D. stared at her like she was trying to break his dick. She grunted like an animal and made ugly faces. It took forty minutes of her riding rough like that to get Number Three.

He took her from behind, face down/ass up. A.D. obeyed her every time she asked for it harder or faster, until their flesh sounded like hands clapping along to an up-tempo beat.

She growled at him, "Smack my ass, pull my hair! Fuck dis pussy like you mad at it."

He snatched her head back by a fistful of weave. Tuesday bucked like a bull trying to throw its rider and A.D. was the cowboy just holding on for his life.

Only after she got her forth nut did she urge him to get his. Tuesday threw it back incredibly fast and forced him to keep pace. Her dirty talk was just a sexy way of saying "Hurry the fuck up!"

A.D. rammed her for another twenty minutes before ecstatic grunts signaled the approach of his climax. Tuesday screamed at him: "Don't cum in me! Don't cum in me Adrian!"

He pumped and groaned a few more times then pulled out as he erupted. The size of his load suggested to her that he hadn't released in a while. He sprayed thick frosting all over her buns like a pastry chef decorating a cake.

A.D. went to the bathroom for a wet towel to clean Tuesday. He collapsed on the bed next to her when he was done.

For a while she lay there with her eyes closed, enjoying the post-sex euphoria until she looked over and saw A.D. staring at her. His expression made her ask, "What's wrong?"

"Feel like you 'bout to drop two hundred on the nightstand."

"You earned five but my money kinda funny right now." She could see in his face that he didn't appreciate the joke.

He rubbed the back of his neck. "I understand this was just me scratching an itch for you—I knew it wasn't nothing more than what it was, but damn. I spent a long time in there fantasizing about you, about what the first time would be like after all those years. It definitely wasn't that."

Tuesday couldn't believe him. "You mean to tell me you been home eight months and that was the first time you got some ass? What about your situation?"

He almost looked embarrassed. "She's born again and fresh off a long relationship. Neither of us wanted to rush the physical part."

Hearing that really made Tuesday feel like shit. Not only did she run a guilt-trip to force a celibate man to cheat on his woman, but the way she had used him was no different than how Marcus had used her when he was distracted by his problems. There was no real connection and she felt like a rubber fuck doll.

"I'm sorry." Tuesday was sincere but matters more pressing weighed on her than A.D.'s chastity. The sex was a much-needed stress-reliever but her thoughts were right back to her daughters. She was haunted by the scene at the Residence Inn; the door kicked in, the whole place a mess, signs of struggle. She imagined Tanisha and Danielle's frightened screams as strange men with large guns barged in and took them.

She borrowed A.D.'s cell and tried to call Danielle again out of desperation. The phone rang seven times and Tuesday was sure that it was about to go to voicemail like it had done all day. Her breath caught in her throat when someone answered.

She sat up on the edge of the bed naked. "Hello? Who is this?"

"Hey bitch, still feel like you're in charge?"

Tuesday frowned at the voice. It was male, a familiar one that took a few seconds to place.

Aaron. Madame Vega's son.

Chapter Forty-eight

"Is you crazy?" was all DelRay had to say in response to Tuesday's request.

"It ain't like they leaving me with no other play. She said come alone and that's what I gotta do."

She had already washed up quickly and dressed in the pants to an Adidas jogging suit and Pistons T-shirt that A.D. provided. She and DelRay were in his old Bonneville traveling within the herd of eastbound traffic on Grand River Avenue.

DelRay understood that saving the girls was Priority One but wasn't cool with her walking into that situation alone. "I'd feel a lot better about this if we still had Silence."

Tuesday agreed that she would as well but didn't see the point of dwelling on what they didn't have.

Aaron had told her to be at the salvage yard by eight and they pulled up fifteen minutes early. Two men with guns were waiting to greet them at the front gate. A semi-automatic was jammed in DelRay's face to emphasize that he had no choice but to sit behind the wheel and watch Tuesday leave the car. She threw him a final nod before she was taken inside.

Her escort kept two steps behind with the assault rifle aimed at her back. This twilight march through the automobile grave-yard at gun point was eerily reminiscent of the same walk she had taken with Face three years before. A lucky break had allowed her to turn the tables and escape with her life. Tuesday recalled the old saying about lightning never striking twice in the same spot.

She was led beyond the small office with the garage stalls. Acidic fluids churned in Tuesday's stomach because she knew, just like the last time, they were going to the rear where the junkers were demolished.

The escort trailed her at a distance of five feet. Tuesday figured she could dip around a corner before he squeezed off a shot and easily lose him in the two-acre maze of stacked cars. However, there was no strategic advantage in doing so. They had her girls which meant they had her cooperation.

They continued to walk until she saw lights up ahead. Five cars too new to be there for scrap were parked in a semicircle. The familiar white BMW X-5 centered the pack playing alpha to cheaper domestics. High beams cleaved the darkness like magic swords and brightened the machines.

Aaron Vega waited with ten more men. As soon as Tuesday was close enough, he grabbed her shirt collar and punched her in the kidney hard enough to fold her over.

"That's for my ol' dude."

Tuesday looked up and recognized the glassy stare of a young wild nigga on Zannie bars. From her knees, she puffed through heavy breaths: "I knew you wouldn't know what to do wit' me, ol' weak sauce ass nigga. I like my foreplay rougher than that."

He kicked her back to the ground when Tuesday tried to stand.

Madame Vega climbed out of the passenger seat of the X-5. "Boy stop being childish."

One of the long-haired Colombians pulled Tuesday to her feet. She held on to her side as Vega approached.

"You weren't totally honest with me the last time you were

here, so I decided we needed to re-negotiate the terms of our agreement."

"Bitch, you playin' a dangerous game wit' me and my children. You already know who my family is."

Vega laughed. "I'm not gonna lie, I let you intimidate me with all that Sebastian Caine talk until a little birdie told me that Caine is dead. That same little birdie told me that you lost the company which means I will not be receiving my ten million dollars.

"He was also kind enough to tell me where I could get in touch with you to discuss any grievances. Unfortunately, you weren't at the hotel."

Brandon. He knew about the deal with Vega and the slimy muthafucka had burned Tuesday with her only potential ally.

Vega nodded to one of her men who pulled Shaun out a separate car wearing duct-tape around her wrists, a bandanna gagged her mouth.

The tiny woman in white pushed her towards Tuesday. "She costs you nothing but your daughters only come back at a price."

Tuesday yanked the rag from Shaun's mouth who immediately started babbling apologies. Tuesday ignored her, addressed Vega: "Where are my girls?"

She directed Tuesday's attention to one of the huge machines; it looked the newest of the three. It was a box-shaped contraption open at the front and rear. This was a highly pressurized compressor that could easily flatten a car into a piece of sheet-metal as thin as a cracker. Tuesday's rented Hyundai was inside.

Tuesday's heart went weak when she saw a small silhouette in the driver's seat roughly Danielle's size. Little Tanisha could not be seen from the distance but Tuesday had no reason to think this was a bluff.

"I don't have money right now but I promise I will get whatever you want. No matter the price, I'll pay it. If I have to rob, scam or kill—I'll get the money."

Standing before her in all white, backlit by headlights, Tuesday thought Madame Vega looked like a spirit.

"I don't want money. Life is a series of serious choices. You are about to make the hardest one you've ever had."

Tuesday was already shaking her head before Vega could explain, already had tears in her eyes.

"This is how my husband died," Vega continued. "I demand blood for blood. *Sangre por sangre!*"

"This some bullshit," Tuesday spat. "Face was a grown man. Those are babies. My girls are innocent."

"Reina cannot be allowed to get your company—that move would give the Rodriguez sisters new life which would be the end of my family. We need to stop the deal and I'm still willing to offer you my assistance for a fee that we will discuss later.

"But first you have to answer for my husband. Your older daughter is on the driver's side and the younger one is on the passenger side. You may go to the car and open one door, take one out. That's the cost."

Tuesday sneered like a rabid animal. "Bitch you must be crazy if you think I'm gone pick one of my girls to die."

"Blood for blood, Tuesday," she said calmly. "You fed my husband to a machine just like this one. I'm not a sick person, and I promise you I don't enjoy this. Killing a child doesn't make this right, it only makes us even."

Tuesday clasped her hands to emphasize the sincerity. "I'm sorry for Face, I really am. But that was three years ago. That was the past. We can move forward, make some real money together."

"We can move forward and will," Vega agreed. "But I'll tell you what. After you listen to the whimpers and cries of your baby girl as the machine crushes her bones. Call me up in three years and tell me if you've moved past it."

One of the men went over to the compressor and hit a button that brought life to the beast. It powered up with a loud whiny motor. A second button next to the first would start the press.

"Please." Desperation made the words spill quickly from Tuesday's mouth: "Dani, she's nine years old and she's so smart. So smart that she takes advanced classes at her school. I haven't been there for her lately—she's mad at me and it's my fault but she's my heart.

"And Nisha's just a baby. She has her father's ways and when she smiles at me it's like a drug. She's the type of girl if you buy her a gift, she's gonna ignore the toy and spend an hour playing wit' the box."

Tuesday got on her knees. "I'm a bitch who ain't never begged for nothing in her life, but I'm begging right now. Please don't hurt my babies."

Madame Vega stared at Tuesday with eyes totally devoid of mercy. "I'm giving you a choice which is more than you did for me.

In one minute we go whether it's one or two girls in the car. Make a choice."

Chapter Forty-nine

Tuesday walked over to the blue Hyundai and peeked inside. Danielle's wrists were tied to the steering wheel, a swatch of duct-tape covered her mouth. Tanisha was in the seat next to her strapped down by the safety belts. She wore zip ties on her tiny wrists and ankles.

Danielle looked up, eyes red and swollen from crying. She looked exhausted but perked when she spied Tuesday through the window.

"It's okay baby. I'm here now."

Her eyes went wide and she tried to fight against her restraints. Her little sister did the same at the sound of her mother's voice.

"So what's it gonna be? Door Number One or Door Number Two?" Aaron imitated a game show host and earned a laugh from his crew.

"Thirty seconds," Vega warned.

Tuesday cried. "I can't do this."

"Not choosing is basically making a worse choice. Fifteen seconds."

"I choose me," said Tuesday. "Let them go and put me in the car."

Madame Vega wagged her finger. "It doesn't work that way."

"You said, 'blood for blood.' I killed Face so I should be the one who dies."

"If this was only about revenge then I could accept that, but you and I still have to conduct business.

"Plus you took somebody I love. It's only fair that I take somebody you love. Dying is easy—the hard part is living with the pain."

Aaron shouted, "Time's up."

The man on the machine hit the start button with the giddiness of a child. The heavy metal slate began to descend smoothly on the car like some medieval torture contraption.

Tuesday freaked out so hard that she had to be restrained. Two men grabbed her when she tried to run to the control switch.

The crusher pressed to the car. Tuesday heard the screams from within.

She panicked. "Stop! Stop! Stop! I'll pick! I'll pick!"

They cut the press a moment before it would've started to smash the roof.

Tuesday went to the car, saw both girls calling to her, pleading for her. Being raised by a bad mother always made Tuesday fear that she would lack a maternal instinct, but in that moment she began to do something so heartless that she didn't even think her mother would be capable of it. She actually began to weigh the pros and cons of each child.

For a few seconds she stood there frozen with indecision.

"Make a choice!" Vega urged sternly. "Once we start the machine again, we won't stop it."

Tuesday spat at her frustrated. "You can't expect any parent to choose between their kids. You're asking me to cut off a limb."

"That's an easy choice depending on if you're a lefty or righty. What you can't afford to do is lose both hands."

"This isn't right. These are just kids."

Madame Vega was unfazed. "I thought it was clear that we

were past the begging stage. Tuesday, go to the car and take out one of your daughters or I swear to God I will kill them both."

Tuesday's heart slammed against her ribs as she took a shaky step towards the Hyundai. Tears blurred her vision.

"Pick me!"

When Tuesday turned around, Shaun was staring at her deadly serious. "If somebody has to die, let it be me."

Vega rejected her. "It has to be a loved one. Somebody she cares for."

"We are lovers," Shaun confessed. "We've been in a relationship for six months."

"If she's married to you-know-who, that would make you just a mistress."

"You're right, I was just a side-piece." Shaun looked earnest. "Tuesday doesn't love me. She spent months wining, dining, and sleeping with me, but when I poured out my heart, she told me to my face that I was nothing to her.

"But that's exactly why it should be me. I told her that her husband would never love her as much as I did, and the fact that I'm willing to die for her kids prove that. She has to spend the rest of her life knowing what I did. The guilt will tear her apart."

Tuesday hissed at Shaun, "Now ain't the time to play some love-sick game. These people will murk you for real."

Madame Vega looked at Shaun as if impressed. "You hardly look twenty-two, but love this woman so much that you would give your life to spare the pain of losing a child? You young, brave, beautiful girl."

Glaring at Tuesday, she said, "I don't think she's worth it, but I will accept your offer only because I think it will hurt her more. Losing a child would devastate her but I will still be seen as the one who took it."

"I will accept her life as repayment for your debt," Vega said to Tuesday. "But only if you take it." She motioned to the second of her two Colombian bookends. When she muttered, *"Deme un cuchillo,"* he presented her the long serrated hunting knife holstered on his belt. Vega studied it for a moment then passed it to Tuesday.

"You have to do it. Right here, right now in front of everybody." Vega then ordered that Danielle and Tanisha be taken out of the Hyundai.

Tuesday frowned at her. "What type of shit you working out of?"

She shrugged. "The children get to leave with their lives, but not their innocence."

The girls were unstrapped from the car and pulled from the compressor. Aaron's young crew walked them over to where everyone was gathered but held them back when Danielle and Tanisha tried to run to their mother.

They all had formed a circle around Shaun and Tuesday, who held the knife in trembling hands.

"Go on," Vega pressed. "Show 'em what their mother really is. Don't be shy now. You've killed here before."

Shaun gave her a look filled with fear and compassion. "Just do it quick. I don't want it to hurt."

Tuesday took a firm grip of the handle. "Dani, Nisha. I want y'all to close ya eyes and turn y'all heads. Do it now!"

Aaron forced Danielle's head when she tried to look away. "No they gotta watch. Either they watch or they go back in the machine, right Ma?"

She agreed with her son.

Tuesday approached Shaun with both daughters' wide, frightful eyes tracking her. Shaun had already begun to cry.

"They'll be okay." Emotion strained Shaun's voice. "They're strong. At least I got to be part of the family."

Tuesday said, "I didn't break up wit' you because I didn't love you. I broke up 'cause I did."

She embraced Shaun in a tight hug. They held each other for a long moment before Tuesday whispered, "And I forgive you. I know we didn't meet in the gym on accident. I know Brandon hired you and I know you're the one who's been helping him steal from the company."

Shaun gasped, but before she could respond Tuesday slipped the blade into the back of her neck, just below the base of her skull.

When her body went limp, Tuesday didn't just let her drop but gently laid Shaun to the ground. Danielle's scream pierced the night. Tears stung Tuesday's eyes.

"Is our debt settled?" Madame Vega's tone was inquisitive but carried the hint of a threat.

Tuesday gazed down at Shaun's face, brown eyes still open.

"For now." Tuesday's tone carried the promise of revenge.

Vega took a step towards her to prove she was not intimidated by her words or frigid gray stare. "What the girl did for you just now—I've never known love like that. Don't insult me or her by pretending you're not secretly happy about it."

Someone dragged away Shaun as Madame Vega headed back towards the white BMW SUV. "Your girls have had an emotional day so take them somewhere and get them fed. Whisper whatever smooth words you can think of to get them to sleep. Then tomorrow you and me will discuss this Guapa business."

One of the men held the door open for her as she looked back to Tuesday. "But if you have a problem with anything that happened here tonight, I'll tell you just like you told me: We can settle our problems when our business is done."

Chapter Fifty

DelRay had waited out front with the car until Tuesday reappeared with her girls. When he asked about Shaun, Tuesday's grim expression offered a grisly overview. It also indicated that she didn't want to discuss the details and DelRay had enough sense not to ask.

She rode in the back seat with her daughters. Tanisha clung to her side, whimpered lightly into Tuesday's shirt. Danielle brooded in silence and Tuesday felt the pain of a heart attack when Danielle recoiled from her touch as if suddenly scared of her. Tuesday did not try to touch her again, especially when she noticed that some of Shaun's blood still stained her fingers.

Tuesday hoped that Tanisha was too young to fully digest what she just witnessed. Her bigger fear was that Danielle might need to talk it out in therapy one day.

A.D.'s girlfriend was at the house by the time they made it back. Under normal circumstances the introduction would have been awkward for Tuesday considering how she had just beastfucked her nigga a few hours before, but the situation at the junkyard was so crazy that everything after seemed tame in comparison.

Her name was Jeanine, an almond-colored girl with a slim build. She was in burgundy nurse scrubs with her hair pulled back into a ponytail. Tuesday didn't think she was ugly, just not a bad bitch.

Tuesday soon felt more guilty about judging her looks and screwing A.D. when she realized that Jeanine couldn't have been a sweeter person. Not only did she not trip about her man's ex popping up with her two kids, she even offered to cook something for the girls when Tuesday confessed they were hungry.

All A.D. explained to her was that Tuesday had fallen upon hard times and had no other place to go. Tuesday hated that it made her sound like a charity case even though it was all true. Still, the woman embraced them with a spirit of generosity that Tuesday didn't think existed in today's world.

Even after a sixteen-hour shift at Henry Ford hospital, Jeanine happily prepared tacos for everybody. They were decent but Danielle couldn't be coaxed into eating. Tanisha nibbled on one and DelRay happily took their leftovers.

A little later, A.D. set Tuesday's family up in the guest bedroom. The exhausting day knocked out Tanisha within the hour. Danielle claimed not to be sleepy.

Tuesday was curled up on a twin-sized bed with both daughters thinking how quickly her world had changed. Three weeks ago her biggest problem was trying to stay awake through a boring meeting. Her new normal had become a nonstop marathon of running in between shootouts and shady deals.

Tuesday was so caught up in picturing Shaun laying in the dirt bleeding from the back of the head that she didn't notice Danielle speaking to her.

"Momma, are we bad people?"

The question took Tuesday by surprise. "No, why would you even ask that?"

She began to shake and sob. "Why do people keep trying to hurt me?"

That hit Tuesday in the chest with the force of a sledgehammer.

She wrapped Danielle from behind, kissed her head. "Baby, you are not a bad person. Your daddy and me used to be bad people Dani. We hurt a lot of people and now some of them want to use you to hurt us. I'm sorry baby, it's our fault."

"I'm telling you this 'cause you said something to me that I gotta respect. You're not a regular nine-year-old and it's time I stopped treating you like one."

Tuesday talked with her daughter, but more importantly, she listened. She apologized for her parental mistakes and explained how they both had to be strong for Tanisha. Then she and Danielle hugged and shared a good cry that purged all the hostility that had grown between them.

That carried Tuesday into sleep and into a weird dream where Danielle got snatched by an evil wizard. All Tuesday recalled from it was Danielle waving goodbye as some dark and mysterious figure flew away with her. Tuesday could only watch helplessly from the ground screaming for her to come back.

Tuesday woke up the next morning in a panic when the girls weren't in bed with her. She rushed downstairs to find them in the kitchen. Jeanine had made a breakfast of waffles, eggs and bacon. Tuesday was happy to see them eating, especially Danielle who didn't have an appetite the night before. She was seated at the table taking in forkfuls of scrambled eggs while staring at Shaun's laptop.

Jeanine offered Tuesday a plate and a mug of coffee. Tuesday nodded her thanks then joined the girls at the table along with DelRay who had slept on the living room sofa.

Tanisha had a sticky kiss for her mother with lips smeared with syrup. Danielle was too absorbed by the computer that Tuesday didn't get her attention until she rubbed her head. "Baby, what you lookin' at?"

"It's your work stuff but these people suck at math."

Tuesday leaned over and saw she was studying department spreadsheets from Abel.

"The permutations are all wonky. The numbers don't add up."

Danielle had to explain to Tuesday who couldn't comprehend. She pointed to the screen. "This says fifteen million, 416 thousand, 292 dollars and seventy-nine cents. But it should be nineteen million, 787 thousand, 929 dollars and thirty-four cents, if you factor in the profits reported here and all the cost deductions listed here," she scrolled down a long list of figures. "And here."

Tuesday bit into a strip of bacon. "What else is wrong?"

"Well, whoever screwed this up must really like that number because they used it like three more times." Danielle took her through a few different spread sheets. Four other departments reported profits that equaled the same wrong number.

Tuesday was finally able to understand that Brandon had been skimming a little from each department then having her sign off on the financial statements. And Shaun was the perfect accessory, a pretty bitch from accounting who would keep Tuesday distracted and help him doctor the books.

DelRay asked, "But why would they keep using the same number, fifteen million, 416 thousand, 29 dollars and seventy-nine cents. He had to know that would look too crazy to be coincidence."

By this time A.D. had joined them. "Because the mistake was meant to be caught. If he was planning to put it on her the whole time, he would want it to be sloppy and obvious."

Tuesday frowned. "Cause a dumb hoodrat bitch like me wouldn't know how to be slick about it."

Tanisha said, "Mommy watch your mouth."

"Sorry baby." Tuesday pecked her forehead.

"Dani, you ain't been to school in a week so here's yo' homework. I want you to go through those files and let me know about anything else that seems off to you."

Danielle gave her a nod with a serious look on her face. Tuesday could see that her little girl was eager to prove she deserved to be treated like an adult and part of the team.

To DelRay, Tuesday said: "I have to meet with Vega in two hours to discuss our play. I'll understand if you don't wanna come with me this time."

"You know I'm down for whatever but after last night can you really trust that bi-" DelRay almost slipped until he remembered the children present.

"I can trust her for right now 'cause we need each other." Tuesday sipped her coffee. "And I hope you really down for whatever, 'cause when the time comes, I'm gonna need you to bait the hook."

Chapter Fifty-one

A caravan of burgundy SUVs left the private air field outside of Los Angeles where La Guapa's jet sat on the tarmac. Four Tahoes escorted the limited-edition Range Rover with heavy tints. The five vehicles traveled single file with the Range third.

Minutes later, they were on the highway that led back to downtown Los Angeles when an economy-class white panel van approached from the rear driving with intercept speed. Once it pulled within ten feet of the convoy, one of Vega's longhaired Colombians leaned out the passenger window holding a fully automatic HK assault rifle.

The van pulled along the left and began spraying bullets at the group, but the drivers of the Tahoes moved to put themselves between the Range Rover and the shooter. These ordinary-looking SUVs had undergone expensive customizations. The rounds scarred the paint but only ricocheted off their reinforced metal plating and special shatterproof glass.

Another van sped down the freeway on-ramp opposite the convoy. The Tahoes took a more protective formation by sandwiching the Range Rover: two in front and back on either side.

A sliding door opened on the left side of the second van to reveal the other Colombian. He motioned for a weapon and someone handed him a Swedish-made AT4 rocket grenade launcher. He balanced the forty-inch tube on his shoulder and took aim.

All together the Range Rover and the Tahoes sped up, trying to put distance between them and the vans. Only their formation took up three of the four lanes on the freeway which caused innocent drivers ahead of them to get pushed out of their path. A tiny red Subaru coupe was spun into the median when one of the Chevys slammed into it from behind.

They cranked it up to a hundred and ten miles per hour, but their souped-up V-8s or even the Rover's supercharged V-10 couldn't put enough distance between them and a launcher that was effective from three hundred yards.

Vega's man steadied himself against the wind and lurching van then fired a rocket carrying four hundred and forty grams of Octol, a highly-explosive anti-tank substance. It streaked to and erupted under the right rear vehicle just as they were approaching a freeway overpass. The blast lifted the Tahoe into the air high enough to flatten it against the underside of the bridge. The wreckage crashed back down, making the white vans and other drivers swerve to avoid the flaming debris.

With one defender down, the three remaining Tahoes adjusted their positions. They slipped back, allowed the Rover to pull ahead and established a three-lane blockade between it and the pursuing vans. The convoy moved together perfectly synchronized, which suggested all the vehicles were communicating and had drivers with tactical training.

The AT4 was a single-shot weapon that took time to reload and this gave them a chance to return fire. All three Tahoes opened their tailgate windows and had black-clad soldiers crouched within. The vans were not bulletproof. So when the clatter of automatic gunfire penetrated their grills and cracked their windshields, Vega's men were forced back a quarter mile.

Freeway traffic condensed when construction funneled four lanes down to two. The Range started to race past an off-ramp but took an abrupt turn at the last second, narrowly missing the orange barrels. The three Tahoes quickly merged back into a single file to follow.

On the surface streets the burgundy SUVs weaved seamlessly into the downtown traffic. Seeing that they had gained some separation from the white vans, they negotiated the drivers, pedestrians and bike riders with restraint. They sought a direct route to the Abel building, which from miles away gleamed like a beacon in the afternoon sun.

The motorcade was stopped at a light on a major street with the Range Rover in front. They pulled off on the green but a huge diesel-powered dump truck with a plow shovel purposely charged through the red light that halted traffic on the cross street. It T-boned the last vehicle hard enough to bend the Tahoe's customized armored frame. People fled with panicked screams when it flipped onto the sidewalk and crashed through the glass front of an ice cream parlor.

Like before, the remaining SUVs pressed on, only driving with more urgency.

Soon the white vans from the freeway caught back up with them. Both groups took lefts and rights while trading short bursts of automatic gunfire.

Another turn put them on a service street that ran parallel to a large boulevard. More of Vega's men managed to get ahead of them because two more vans appeared at the end of that block to box them in. The Colombians formed a road block. The shooters jumped out and took up positions behind the vehicles. Two of them ran partway up the street to throw down a police spike strip.

In one motion the Range slowed, veered right and let one of the Tahoes pass on its left. Once in the lead, the Chevy sped up as if they were going to ram their way through the road block.

But halfway down the street, the driver cut the wheel and hit the emergency brake. This sent the SUV into a skid as well as a slow ninety-degree spin. It was moving forward but turned sideways by the time it hit the spike strip, so rather than roll over the sharp pins, the tires swept the entire strip out of the road. The Chevy slid down the block while the Colombians sprinkled it with bullets. At the corner, the Tahoe slammed laterally into the parked vans with enough impact to push back their barricade.

This cleared the path for the Range and its final escort. They hung a left at that corner and escaped along the intersecting street.

The two remaining SUVs weaved their way through the downtown streets with the vans giving chase. It wasn't long before all the shooting attracted the police whose sirens swelled in the distance.

Vega's men didn't keep the group from reaching their destination. The Range and the Tahoe sped into Abel's underground parking structure with squealing tires. Building security had obviously been alerted to the threat because they immediately lowered the railing to close off the garage once they entered.

They screeched to a stop and the men hustled their queen out of the back seat. She stepped out wearing a tan business suit, big sunglasses, and a large stylish hat.

Her team escorted her to the open elevator where Brandon waited with two of his own blue-shirt rent-a-cops.

He extended a hand. "Reina, a pleasure to meet you in the flesh finally. Your reputation for being a shrewd businesswoman is well deserved." He added with a smile, "As well as the stories of your stunning beauty."

She refused his hand. "You've been a tremendous help in removing any obstacles to securing this acquisition. My associates and I are extremely grateful."

"So grateful that you'll remember me when you are sitting at The Table?" he asked with raised eyebrows. "And speaking of obstacles, I hear you faced a few trying to get here."

She was dismissive. "Nothing we didn't anticipate. Apparently the hoodrat made a new friend—a low-level gun smuggler my family has history with. I plan to deal with that no sooner than our business here is concluded."

Brandon shrugged. "Then let's conclude our business. Once the papers are signed there will be nothing the hoodrat or the smuggler can do."

She looked around to notice that the parking garage was empty for ten a.m. on a Wednesday.

Brandon explained: "In anticipation of our deal, I closed the building to any inessential personnel. Any employee not important to completing the deal or keeping the lights on and toilets flushing is enjoying a mandatory vacation day."

The two boarded the executive elevator; he pressed for the top floor where the legal teams waited with the final paperwork. She had two of her guards come along, left the others outside to defend the garage.

While they rode up, Brandon boasted that the Abel tower was essentially a seventy-story fortress. The building was in total lockdown. Ninety-eight percent of the staff had the day off but security was doubled. Armed men in blue shirts were posted at every entrance and exit with pictures of Tuesday. More roamed the building on foot or cruised the perimeter and subterranean garage in patrol cars.

She loudly sucked her teeth as if unimpressed. "Have your men coordinate with mine. Tell them to sweep every floor, starting with the top, and work their way down."

Brandon looked confused. "I understand your caution but—"

She cut him off. "Do you know the difference between a leader and a shepherd?"

He assumed the question was rhetorical.

"A leader stands out front and demands to be followed. A shepherd skillfully guides and pushes the flock from the rear—it's why Jesus is called the Good Shepherd."

Brandon figured her point was somewhere in the making.

"The hoodrat is more clever than we gave her credit for. Everything that happened on the freeway and the street was only for trimming my numbers. She wasn't trying to keep me from getting to the meeting. I was being herded here."

She folded her hands behind her back, calmly stared up at the digital display that counted the floors. "Our enemies are already in the building."

Chapter Fifty-two

Brandon had made that call by the time they reached the top floor. He thought it was impossible for Tuesday to be inside the building with all the security in place, but did so to placate his guest. He ordered teams to start sweeping each floor. He even moved the signing from the easily accessible conference room into the CEO's office because it was more secure. He posted four men outside the door.

Inside she, Brandon, and three lawyers hovered over the desk he had taken over from Tuesday when he assumed control. Upon it was a stack of legal documents two feet high. They sped through it while the trio told them where to sign or initial.

Brandon's phone rang just as he was scribbling his name for what could've been the hundredth time. The caller ID read "unavailable," but he answered to the sound of a woman's voice. He touched his associate's arm to let her know it was Tuesday on the line.

"Where are you? Reina thinks you're in the building."

"I'm not even in the state. I would've loved to be there in person but had more important business elsewhere so you'll just have to settle for a conference call."

He said, "You're too late. I'm signing the final paperwork as we speak that transfers ownership of the company, the building and the majority share of the stock. It's over."

She sounded calm. "You sure 'bout that?"

He said, "In the ghetto you're a queen, but you never had the mind to play on this level. Here wars are fought in the boardroom, not in the streets."

"I was blind to a lot of things. It took Danielle of all people to understand exactly how you were stealing from the company, setting me up to take the fall."

He smirked into the phone. "Sounds like you're trying to get me to admit to something."

Tuesday said, "It's also because of Danielle that the big ass stack of papers you and your friend just signed don't amount to shit."

Brandon placed his signature on the line where the lawyer indicated. "You sound desperate and pathetic."

"You couldn't take the company or the stock majority from me because it was never mine. You were the one who explained how the moment we declared Marcus King dead the company immediately fell into the trust."

He countered: "I also explained that as the girls' legal guardian, you were the custodian of the trust which gave you powers over it. But you signed those powers over to me—which I thank you for, if I haven't already."

"Here's where it gets tricky. I did sign it over to you, but I didn't."

Brandon scrambled to pore through the drawers in his desk. After a rushed search, he located the file and thumbed the pages until he found the trust agreement.

He said, "Nice try but I'm looking at your signature right here. All perfectly legal."

"Look closer. I almost missed it myself but Dani didn't. I guess I can thank you for giving Shaun a digital copy of the agreement to keep on her computer."

It took Brandon a full minute of scanning the document before he understood what she meant. He ran his hand over his gray curly hair.

She said, "Tabitha King was the CEO of Abel and on papers Tabitha King is the girls' legal guardian. But Marcus, whether accidentally or on purpose, made Tuesday Knight the custodian. I signed the wrong name, which technically means I didn't sign."

"Bullshit!" he spat, even though the proof was right before his eyes. At the top of the document TUESDAY KNIGHT was typed in all caps as overseer of the trust; however, Tabitha King was inked at the bottom in Tuesday's sloppy script.

She taunted him. "I might not know much about corporate law, but I know that one person can't give away something that belongs to somebody else. I might as well have signed Mickey Mouse."

His business partner had been watching his conversation with growing agitation. Brandon waved a finger to indicate that nothing was wrong.

"If this was your great master plan then I am hilariously disappointed. You really think I'm gonna let the wrong name on a few sheets of paper stop me from collecting a three-hundred-million-dollar check?"

Tuesday said, "Some wars are fought in the boardroom but the rules are the same for fighting in the street. When a nigga pull a gun, that change everythang."

Suddenly the phones chirped on all three members of Brandon's legal team. Without checking them the trio of suits opened their briefcases to reveal semi-automatic M-11s.

The lady seemed less surprised than Brandon. "You walked us into this simple trap. The real lawyers are dead or in the Bahamas."

One of the suited gunmen took the phone from Brandon's ear. He placed it on the desk and switched it to speaker.

Tuesday's voice crackled with distortion. "You were so eager to get this deal done that you didn't pay attention to the men handling the paperwork. I'm willing to bet you didn't pay attention to what you just signed either."

Another of the fake lawyers pulled out a document hidden within the large stack they just signed. He passed it to Brandon and allowed him to study it.

Brandon snorted when he realized he had put his name to a typed confession that detailed how he had aided in the disappearance of Marcus King, embezzled Abel funds, burned down her home and killed two men during the staged kidnapping.

He laughed out loud. "You really think this weak shit is gonna hold up in court?"

"Don't need to 'cause yo' ass ain't 'bout to see a judge."

The third gunman opened the office door. The massive man who stood on the other side was dressed head-to-toe in black. All four guards Brandon had posted there were sprawled at his feet unconscious in awkward poses.

Brandon's eyes went wide when Silence stepped inside and closed the door. He tried to keep Tuesday from hearing the fear in his voice: "How does a massacre in the CEO's office send everything back to normal at Abel?"

"It's not gonna be a massacre. Show 'em the other thing."

The second suit brought Brandon's attention to something else he had signed in haste, a letter in his own handwriting.

Tuesday explained: "You said you were tired of playing the role of Brandon King so here's how it ends. The note along with the confession tells the story of a brilliant man and successful entrepreneur momentarily so blinded by greed and jealousy that he betrayed his own son. His conscience convicted him much worse than a jury would have."

Brandon scanned what was supposed to be his suicide note. He stroked his head nervously. "Nobody's gonna believe I killed myself in the middle of the biggest deal of my life. And in front of La Guapa? You didn't think this through Tuesday."

She fired back: "Naw nigga! You didn't think shit through when you betrayed the fam. I'm still CEO 'round this bitch, and effective immediately, yo' ass is terminated. Please show this bitch out my building."

One of the gunmen went through a short series of quick hand gestures that Silence received with a slow nod.

The mute man flexed his gloved fingers, then walked over to Brandon who tried to pull a pistol concealed under his jacket. The goon easily deflected Brandon's arm as he squeezed off a shot, twisted it behind Brandon's back like a chicken wing, and made him drop the gun.

The first suit opened the sliding door while Silence pushed a dancing and hop-scotching Brandon towards the balcony.

Brandon yelled, "I should've killed you bitch!"

Tuesday said, "You ain't the first to make that mistake."

With a mighty heave Silence tossed his thin body over the railing like a bag of garbage. Brandon flailed like an uncoordinated swimmer. His screams echoed as he dropped seventy stories.

Afterward all their attention was turned to the lady. She just stood by the desk calmly as Silence stepped back in from the balcony.

She hovered over the phone. "So what happens now? Did I just sign a suicide note too?"

"You already know what's 'bout to happen," Tuesday said through the speaker. "The only question is, are you gonna be okay with it, Rose?"

Chapter Fifty-three

At Villa Bella, Reina was at dinner in the formal dining room. The staff served a fantastic rendition of *cabrito,* goat roasted over open flame. She ate modestly although everything was to her liking. She and Roselyn rarely dined together as her twin sister was more into vegan dishes with soy replacing the real carne that accompanied authentic Mexican cuisine.

Her phone sat on the table receiving more attention than her plate. She was supposed to get a text as soon as the papers were signed. The phone mocked her with its silence and repeated calls had gone unanswered.

Brandon had assured her that their lawyers would have the Abel deal finalized before noon. Within two months she and her partners planned to be moving several metric tons of product. Their newly-acquired fleet of shipping freighters would sail right around the president's border wall, and soon the profits would bring the Rodriguez family back to full strength.

Only it was after eight p.m., and she still hadn't heard from Brandon or Roselyn.

Reina typically kept two sets of plans in her head. One for how things should go and the other for how they shouldn't.

She was so wrapped in her own thoughts that she hardly noticed dessert being brought in. The cute young chef wheeled out a cart with a large three-tier yellow cake.

Reina frowned skeptically at its bizarre decoration. The cake was capped with candles and a macabre Barbie doll whose head had been replaced by a tiny skull. *Feliz Dia de Muerte, La Guapa* was written across the front in red icing.

The newest member of her staff tried to rush back to the kitchen until she called after him. Reina noticed his nervous glance, shifty movements. His face was glazed with sweat. She cut her eyes to the cake then back to the chef. Without a word, they both bolted out of the room in opposite directions.

She turned into the hall and threw herself to the floor. She expected a blast that would kick the doors off the hinges and drop the roof on her.

But there was only a hollow pop. She peeked back inside to see that the cake had exploded but with hardly any power. Lemon frosting and crumbs splattered the walls but the room suffered no structural damage. This could've been the work of a child's firework rather than lethal explosive.

She climbed to her feet wondering if this was somebody's idea of a joke, then she heard men outside yelling to each other in rapid-fire Spanish. This was followed by rapid-fire snaps that clearly weren't fireworks.

Suddenly a real explosion shook the foundation of the house. It echoed from somewhere in the rear, but the impact was strong enough to knock her off her feet.

All the power winked off, sank everything into darkness. The pitch of a rural Texas night shone at the windows which told her that even the exterior lighting had been knocked out. When the backup generator didn't immediately spring to life, Reina knew the bomb had been strategically placed.

She got to her feet and took a moment to steady herself. Her ears rang, she was dizzy, her vision shifted the world in and out of focus.

The white walls offered a meager amount of ambient light so she staggered forward dazed and half-blinded, touching them for support. She needed to get to her room or maybe an exit.

She turned into the main hall and ran into the huge silhouette of a man. He was a faceless shadow like something from a horror movie. She backed away, put up her hands in defense.

"La Guapa, *estas bien?*"

His voice caused her to let out a breath she'd held since bumping into him.

Before Reina could speak, he confirmed what she already knew: "Colombians breached the house. At least twenty men, heavily armed. Not many of us are still alive."

Reina told him about the traitorous chef and they both surmised that he had helped the intruders get inside.

"Get me out and I'll suck your dick on a pile of money."

He wasted no time with a response. He led the way holding a weapon that looked fully-automatic. She held on to his shoulder and allowed herself to be guided.

She trailed him down the hall but he held her back at the entrance to the foyer. His hand gesture indicated that there were men standing between them and the front door. He crouched, took aim from around the corner. Reina flinched when he let out three short bursts from his rifle. When he urged her forward again, she saw the shapes of two bodies on her hardwood floor.

Warm light brightened the windows at the front of the house but only because the three of the house vehicles were engulfed in flames. There would be no escape from the front door.

He pulled Reina back the other way, towards the rear via the main hall. They passed through the dining room where the scent of cordite and brown sugar mingled in the air.

They encountered another gunman in the short hall that connected the dining room to the kitchen. He was crouched against the wall concealed by darkness. The blood that pooled underneath him proved that he was already shot. Reina spotted him first and froze at the sight of his gun.

He had her in his sights, but hesitated and retrained the gun on her escort. A moment too late though, because a quick rat-a-tat from her protector slumped him against a curio table, knocking over the ceramic Virgin Mary.

He waved Reina back and put a finger to his lips before he crept to the nearest corner. He peeked around but apparently didn't like what he saw. He returned and gave a slow head shake.

"Guapa, I have to get you somewhere safe. Hide you until I can come back for you."

Reina agreed. She led him to what she knew to be the safest place in the house. After a few turns, she was at the hidden door to her father's office. She undid the latch and stepped inside to the pitch black windowless room.

"I'll come back soon as I can," was the last thing her faceless hero said before closing the door on her.

Her father's dated masculine theme and the overuse of dark wood meant no ambient light for her to see by. Reina had to feel her way forward until she reached the desk.

Suddenly a phone light blinded her, held by somebody sitting there. She was startled like a deer in the road.

"Hey, Pretty Girl. Didn't I tell you I'd get us in a room all by ourselves?"

Tuesday turned the screen on itself so Reina could see her gray eyes flicker in the light. "Alone at last."

Chapter Fifty-four

"How did you know Rose was a decoy?" Reina asked.

"Because you're a chess master. A good player will always sacrifice the queen to escape a tight position."

Tuesday typed a text into her phone. A second later the lights came back on. They both squinted hard, needing a moment for their dark-adapted eyes to adjust.

Reina shook her head, wearing a smirk. "The darkness and explosions—disorientation and distraction."

She remembered the man they found slumped over in the hall. He pointed his gun at Reina then immediately turned it on her escort.

"My friend there wasn't killing intruders to protect me—he was the intruder killing my men right in front of me. All the while every choice designed to lead me right here."

"Didn't think you would recognize my man DelRay," Tuesday said. "Now all your men are dead—your numbers were already low, but the losses in Detroit and L.A. left you too weak here. Sun Tzu said that the best way to defeat a large army is to divide its forces."

Reina looked impressed. "You studied *The Art of War*?"

"Just read the book, but been studying it my whole life. To be honest, really didn't tell me shit I ain't already know.

"Bitch like me didn't go to Oxford or come up in a big house with a rich daddy. All the strategies and military tactics you learned from books and games, I had to live in the streets."

"My sister. Is she dead?"

"I gave her a choice and she made it."

"While Brandon was betraying you, Rose was betraying me. Probably been helping you long enough to plant the new chef in my house. The cake was a nice touch."

Tuesday shrugged. "Someone once said 'in this game people either die loyal or live long enough to betray you.' After the way you dangled her as bait, I can't blame her."

"Did I dangle Rose or did she dangle me? I bet she fed you some sob story about being the unloved twin who was always stuck in my shadow."

Tuesday nodded towards the case with all of her trophies and awards. "Pretty clear who Daddy's favorite was."

When Tuesday stood, Reina saw that she was wearing an Adidas track suit and matching sneakers. She walked over to Reina who did not retreat from her approach. For a second they just measured each other with a stare.

Tuesday grabbed her, forced her body into hers and jammed her tongue into Reina's mouth. Reina was stunned at first but quickly gave in to the kiss. What they shared was slow and passionate and lasted for about twenty seconds before each one needed to catch her breath.

Reina had something in her eyes that resembled victory. "How long have you been wanting to do that?"

"Since the first time I saw you at the restaurant." Tuesday whispered this as if ashamed to confess it.

She matched Tuesday's tone: "And what did you think the first time you saw me?"

Tuesday hesitated. "She da baddest bitch I ever seen."

Reina smiled, wet her lips seductively. "And what else have you been wanting to do to me?"

Tuesday stepped back, slid out of the Adidas jacket revealing a crispy wifebeater with no bra. She pulled a ponytail holder from her pocket and used it to tie back her hair.

Reina looked amused. "Is this what we're doing? Are we supposed to take off our earrings and fight like two chicks in the middle of the projects?"

"Y'all like to keep reminding me that I'm just a hoodrat. I promised I was gonna beat the shit outta you then choke you to death for Marcus. You can try to fight back."

"I have two Ph.Ds. and an I.Q. of one-ninety. Ironic that I'm about to die because I never learned to fight."

"It's the first thing you learn where I'm from."

"Before we start do you mind if I enjoy a final sip of that tequila and one of those good Cubans?"

When Tuesday agreed, Reina walked over to her father's desk and poured two glasses from the crystal decanter. She lifted the humidor and offered Tuesday a smoke.

She accepted the drink and cigar. She leaned forward and accepted a light when Reina presented a platinum Zippo.

They had switched positions. She sank into her father's chair while Tuesday stood before the desk.

For a few minutes, neither woman spoke, they sipped and puffed thick tobacco clouds in silence.

"This is good," Tuesday said holding up the glass. "The cigar is a little harsh though."

"The tequila is from a small village in Mexico close to where my father was born. He says they age it seventeen years before bottling it, but I don't know if that's true."

"Could be," Tuesday said after another swallow. "It's clearly the best I ever had."

"My father wasn't educated either but he had good taste. He was also a very prudent man."

"Marcus told me he was super-connected."

Reina blew smoke. "You have no idea what this is really about. Brandon crossed Sebastian for the same reason Rose crossed me. When my father died it left a vacant chair. Everybody's jockeying for that seat at The Table."

Wrinkles creased Tuesday's forehead. "Whose table?"

Reina laughed. "They're people out here with power on a level you couldn't imagine—compared to them I'm just a peon. I only want to sell a little dope and make a few billion, but they're actually playing chess with the planet. Tuesday, your world is about to get a lot bigger and a lot more complicated."

While she spoke, Tuesday noticed her hand slip out of view.

"Don't even bother searching for that pistol your very-prudent father hid under the desk." From her pocket, Tuesday pulled a shiny chrome single-shot .22 Derringer. "I had enough time to do some snooping before you came in."

That was when something like defeat showed on Reina's face.

Tuesday sucked down the last bit of pale liquor and butted the remainder of the Cuban. "You ready?"

"As I'll ever be." Reina stood after one last pull. She stepped around the desk and presented herself to Tuesday like a prisoner awaiting execution. Nothing in her body language suggested that she intended to fight back.

"Rose was right. I should've never underestimated you."

Tuesday countered, "You should've never fucked with me!"

"I'll tell you a secret about my sister, something my father never knew. She scored a lot higher than me on the I.Q. test and was the only person who could consistently beat me at chess. She's good at playing the victim but is actually a predator."

Tuesday's face indicated that she was done talking. She made a fist, motioned like she was about to swing but Reina flinched so hard that Tuesday paused.

She raised her hands in defense. "Please, not in the face."

Tuesday looked at Reina and almost pitied her. "This was never s'posed to be your life. You're not a gangster, never had to get your hands dirty. You're just a spoiled little daddy's girl who should've been in a lab somewhere curing cancer. I'm sorry for what Marcus did to your brother."

"He broke my heart—it's what he does. He would've broken yours too—"

Pop.

That shot to the chest silenced Reina mid-sentence. Tuesday watched the pretty doll sink to her knees then ease onto her side. She reclined against the case that held the evidence of her beauty and intelligence. Her head rolled to the side; her eyes were open but seeing nothing. To Tuesday it was as if she had purposely posed herself even though she had died instantly.

The .22 bullet had stopped her heart which meant no blood would pool around her body. No bruise would appear on her exquisite face. La Guapa would be as beautiful in death as she had been in life.

Tuesday looked down on her for a moment then returned to the desk. She helped herself to another glass of tequila.

Chapter Fifty-five

Three weeks later DelRay pulled back into the junkyard on Detroit's Westside. He was driving the brand new Escalade ESV Tuesday had bought for him. It was her first major purchase after the feds released Tabitha King's bank accounts. Silence was in the passenger seat and Tuesday sat behind him.

Madame Vega, her son, and a few of their men were already waiting. They stood outside the white BMW as DelRay pulled his Escalade nose-to-nose. The shiny new vehicles stood out among the rusty and twisted metal.

Tuesday, DelRay, and Silence all stepped out to greet the woman in white.

Vega said, "I didn't think you'd want to meet like this now that you're back to being all corporate again."

"Believe me, this is the last time. And it's the last time you speak to me directly." Tuesday nodded towards DelRay. "From here on out, you deal with my right hand."

"So how did it feel to kill the woman who killed your husband? I'm curious to know."

Tuesday didn't blink. "When our business is complete you'll get your chance to find out."

"That play you put down cost me a lot of men and material. I'm thinking we need to restructure the terms of our agreement."

"I don't wanna hear that shit," Tuesday snapped. "You 'bout to come up fuckin' with me. Don't try to get greedy."

"I'm supposed to shoot my shot," said Vega. "Saw a big thing on the news about how Abel Incorporated is moving to Detroit. Breaking ground on a new high-rise downtown next year. Supposed to bring about seven thousand new jobs to the city. You're doing big things Ms. CEO."

Tuesday didn't entertain her. "Did you get the list?"

Vega flashed a folded slip of paper she pulled from her purse.

Tuesday said, "Before we can get started we need all those positions filled within the U.S. Customs Agency, the Port Authority, and within my company."

"I have a list of applicants." Vega pulled a separate sheet of paper and passed it to her man who walked it to DelRay. "Loyal, dependable, ambitious. People who will do what they're told and not ask too many questions, as long as our gratitude is reflected in their pockets."

Tuesday received the list from DelRay. She scanned it for a moment, then folded it into her pocket. "It'll be suspicious if they're all Latino. Think diversity. And it goes without saying that they all gotta have clean records."

Vega agreed. "Once we get everybody in place, how soon can you start making deliveries?"

"I figure the first can happen within six weeks of being staffed. One shipment every ninety days after that for twenty-four months. Eight total. Then we're done."

"You're gonna make so much money on this deal that you might want to extend the time period."

"That's not gonna happen," Tuesday frowned. "I'm already caked up—I'm not doing this for the money. I'm just keeping my word. Eight shipments, that's it."

Vega smiled. "You look so serious. That's a different look in your eyes from the one you had the last time you were here."

That comment drew laughter from Vega's son Aaron who added, "Your girlfriend is buried out back if you ever want to come pay your respects."

Tuesday took a step towards them. "I'm back home now and 'bout to put my hand down in a big way. You better use these next few years to get your house in order. Go every place you've ever wanted to go, eat all your favorite foods, fuck every nigga you've ever wanted to fuck. Hug and kiss that little funny-looking ass boy there as much as you can."

That scrubbed the smirk from Aaron's face.

"Put together that bucket list and start checking shit off," Tuesday continued. "Because as soon as I make good on my promise, as soon as I deliver the last shipment, I'm at yo' mutha-fuckin' ass, bitch. Please believe it."

Tuesday motioned to DelRay and Silence who all turned to leave when Vega called out to her.

"I just have to know—one mother to another—who did you pick? Before the girl gave up her life in that beautiful and selfless act, I know you made a choice. Which door were you going to open, Tuesday? Which daughter were you going to save, which were you going to leave in the car?"

Tuesday climbed into the Cadillac and glared at her through the window. There was nothing but fire and steel in her eyes. "Two years then we WAR!"

Chapter Fifty-six

Tuesday had to fly out to Los Angeles that night with plans to stay for three days before returning. A tedious marathon of meetings with bankers and lawyers was necessary to transfer some of Tabitha King's personal interests to Michigan. She also had to transfer Danielle to a school district in Farmington Hills—an affluent suburb outside of Detroit—where Tuesday had already begun searching for a new house.

DelRay had never flown commercial before so she was eager to take him up on the Abel corporate jet. With the move to Detroit pending, the company had already leased a private hangar at Metro Airport for the G-650.

DelRay was behind the wheel of his Escalade, and Silence, who Tuesday paid to retain his services indefinitely, sat in the passenger seat. She was in the back with Tanisha sandwiched between her and Danielle.

Tuesday's phone had been blowing up on the ride to the airport from an unavailable number. She refused to answer and they refused to leave a voice mail.

The parking lot was near empty when they pulled up at Metro. Inside they walked past ticket booths with no lines and saw only scattered groups of individuals entranced by their mobile devices while waiting for boarding calls.

Inside the private hanger DelRay marveled at the white bird with red striping, Abel Inc. across the fuselage in block lettering. Tuesday recognized the look of nervous excitement, the look of a kid about to ride his first roller coaster.

After Tuesday looked around, her expression reflected her concern. While the door on the jet was open, the large hangar door was still closed. The captain and copilot were typically on hand to greet her and load any baggage, but neither of them were visible.

Beef with La Guapa still had her cautious. Her mind was screaming: *Trap!*

"Ms. Knight, you and I have a few things to discuss."

Tuesday turned to the direction of the female voice. From the opposite side of the hangar, near a separate service door that led outside, Ms. Jackson approached with another male agent.

DelRay looked confused, but Silence took the stance of some-one ready to bang it out. His hand hovered near a pistol tucked on his waist. It was clear that he was prepared to separate spirit from body before being taken back into custody.

"It's okay Big Man, nobody's here for that." The woman with the short afro limped forward favoring a cane, one palm up. "I'm only here to talk and she wasn't answering the phone.

"If I wanted you in a cell, you'd already be there. I know about you . . . and your father." She punctuated that with a look that in-dicated a history both understood and neither needed to explain.

Message received, Silence moved his hand away from the gun.

"Tuesday, the gentleman at my side is Agent Morrison." She motioned to the light-skinned dude next to her with the bald head and crispy-trimmed goatee. "He's one of my most-trusted colleagues. You and I are about to discuss topics that may not be age-appropriate for you daughters. Do you mind if he takes the girls back inside to the frozen yogurt kiosk in the food court?"

Skepticism pinched her face.

Ms. Jackson said, "I am aware of the ordeal they recently endured and can assure you they're perfectly safe with him."

Tuesday thought for a second then sucked her teeth. "DelRay, go with them."

Jackson paused for a moment before giving a slow nod. "That is acceptable. Mr. Royce can join the girls."

Her daughters looked to Tuesday for approval before they accepted DelRay's large hands. He and the young agent walked them back towards the service exit that led back into the airport.

Once the door closed behind the children, the three remaining adults faced each other.

"Congratulations Ms. Knight, on getting your company back. Me and other interested parties were watching from the side."

She sneered. "Now it's congratulations? Last time we spoke you was talking 'bout locking me up for a hundred years."

"I could lock you up for five hundred," Jackson shot back. "If you factor in what happened here, California, and Texas—you actually had men firing a rocket launcher on the Los Angeles freeway. Fuck murder," she scoffed. "I could bring you up on terrorism charges."

Tuesday folded her arms. "Then why I'm still walking 'round free? Especially after I ghosted you at the First Precinct."

"Don't look so smug, Ms. Knight, 'cause you're not half as slick as you think you are. Do you think it's a coincidence that no law enforcement agency, local or otherwise, has kicked in your door after all that chaos? Don't you find it odd that the insurance company paid out so quickly for your house in Beverly Hills and that the Abel investigation wrapped up in a flash to unfreeze your accounts? What about how easily the case closed on Brandon King's 'suicide?'" She used her fingers to mimic quotes. "Who do you think's been running behind you, scooping up your shit like a dog walker?"

Tuesday's face revealed she never even considered it.

"Making police reports disappear, witnesses changing their stories, even bodies vanishing from the coroner's office. Pulling strings on the Detroit city council to fast-track Abel's move without all the typical red tape." Jackson tapped her chest. "All me, babygirl.

"And for the record, you never ghosted me. Do you really think we are so incompetent that we would put you in the wrong holding cell?" She glanced at Silence. "Or forget to properly lock your handcuffs?"

That raised Tuesday's eyebrows.

"Now you're starting to see that you're not lucky, Ms. Knight. You're protected." Ms. Jackson twisted the strange triangle-shaped ring Tuesday noticed in the interrogation room.

She asked, "Protected by you?"

Jackson looked to the jet. "Would you mind if we finished our conversation inside? Chemo did a number on my bones, can't stand for longer than a minute before my knees start aching."

Tuesday and Silence led her up the boarding stairs. The G-650 was the largest and most-equipped in the Gulfstream series. It was not like the smaller business class jets that only sat eight and didn't permit passengers to stand up straight. The interior was spacious with a ceiling high enough that even the six foot, five inch Silence didn't have to stoop. To the left was an empty cockpit and to the right comfortable seating for fifteen, beyond that a small galley where a single stewardess could serve precooked meals, and at the rear, a small suite with a half bath.

Over the years, Tuesday had flown on the corporate jet many times and was accustomed to the plush leather seats; the 24-karat gold trimming, handles and fittings; the polished Brazilian Cherrywood tables and inlays.

What made Tuesday's mouth drop to the floor was the dark-skinned gentleman staring at her from the third row of seats.

Marcus.

Chapter Fifty-seven

Ms. Jackson dropped herself hard into one of the port-facing bench seats. She sucked air between her teeth while rubbing her left knee. The pain appeared to be genuine and not purely for aiding in Marcus's dramatic reveal.

Over a dark suit with a black button-up and tie, Marcus wore a black full-length cashmere coat with a mink collar. The same animal had been slain for the hat.

His beard had grown in full; he obviously hadn't shaved since the day he left. It worked well with the fur, a bossed-up manliness Tuesday was feeling.

She spent two minutes stuck in the same position from when she first saw him. Tears moistened her eyes but didn't fall. She stared at him with some blending of rage and relief.

She hissed, "You sonofabitch."

Marcus said, "I can explain everything."

She repeated, "You sonofabitch."

Marcus stood to greet Silence and initiated a quick series of hand gestures that caused the quiet killer to respond in kind. Tuesday watched their exchange in disbelief. The fact that her husband was fluent in sign language was just another in his long list of secrets.

Their nonverbal conversation went on for a while before Tuesday couldn't resist butting in. "What y'all saying?"

"Nothing much. Just a mutual appreciation for each other's work." Marcus shook his hand then directed Silence to a seat before taking his.

Tuesday shook her head. "On some level I just knew it."

He turned to her. "Before Rene died we had a long talk about Rico and the past and everything that happened with me and the Rodriguez family. But the real conversation was when we talked about the future.

"After the funeral, Reina made her play but used men who were loyal to her father, men who knew the old man had already pledged me. So she thought they put a bullet in my head and took to me to a hog farm when really these kindly gentlemen took me to the airport to board an international flight. Even treated me to McDonald's on the way."

Tuesday flopped into a seat. "So while you were busy laying low—hiding on some island or in some cave, you left me here to deal with all this shit by my muthafuckin' self, again!"

"Not an island this time—Cairo. After Egypt then Russia."

Tuesday peeped his swag was like a Siberian mobster.

"I was so proud of how you handled yourself. Even after you lost everything, was all the way down, you bounced back and took care of business. Protected the company and family."

"Be careful not to press a desperate foe," she quoted.

He smiled. "That's my girl."

"And it just so happened that the guy in the next cell had a copy."

"I figured you could use it," said Jackson. "I also figured you could use a little time to think. I cleaned up for you but it was important that you solved your own problems."

Marcus leaned back in his seat, scratched at his new beard.

"You know how important it is to me that Abel stays legitimate. I wasn't happy 'bout you putting us in that position with the Colombians." After a pause he added, "But I understood."

It didn't surprise Tuesday that he somehow knew about the deal she made with Vega. "I owe her eight shipments of illegals from Central and South America. Supposed to be hard working immigrants who just want an opportunity to do better in the United States. No criminals, no drugs, no guns.

"If you want I can shut it down. I plan on taking a look at her as soon as we're done anyway."

Marcus contemplated that for a second then shook his head. "Honor your word, but make sure she understands there will be penalties for trying anything slick. If we should find somebody carrying a duffel bag of AK's or a mother with heroin stuffed in her baby's diaper—" He didn't need to finish the threat.

Tuesday nodded solemnly. "I'll make sure she sticks to the agreement."

Tuesday didn't see how she first missed the massive ring on his right hand. It was similar to Ms. Jackson's, only larger, more detailed. What she thought was a simple triangle was actually a pyramid with tiny hieroglyphs on the face. It was gold and set with dark stones that Tuesday's trained eye knew were not onyx but genuine black diamonds.

Jewelry like that was typically too gaudy for her low-key husband's tastes. Tuesday knew it was a symbol, something worn because it meant something, and not because it looked good.

"What are you involved in?"

"Something bigger than both of us."

"Are you saying you're back in the game?"

"A bigger game with higher stakes."

Tuesday recalled her conversation with Reina and was able to put things together. "Rene gave you his seat at The Table."

He explained: "Rene Rodriguez was a Brother in Good Standing but his seat was at a much smaller table. Brandon was, and a few others still are, lobbying for that seat. I had been a Brother for years, just not always in good standing."

Tuesday thought back on the rings she found cleaning up the closet. The connection had eluded her.

"Rene nominated me for the seat he would've been promoted to if his health hadn't been bad. A seat at the Big Table."

Tuesday looked lost.

Ms. Jackson helped her. "Each new level requires another initiation. The process takes eight weeks, and during that time there's no contact with the outside world. That's why he couldn't call, couldn't be there, but he made sure I was.

"Now your husband sits where esteemed Masters have sat before him. W. E. B. Dubois, Carter G. Woods, Madam C. J. Walker."

Marcus checked her with a look. It told Tuesday that the woman had said too much. More than the sizes of their rings, it also told her that whatever they were in together, Marcus was clearly her superior.

"Look, I don't care where you been, or why you been gone. I don't even care how we'll explain it to the girls. I just want you back. I just wanna sit on the couch and tuck my cold feet under you. I just want everything back like it was."

He lowered his gaze. "The responsibilities I have don't allow me to be Marcus King anymore. They don't allow me to be your husband."

Tuesday looked to Silence and Ms. Jackson as if she needed witnesses to confirm what she was hearing.

"When are you coming home?"

He delivered the bad news with his eyes.

Tuesday's jaw tightened, anger made her hands shake. "That's why you didn't want the girls to see you. Yo' ass too much of a coward to say goodbye to their faces.

"I'm not doing your dirt for you this time. I'm not protecting your memory. I'm gonna let them know you abandoned this family so you can fly around the world and play toy mafia."

"Toy mafia?" Jackson said indignantly. "The Great House of Kamku has been directing the path—"

Marcus again silenced her with a look. "Let me speak to my wife in private." His tone was more command than request.

Silence got up immediately but Ms. Jackson's arthritic knees took her a little longer to ease out of her seat. As soon as they left the plane, Marcus said: "I am a part of something huge, organized, and global. You think I would choose anything over you if it wasn't extremely important? I am about to run all the legal and illegal business in three countries: Canada, Mexico, and the United States. I now overboss the entire North American continent."

Tuesday fell back against her seat.

He flashed the ring again. "Not a toy mafia, not a few thug niggas who gang bang. I'm talking judges, politicians, captains of industry; this shit runs all the way to the top."

Tuesday finally caught on. "A secret society."

Marcus took the seat next to hers and leaned into her ear. "I'm in violation for even telling you this much. For centuries, small groups of extremely wealthy and powerful white men have worked to put their people in position. Pulling strings from behind the scenes.

"About one hundred years ago some very smart black folks, a few you might even have heard of, decided that if we were gonna have a chance we needed the same thing. You think people like Thurgood Marshall, MLK, or Malcolm X have their impact without somebody behind them? What about organizations like the Nation of Islam, the NAACP, the Historical Black Colleges?"

She cocked her head a bit. "This Kamku thing—you're the black Illuminati."

He nodded. "Literally. Kam means black and Ku means light. And we're stronger than ever right now. Think about the athletes, entertainers, and entrepreneurs; there are more black multimillionaires and billionaires than the world has ever seen—many are Brothers in Good Standing. We are making sure that, not just black, but all people of color get their fair share.

"That's why it's so important that you take care of Abel. Our scholarship programs make sure young minorities get educated, get more doctors, lawyers and businessmen into the fold."

It was another one of those teachable moments where Marcus made Tuesday feel stupid without trying. During their marriage she had been concerned over frivolous stuff like losing the baby weight and quitting her job to open a clothing boutique. Meanwhile he had been viewing things from a broader perspective.

He said, "Making you run the company, leaving you to fight these battles. Deep down you've always known I've been grooming you for something. The only reason I'm telling you all this is because one day there might be a seat for you at The Table."

Her eyes widened with excitement but he stopped her before she could ask a thousand questions. "It won't be soon. Abel needs you, Tanisha needs you, and to be honest bae, you're not ready. There will be more tests but you have to take these next steps on your own."

Tuesday took a second to absorb it all. "What you're doing is big and so important for our people. But I still don't get why you can't do this with us. Why do you have to go away?"

He took her hands into his. "It's not because I want to. But there's a reason why coaches stand on the sideline. I promise one day you'll understand."

They met in a kiss. It was slow and sensual, not charged with their usual sexual energy—a display of their love and not their lust.

He rested his forehead against hers, and for a moment they just stayed like that, holding each other, eyes closed. When he pulled back, Tuesday didn't like his expression. He had the look of someone bothered by an ulcer.

"What is it?" Tuesday knew her husband well enough to see he still hadn't delivered the worst of the news.

He took a deep breath and blew it out slowly. "I'm taking Danielle with me."

Chapter Fifty-eight

"No! No! You are not taking Dani."

Marcus looked as if he expected this response. "The most important thing we do is find young talented people and put them on a path that will do the most good. We've already discussed this at the Big Table."

"I don't give a fuck what y'all talked about. Ain't nobody talked to me. And my daughter ain't goin' no fuckin' where."

"Tuesday, you're rich, but even you don't have access to the resources I have now. Dani is too gifted to wind up stuck with three kids, married to a mechanic and teaching high school algebra. I need her with me."

She became defensive. "You act like I'm a bad mother."

He frowned at her. "You know that's not what I'm saying. With you, Dani will grow up to be a fine, well-adjusted member of society. The problem is that we need her to be more."

Tuesday folded her arms across her chest. "And what does the Big Table need her to be?"

Marcus took a breath then began: "Dani is going to travel the world with me, being exposed to different cultures—with the aid of a series of highly-skilled tutors, she's going to be fluent in six languages by the time she is thirteen. By fifteen she will get accepted into Harvard, where her math skills are going to help her pursue degrees in business, particularly high finance, with a minor in Political Science. By eighteen she'll have her MBA, by twenty a Ph.D. in Business.

"Shortly after that, she'll begin interning at Goldman Sachs or J.P. Morgan, one of the large banking institutions. She will pay her dues, make her way and rise up through the ranks. Soon she'll be their most successful broker and by twenty-nine, will be the youngest junior partner in their firm's history.

"She'll start her own investment company by thirty-five where she's going to make a lot of money for herself and other important people. Her uncanny ability to spot trends and forecast the market will make her one of the most influential people on Wall Street. For fifteen years, her company will enjoy ridiculously high profits, growing her bank account, but more importantly, growing her reputation.

"But sometime during her late forties she will feel the urge for public service and gravitate towards politics. A senate seat will become available in New York, and with the support of all those people she made rich in the private sector, she'll win it by a narrow margin.

"She'll spend the next six or seven years gaining momentum within the Democratic Party, and when the next election cycle happens, they're going to be begging for her to run. By that time, the country will be in a deep recession. People will be struggling so bad that they're going to want somebody who can fix the economy, a smart businessman—woman in this case—with a proven track record. She'll get nominated and humbly accept.

"She's going to steamroll her way through the primary but the general election will be much tighter. She will get clobbered at first just to make it look good. Her opponent will be ahead in the polls by eight or nine points in early July, but a scandal involving his campaign funding will allow Dani to rally late."

The whole time he spoke, Tuesday just listened with her

mouth hanging open. "You're saying Dani's gonna be the president one day? Fifty years from now and y'all already worked it out."

"It's not just going to be handed to her," he said. "You know me, I'll make sure there are tests but things will always seem to fall in her favor. To the public it will sometimes look like brilliance, sometimes dumb luck."

"But it will be the Kamku behind her pulling all the strings." Tuesday shook her head. "That makes her a puppet."

"She's going to do a lot for our people, out front and behind the scenes—a lot for the country. Our baby girl is going to be revered like Lincoln. They're going to build statues of her." He smiled at the thought. "If they still have cash by then, Dani's face will be on their money."

"You've planned her life down to the smallest detail but what if Dani has her own plan? What if she wants to be a school teacher, wants to fall in love and have those three kids?"

"Tuesday, this has already been voted on at the Big Table."

She countered, "But Dani didn't get a vote, did she? Marcus what y'all doing sounds like some James-Bond-mad-scientist shit. This is our daughter, dude. You raise your kids and enjoy watching them turn into the people they're gonna be. I'm not with all this programming and planning."

"Leaders are not born, they're made!" he snapped with frustration. "Two brothers may be born of royal blood, but the one who will get the throne is taught from Day One to walk, talk and act like a King. Dani's training must begin now."

Tuesday measured him with a curious glare. This bearded man in the black suit and gold ring was wearing her husband's face but like a stranger to her. "I don't know what they did in that initiation but it's almost like they brainwashed you. Please baby, don't do this. Let them muthafuckas run the world. Just help me raise both our daughters."

"It's going to be a hard adjustment for all of us but we can't be selfish. We have to make a sacrifice for our people."

"No. I won't let you take her." It was the first time she openly defied her husband and it took all her strength.

His face mirrored the pain he saw in his wife. "You know I'm not doing this to hurt you right?"

The tears she fought back earlier broke free, raced down her cheeks. "I'll fight you on this if I have to, Marcus. I'll do what I gotta do for my daughter."

He rubbed her leg. "I know you will, but you'll lose. There's not a cop, lawyer, or judge from California to Florida that I can't put a battery pack in. This isn't some normal custody dispute that's going to play out in family court. I was too powerful for that before, but now I'm practically a god. Don't try to fight the Kamku, Tuesday—you're in a canoe throwing rocks at a battleship."

Her eyes shifted from green to gray as she showed no fear or sign of backing down. "Even the Titanic sank."

He laughed. "Damn, you making my dick so hard right now."

Tuesday didn't find him funny.

He said, "You're not gonna be able to fight me 'cause you're not gonna be able to find me. And besides, you're gonna have your hands too full with your own enemies to worry about me."

Tuesday said, "I can crush Vega anytime I want."

"But what about Rose? You think Reina was a problem, believe me Rose is much more dangerous."

"I have no beef with Rose."

"But you will at some point. I can promise you that."

She sneered. "You manipulative sonofabitch, you would put me in a war with Rose just to keep me off your ass."

He patted her thigh again. "Not just to keep you off my ass. Remember, tests are necessary for getting you ready."

This time Tuesday moved his hand. "They might have fucked you up but ain't nobody brainwashing me. I'll never join the Kamku and neither is Dani. You are hands down the smartest man I've ever known, but don't underestimate me either, Marcus."

"I would never do that." He looked at her, his eyes sincere. "But don't call me Marcus, my name is Sebastian."

Tuesday nodded. "So my husband really is dead."

He whispered, "You deserve somebody on that couch with you keeping your feet warm. I love you more than anything." Then in a clear and distinct voice he said, "Do it now, and if you hurt her I'll kill you."

Tuesday looked back to find Agent Morrison standing behind her. The young fed who had taken the children for frozen yogurt had slipped back onto the plane and snuck up behind her.

Before Tuesday could see what he held, he hit her with the Taser. Fifty thousand volts short-circuited her body and brain. Tuesday flopped like a fish out of water then sank into her seat unconscious.

Chapter Fifty-nine

Tuesday snapped awake like somebody coming out of a nightmare, looked around wide-eyed and panicked. The jet was cruising at thirty thousand feet, en route to Los Angeles. Tanisha was strapped into the seat next to her watching *Toy Story 3* while enjoying her frozen yogurt. DelRay was in the next seat, snoring loudly, most likely out from being tased.

Danielle was not on board.

Neither was Silence who Tuesday began to suspect had been working for Marcus the whole time. Silence had the type of skillset that would make him someone her husband kept in his phone. She couldn't imagine anybody but him carrying DelRay's four hundred pounds of dead weight up the stairs to the plane.

The Kamku began its work immediately. The very same day, Tuesday realized they began scrubbing any trace of Danielle from the internet. All her social media accounts had been deleted; they even hacked into Tabitha King's Facebook and removed any photos of Danielle Tuesday had posted there. By the third day, a Google search turned up zero items found for Danielle King.

Tuesday considered going to the police but realized how futile that would be. The King family had only been a clever illusion. So every time she played the conversation in her head, it sounded ridiculous even to her. Her husband, who never really existed, stole their daughter, who also never really existed or belonged to either of them, then vanished with the help of a secret society who was trying to take over the world. The average cop would think she was insane.

The only ones who would possibly believe her were those already corrupted. In Ms. Jackson, Marcus had a high-ranking member of the FBI who was basically his lackey; Tuesday figured he had even more planted within the CIA, NSA, and local law enforcement. Tuesday pictured herself being invited into the captain's office at the First Precinct just to find herself talking to an old black man wearing a triangle-shaped ring.

Tuesday knew it would be up to her to find Danielle but had no idea where to begin. How could she possibly find somebody as connected and elusive as Marcus when he was determined not to be found? He had spent twenty years with the nickname The Invisible Man for a reason.

The next three weeks were hard for Tuesday. She fell into a deep depression. She mourned her missing daughter who was somewhere being prepped to be a Manchurian Candidate. Tuesday would crane her neck and stare each time she drove past a girl on the street who resembled Danielle.

The hardest part was consoling Tanisha when she started to cry for her big sister. Tuesday felt the pain of watching her baby cope with the loss of a father and sibling in the span of a few weeks. Worse was that Tuesday had no creative way to explain the vacancies in their family.

Tuesday also mourned for Marcus, whose death felt more real this time even though he was alive. She had fallen in love with a reformed drug dealer, an idealist who only wanted to rebuild the same communities that he had helped to destroy. During their last conversation he sounded nothing like that man. She didn't know if he had been seduced by this new level of power or if that's who he had been the entire time. Had the personality of Marcus King been as phony as the name?

I was too powerful for that before, but now I'm practically a god.

Whenever she thought of him, those words would echo eerily in her mind. He didn't say this like a boast or mean it to be intimidating. He stated this like a plain fact, and to Tuesday that made it much more frightening.

It was during those first three weeks that Tuesday was at her lowest. She spent a lot of time in bed crying, or sleeping when the crying exhausted her. She hardly left her suite at the Athenium Hotel, rarely got dressed. But at some point she picked herself up. Tanisha still needed a mother, and Abel still needed a CEO. Plus she had never been the type of bitch who stayed down for too long.

Over the next couple of months, Tuesday got herself into a rhythm. She dropped six million on a house in Farmington Hills, and asked DelRay to move in until she and Tanisha got settled. Tuesday had relied on him heavily during that difficult transition; DelRay never left her side and she came to view him like a brother. Their new house had twelve thousand square feet, five bedrooms, and seven baths. Tuesday didn't know if it was hope or delusion but still decorated a room for Danielle.

Tuesday offered to replace 24 Karats, but DelRay passed on owning another strip club. Inspired by her to do better, his vision was more family-friendly: a Dave n' Buster's-style restaurant with liquor for adults and games for kids. He and Tuesday had already started searching for a building.

Her new family slowly fell into a routine the way families do. She ran Abel from their temporary headquarters in Detroit and flew out to Los Angeles when her presence was necessary there. The first two shipments of Vega's illegal immigrants passed through without a problem. Tanisha seemed to adjust to their new dynamic and was about to start kindergarten. DelRay's new eatery was scheduled to open the same fall.

She occasionally saw A.D., who still volunteered at the church. She offered to buy him a new house, to give him a job at Abel that came with a decent salary and benefits. A.D. refused what he considered to be a handout. He wouldn't accept her help but his church accepted five new vans donated by an anonymous benefactor. For Abel it was a simple tax write-off.

At some point, Tuesday gleaned the truth behind A.D.'s lucky break. A lawyer who comes from nowhere, agrees to work for free and gets him off a life-bit like it's nothing—Marcus had that type of pull even before the Big Table.

Her husband was a man always thinking twenty steps ahead and had a history of recruiting people to fill positions within his surrogate family. If he knew he would be leaving soon, Tuesday could see him finding a stand-in even for himself. He made A.D. available: the only other man she ever loved. Marcus had even given her a clue on the plane when he said that comment about deserving somebody on that couch with her.

The miraculous exodus was the cornerstone of A.D.'s newfound faith and Tuesday didn't have the heart to tell him that The Lord wasn't responsible. The praise belonged to a dark and manipulative god who was also willing to sacrifice his own child.

She also didn't try to get back with her ex, despite what Marcus had planned. A.D. was looking for a simple life and Tuesday wanted him to have that. He deserved the type of woman who could attend church with him on Sundays. The type of woman unburdened with the threats of gun dealers, cartel bosses, and secret societies.

With Marcus and Brandon dead, the King family fortune officially passed down to Tuesday, and in her spare time she was using a large portion of that considerable wealth to become a real estate mogul. A few billionaire investors like Dan Gilbert and the Illitch family had built up downtown Detroit with new condos, casinos and sports venues, but left the inner city looking like a third-world country. Tuesday focused there: renovating entire neighborhoods filled with abandoned homes and apartment complexes to provide affordable housing. The dozens of empty buildings left in the wake of school closings were being transformed into shelters for the homeless and abused, and halfway houses for prisoners trying to reintegrate into society. The derelict factories left to rust after the flight of the auto industry were being resurrected for new purposes. Tuesday was determined to bring her city back, and was spending a lot of money to do it. Abel Incorporated's Tabitha King was quickly making a name as a shrewd businesswoman and great philanthropist.

That mission gave Tuesday purpose, and that purpose provided enough of a distraction throughout the day to lessen the pain. The nights were a little harder as she couldn't get used to sleeping alone again, but time was making that easier. Life continued to move on, the way it does, even after a serious loss.

Then one day while riding shotgun with DelRay in the new Bentley Mulsanne insurance replaced for her cars lost in California, her phone rang from an unavailable number. She ignored it at first but the caller was so persistent that she dug into her bag only to silence it.

She read the text: "We are never that far from home."

Two photos popped up on screen. The first was just a shot of the Eiffel Tower taken from a hotel window in Paris. No person appeared in the picture.

The second was of a girl in a rose-colored hijab, the hooded scarf worn by women in Muslim countries. She was seated on a camel somewhere in the desert. Even though the picture was taken at a distance that didn't give a clear view of the girl's face, Tuesday could tell it was Danielle.

Her heart thumped in her chest, it became hard to breathe, she felt like she was having an anxiety attack.

While Tuesday stared at her phone in shock, a second text appeared: "Another test coming soon. Get rest, you look tired."

Tuesday didn't bother looking around because any of the

other cars surrounding them on the freeway might have a Kamku spy watching her with a camera. He might even be looking down on her with a satellite somewhere in orbit.

Tuesday didn't even consider taking the phone to the police so they could trace the call. She knew it was a burner that wouldn't be registered to Marcus King or anyone else she'd ever heard of.

She simply typed back: "Will make sure I'm ready; you better do the same. Coming for my girl."

Tuesday put the phone away.

Marcus's first test had come three years before, when he allowed Tuesday to deal with her former team on her own when they kidnapped Danielle. Back then, Tuesday had learned to think on the level of a hood boss.

Tuesday had no doubt that Marcus knew ahead of time that Brandon would betray her and Reina would make a play for the company. The second test had required she learn to think on the level of a corporate boss and military general.

Tuesday didn't know what would be required for his third test, but was done playing his game. It was time for the student to become the Master.

Tuesday was preparing herself to face her most dangerous opponent ever. She was about to go to war with Sebastian Caine.